VICTORIA ANTOINETTE

Mother-Hood

Contents

1

Malachi

Welcome to London, the city of opportunities where the best place to be stabbed is in a bus lane; those cameras are always on. Getting kicked out of school means going to a Pupil referral unit where you can mix with your own, and make contacts that will serve you well in and out of jail. You see, we are not ever going to have a happy ever after. We have no inheritance of homes or money waiting for us. We only inherit poor health, bad teeth, and addictive personalities.

I knew from a very young age that to make anything of my life I had to be good at being self-sufficient; you see, I just genuinely didn't give a fuck. The rising cost of living sent us all spiralling into a hundred different directions, to make money fast.

We were suffering and hungry; if the drugs or drink bug hadn't bitten you, you were desperate to get out any way you could. I wasn't going to be the one with the BMW and new Nike trainers sitting on a council estate that just wasn't my bag, you drew too much attention to your flash lifestyle and that's when you start

1

to pick up enemies.

And picking up enemies while sitting on a council estate is not the way to go; if you're going to operate here, do it quietly and keep your business to yourself. Women on these estates have low-cut tops, thick skins and low morals. Bitches try to reproduce with you if you have a bit of cash or status about you. There was no way I would get sucked down into that crazy life that I see my own Mum live, fuck having some snot-encrusted kid hanging around my knees. I made myself known and then was silent.

I disappeared and walked a fine line between light and dark, and I was crazy I was spontaneous I was your worst nightmare if you caught me on a bad day.

I was managing a team of 35 soldiers on our estate, we took over flats and we sold drugs we moved weapons all up and down the country and most of all I got to the top table by just my sheer inability to not give a fuck about another human being, and of course, my Dad being who he was helped.

The man I believed for 23 years was my Dad Nico, my link to the big time. He was a well-respected middleman who was the in-between guy for the European gangsters that shipped cocaine and heroin to our UK shores. You see my Dad was old-school East End from the 80s a crazy bastard with a good nose for business. He managed the unruly East End hungry teenagers, the youth that thought they were tough, but they were the idiots driving about with bags of drugs and doing all the dirty work. At the same time, the real Gangsters were the ones sitting in their semidetached mansions in Chigwell with the cleanest hands. The little plastic gangsters were on their council estate rapping about drugs, gangs, knives and women but trust me no real gangster ever lived on a Council estate. I mean I moved to a

2

luxury flat in Canary Wharf so I was out but still in if that made sense.

I believed in relying on no one and every human being in my life was expendable whether they knew it or not. I blended seamlessly into society I was mixed race; always beautifully dressed. You see me I look like a banker, I only wear a tracksuit when I go to the Gym. I have connections at my fingers that you could only dream of. I was born into this and My Dad dragged me further into it; I'd spent way too many years in second-hand clothes and with a Mum that see me as a product of a big fucking mistake. Imagine how that made me feel. This life It's precious to me, I fought hard to get here, so you aren't taking anything away from me without a fight.

I'd seen people get killed or end up in prison like my Dad except I would find out 23 years later the Mum who had pushed me out into this world had been lying. Nico was not my biological dad. The night Nico got nicked I felt like my fucking heart had been ripped from my chest. Dad took me in when my Mother left. He had me packing drugs as a child and taught me how to be a proper man. When I first moved in with him I was 12, years old. A few months into secondary school, after the Easter Holiday, I remember him sitting me down and saying I could either plug the drugs stick them up my ass, or stick them to my body with that strong Gorilla tape. I opted for the tape but turns out that strapping their packages to your leg and then ripping it off is fucking painful Sticking it up your ass was better with a bit of lube. There I was, a child in my School Uniform running these packages up and down the M25 with my Daddy; we looked good together, Dad and Son. I was 12, and suddenly my Dad made me a little don. If any kid even looked at me twice I'd take their fucking eye out.

Visiting my Dad was tough, the smell of the prison and the confined space made me feel sick. I knew that for me a prison sentence would be intolerable. I sat and thought long and hard about my life choices and the consequences of living by the sword and to die by the sword. Did I want something more? Because now I had the money to achieve it. The fucking thing was Dad had the opportunity to send all the top level down, the older white bastards that lived out of the Estate in their white areas and gated houses. He kept quiet, he did his time, and he handed the baton over to me.

I contemplated what I wanted and on a sunny day, while I sat drinking a cold beer I decided I wouldn't become my Dad. If I went to jail nobody would be coming to see me. I had no intentions of trusting or loving another human being if my own Mum didn't want or love me then how could I expect someone else to?

I lived a solitary life but at least that way, you don't get hurt do you? Then something so small and stupid happened; we always record these girls being passed around and use it as a threat; no girl wants those recordings of them being made public. But for some reason, my mate sent it to a man called Jerome who was no word of a lie a fucking insane human being, a certified lunatic, properly mentally ill and my fucking biological Dad I just didn't know it at the time.

Now the girl in that recording was an estate girl -Amelia running one of my trap houses, her mum Louisa was a good woman she was clean, hardworking and one of the few British born people that kept in with the immigrants to Newham. She was good mates with them all whereas the local British women were more wary of people they didn't understand.

So to wind up Jerome my mate sent this recording of Amelia

4

being degraded in the worse ways a Dad could have seen his Daughter.

How my Mum see the footage, I don't know; turns out some other person on the block must have known her secret that Amelia was my half-sister!

So when I get that call from my so-called Mother, out of the blue I was surprised because she has not had anything to do with me for years; the last time I see her Id traveled by train to her in Southend to see my new Baby sister. I wanted to live back with Mum because I knew my Dad was into this new woman and she was on about having kids so I knew a teenage me would be shipped out. This new Baby sister well she was half me, I was curious.

My mother's new partner some racist junkie and me got into a fight; he was calling me a black bastard and I kicked the shit out of him. Mum was screaming at me to stop then she looked into my eyes. "You see Malachi you're always causing trouble; I don't want you no more. I never did. Just leave and never come back".

Well, I never did go back; that train journey home to London with my knuckles grazed and bloody from punching that man in the mouth was a sobering journey for me. That taught me, blood means fuck all, the people that can care for you can turn out to be your worst fucking enemies.

So this so-called Mother of mine calls me saying she has seen the video from a friend and she said you're hurting your sister and it's wrong! I'm like what the fuck is this bullshit, but Mum is one year sober and has been in rehab and turned her life around. She has not got her daughter back. She was adopted and she has not bothered with me, I told you some women are cunts.

So I'm taking all this in and thinking what bullshit is she filling with me now, what does she want from me? I could hear in her voice the truth; as soon as she uttered those words I knew she wasn't bullshitting me. "I know it's been a while, son; I've been getting clean. I'm calling because I need you to stop all this stupid gang shit you're involved in, stop hurting others... Malachi, that girl in that Video, little Amelia, is your half-sister; Nico was never your real Dad."

I sat back in shock as she continued to speak; a million things were going through my brain. Nico was my Dad he had been the one that schooled me in Gang life; his connections got me to places I never would have. He trained me as his only bloodline son in taking over from him when he was jailed; being his child I was trustworthy and loyal. If my Mother had spoken those words before me I would have ripped her throat out or stabbed her. And I know if Nico ever learned the truth he would have her killed for the years of deceit in making him think I was his son.

"Jerome was your real Dad Malachi, so listen to me... Amelia, she is your half-sibling...you were hurting your own blood"

"Why the fuck should I believe a word that comes out of your fucking mouth? Where are you? I'll fucking kill you with my bare hands" I could feel myself becoming hot and my temper rising.

She exhaled. "You won't ever find me Malachi, but I needed you to know and keep away from that girl, I could never allow Jerome to be your Dad he was crazy, mentally not well, I'd been seeing Nico too and I knew out of the two who would be the better one to be your Dad, I was young. I was scared I didn't know what to do, I did the thing that I believed would be best for you. For us. You have to, believe me, I did this for you"

I hung up the phone, I didn't even know how she got my number, I didn't know if she even knew Jerome was dead, I thought of all the times I had taken the piss out of Jerome. Sold him shit drugs and took his money laughing at him.

But what hurt me the most was Amelia. She was a girl that I had taken out and abused so badly, and she was half me,my sister. I felt sick because I knew when I was around her, she reminded me of someone and I liked her eyes; turns out she reminded me of me.

The only other fucking human being in my life that if I had known was half mine I would have taken her under my wing in a whole other way. But what the fuck had I done. I was so used to not giving a shit about anyone or anything I was cold believe me, utterly fucking devoid of emotion but this! This was like a cut that was open and wouldn't heal I tried to let it scab over but it played on my mind.

I know Amelia's Mum Louisa was one of the few English born on the estate that worked. And I know Louisa had a really shit start in life; dunno how I am ever going to make it   up to them because they have disappeared. And that's the thing with good women. They have this Mother-Hood stuff worked out well. They protect their kids in any way they know how. I hope Louisa knows just how much of an amazing Mum she really is Amelia is blessed to have her, a good Mum is like a precious stone, you have to treasure them. My own Mum was like a rock she was cold, hard and would only weigh me down.

2

Louisa- Poverty the circle of life

There must be a reason why what you're trying to escape is the one thing that you're drawn deeper into. It's like the universe attracts what you are trying to avoid. That the energy of your thoughts can somehow influence your physical reality. But it's hard to get into that mindset when I have £10 left in my pocket, electricity to top up and an empty fridge, it's eat or heat. No amount of visualising myself in a comfortable, warm home with enough food, money or a garden will change where I am and that's in a high-rise tower block with a hungry belly. My name is Louisa Mary Doherty, and my life has gone full circle and repeated the same pattern as my Mum before me. I was raised in the same tower block I am living in now. The only difference is that my Mum Karen, raised me on the first floor, and now I'm on the seventeenth floor. You see – the higher you rise up the block, the more of a fuck up you are. I can't tell you how many nights I spent as a teenager looking out over the same skyline watching changes happening everywhere except in my life. I'd climb to the top of the tower block, get out of the fire escape, and feel like I was on top of the world. I would look out across the vibrant landscape of East London. New builds, shopping centres, and much of East London caught up in gentrification, except for my life and surroundings which stayed poor and always the same. Urban regeneration is excellent if you're part of the process, but our tower block was like the big ugly sister dwarfing over the new part of Stratford town centre, where everything had stayed the same from when it was built in the 1970s. It was shit in the 1990s when I grew up there, and it's shit now, years later.

The building has been condemned many times, and then after consultations, a lick of paint and building work to make it look better. But look beyond the surface, and the flats were full of dampness and squalor, like the souls of its inhabitants.

As a teenager, the top of the blocks spelt freedom, where we went to escape our piss-poor lives. We took whatever alcohol we could get our hands on and listened to the pirate radio stations banging out tunes. I used to sit up there and look at East London being transformed, and it filled me with hope. The skyline was forever transforming, with the bright lights of Canary Wharf -the new financial district a glowing beacon with some of the poorest neighbourhoods in its shadows.

I always aspired to get a good job and get out, and I always felt that I would one way or the other. But I wasn't good at school; I liked it, but I'd spend many days skipping class, so how I would rise higher to have a better life was a mystery. I was always waiting for the lottery win or a man that might lift me out of the shit I was in.

I spent my early years learning quite quickly I had nobody to rely on but myself. I was the product of a broken family daughter

9

of a single parent. My Mums family had disowned her because my Dad was from Pakistan. My Dad, a newly arrived immigrant to London and Forest Gate, was dazzled by my pretty blonde and blue-eyed Mum.

So my start in life set the scene for how I'm constantly feeling; not quite sure where I belong, and no one seems to want to take ownership of me.

My Mum was 17 when she pushed me out into the world, a concealed pregnancy until six months when she had to reveal her predicament. She came from a white working-class family in Canning Town, petty thieves who supported the British National Party and spent their evenings in the local working man's club, pissing away their ill-gotten gains.

The East End was a very different place back then; very white and hostile to outsiders; anyone different was not welcome, including black people, Indian people and Millwall football fans. It was all Pie and Mash, jellied eels, and West Ham ICF supporters. Coming home pregnant by a Pakistani boy went down like a lead balloon.

Mum and my elusive Dad weren't a love story – far from it! I was a mistake, and my Mum has never let me forget that fact. They met while Mum was selling West Ham programs outside Upton Park Station, and he was selling fruit bowls at a market stall.

He found Mum quite exotic, and what did she see in him? Danger, perhaps, or rebellion? We will never know because my Dad was never a happy topic of conversation. All I knew was that he was young, beautiful, and shipped back to Islamabad as soon his family heard he had got Mum pregnant.

I was born at Forest Gate maternity home - a little dark-haired baby with olive skin looking nothing like my Mum. I was labelled void. Mum would often recount how when Nell, her own Mum, came to visit her and took one look at me, she shook her head and told Mum, "You're on your own now" and shut the door on us. I didn't look white, I would not fit in, I spoiled their bloodline. Mum and me ceased to exist to her whole family after that.

My Mum found solace in Heroin, drink, and bad men. She could still work in the local pub and ensure I looked clean for school, so we avoided local authority involvement.

Mum was a functioning addict, and she could appear normal, visit the school, turn up on time to collect me, smile at the class assemblies, and work in her shitty job but still be addicted to anything that gave her oblivion from her life.

The only drugs I liked were prescription medications – a few sleeping tablets or anti-anxiety drugs, but they're still drugs, really, just government-approved ones, so maybe I was a hypocrite. But the fact a Dr signed the prescription and you got it from a chemist made it justifiable.

Therefore, my Mum moved into temporary accommodation where she would start her life cycle in poverty, second-hand sofas, second-hand beds – it was rare for us to have anything new. Even our towels were hand-me-downs, and our furniture was a mishmash of things we found along the way.

It wasn't easy for my Mum as she never had a family to call her own after that. She was incredibly street-wise and a great shoplifter. You can guarantee she would be involved if a scam was going on. It's a shame she didn't put her intelligence to better use and study, as she could have done so well.

Most of Mum's life was spent winging it, and I now know how hard it is being a Mum, and when you're doing it all on your own, even harder.

I can't blame her for escaping into a void of drink and drugs,

11

but I would never follow that path; seeing her descent into the black hole was enough to put me off drugs and to rely on anything for the rest of my life.

I watched my Mum bring home all kinds of men, but she always hoped they were a way out of our struggle. A man can be the next best thing when you have no education and no escape route. The jobs you qualify for don't pay good money, and it's better to work part-time or not at all to ensure that your rent gets paid by the government. So you become trapped in a cycle of poverty and poor choices. And when you're poor, everything else is just so expensive, your electricity meter, your pay-as-you-go phones, your oblivion cruxes drink, fags and drugs. In my early childhood, I learned to be quite content on my own., Mum was a barmaid; her hours meant she worked from 7 pm-11.30 pm, so most nights, I put myself to bed learning to ignore the sounds of her drunkenly coming home late. I had developed a skill of putting an old wooden chair under the door handle. I had an old rubber hot water bottle for warmth; heating was never an option, and a bucket to pee in so I never had to leave the room. This was my safe space where nobody could get in. You know some kids dream of monsters under the bed? I was home alone in a tower block with monsters all around; it wasn't the imaginary monsters I was scared of but the real ones.

The benefit of working in a Pub for her was free booze and access to desperate men.

Some of the men Mum brought home were nice, and some were utter bastards. Some had regular manual labour jobs, which was always good as Mum could get them drunk and steal money from their wallets, then act nonchalantly, blaming them for being drunk and losing the cash.

Not always with a happy ending, as a drunken man losing all

his wages could become angry. Mum had been on the receiving end of many punches over the years. I was lucky, and I only ever got hit once, right across the face, and it shocked me; I felt my teeth rattle in my head and was scared I might lose a tooth. But the amount of money and gold she had managed to steal over the years far outweighed the punches and the black eyes.

As a result, the older I got, especially when I entered my teenage years, the more reluctant I was to go home, as I never knew what awaited me. Arguments, drinking, and fights would result in me pushing my cheap second-hand wardrobe against the door to stop the men or Mum drunkenly trying to get into my room. The older I got, the larger the objects against the door. As time passed, the more I felt my Mum resented me, so many times Mum would tell me how I had destroyed her life and her size 8 figure, it was easier as a child to ignore, but as a teenager, it was harder and harder to tune out. With my teenage hormones kicking in, I would argue back; no longer was I the little girl that could be her emotional punchbag.

I grew up thinking a crack pipe was an ordinary piece of kitchen equipment! A plastic bottle with a straw through it and the foil on top, what do you mean that's not normal?! And scraps of foil around the table with dried brown stuff on, Heroin Chic, she wore it well. I had no boundaries, but in the 90s, there weren't gangs like there are now. We were terrible but no way on the level of kids of today. We stole, we would fight, but nobody died, and the only territorial boundary was the River Thames. I never felt at ease south of the river, and East London was my home; you never went across to the South side; you stayed East.

I would cycle the whole length of the Greenway from Stratford to Beckton – a vast cycling strip built over a sewer bank, with the wind in my hair. It was absolute freedom; today's kids will never know how good that felt. I only had to worry about getting a flat tire on my bike.

It was no surprise that older boys started appearing on my radar because boys my age didn't have the stability I was craving. When you don't come from a close-knit family, and you have never known the blessing of having other people to rely on, there can be an urgency in some to create their own families. It was never my plan, but then again, maybe subconsciously, it was as If I knew having unprotected sex could result in a baby.

They say girls that have disrupted childhoods get pregnant younger, which was undoubtedly true on our block; many girls came from broken homes and had disrupted lives. I didn't intentionally sit and think about getting pregnant, but there was a part of my brain that did want someone to call my own and to be mine, for me to build my own family, the family I didn't have.

As a child of a broken home, you build homes with unsuitable ones because you are desperate for stability. It sometimes means you stay in an unhappy situation or rush head first into a romance because you want the home and the Man and the kid. The cycle begins; the foundations are cracked before you even start building.

I met my baby's daddy, Jerome, while I was skipping school, sitting in the park drinking a nasty large bottle of Cider that my friend had stolen from the local supermarket. He was 6ft2 and built like he had spent all day in the gym. He spoke with a strong Jamaican accent, which I have always found strange seeing as he was born here and had never set foot in his mother-land. He was like a big protector with a beautiful smile, and his interest

14

in me made me feel on top of the world.

I was a young girl still in school uniform, glazed eyes from the drink. I was sitting looking pretty, ripe for the taking. He was 19 and had his own home, bingo! He had money, he was clean, and he was handsome. I suddenly felt wanted and needed; he had chosen me! I was the envy of my girlfriends and even some male friends because he had his home! It was big for us little hood rats, spending our days on top of tower blocks or park benches. We now had a place to chill, drink and be merry.

An ordinary man with a 9-5 and comfortable home would never be interested in girls from the estate. And in reality, I don't think I even knew a man like that; no one like that had ever been on my Mum's radar. Unsurprisingly, I ended up in love with a man who gave me a snapshot of a clean, warm home and fridge full of food, things I had never had.

And the fact he was bat-shit crazy and kept me in fear with his moods, well, I was used to living on the edge, waiting for the next argument. I had done it all my life; it was normal.

Our relationship unsurprisingly revolved around sex; I spent most of my time in his home getting drunk, having sex, or eating cheap chicken and chips. Jerome had a very high sex drive and was crazy in more ways than one. He had his home, money, and food in the fridge because he was mentally unwell. Jerome was a care-in-the-community patient, suffered from Schizophrenia, and had been sectioned numerous times. He had a social worker and a Carer who ensured that he remained functioning in the community.

Jerome had many different ideas and theories about life, from corrupt governments, aliens, and paranoia that would result in him putting tin foil around his windows to keep a spying signal out.

Not one professional ever questioned the fact he was becoming more unwell. I was never around when they visited as he pretended he was working undercover and they were his colleagues. I didn't understand his ramblings at times and knew the best way to appease him was to get him into bed, drunk or stoned.

But despite his crazy ways, I thought I was in love with him; I was a school girl; I knew if he was caught with me, shit would hit the fan as I was underage. I would lay in his bed with my school uniform all over the floor. I didn't want to lose him, so I kept quiet, did as he said, and ignored the boxes of tablets and the crazy ideas because for the first time in my life, I had a comfortable sofa and warm place to crash and I was the envy of my friends. I was the talk of the class - I had a man, there was no way I was giving him up, and for the first time in my life, I felt wanted and needed; it felt good I was part of something.

The sweet-talking ended up, unsurprisingly, with me becoming pregnant. Jerome hated to wear condoms. He believed he was put on this earth to reproduce and promised me the withdrawal method was safe! He said latex was impregnated with chemicals that would lead to infertility-work of the devil conservative government – yes, alarm bells should have rung for me then, but I was too in love.

I didn't know much about mental illness, but by then, I was scared to look any deeper because I was now too involved with Jerome and couldn't handle any more disappointment in my life.

I was a teenager on the cusp of young adulthood with a neglectful Mum, no prospects, and no real direction. I was still determining who or what I wanted to be. I wanted to belong somewhere and feel loved. No career adviser at school could conjure up a job like that, but in my mind, there was one job that would fill at least a little of that gap- Motherhood- the biggest blessing and the biggest curse all rolled into one. It was happening, and I suddenly had a life growing inside me that would love me, and I'd create the family I never had somehow.

3

Louisa-Morning Sickness and Hangovers

I discovered I was pregnant on the 16th of January. I remember the exact date because I had been vomiting, not my usual morning hangover, as this was late afternoon. The smell of the local chicken and chip shop sent me heaving into the gutter. My friend had stolen a pregnancy test from Pound land during our school lunch break, and I had rushed home eager to await my fate.I arrived home to find my Mum stuffing all our belongings into black bin bags and the ugliest man I have ever seen eagerly helping her.

I knew him from the area as Scarface Ron, an old ex-bank robber who lived in Canning Town and had a large scar across his face making him look like he was smiling. They call these types of scars Chelsea Smiles, typically reserved for grasses. I don't know Ron's story, but I knew he was one of the old faces around the manor. I had seen the pile of important-looking letters that Mum had been ignoring. Final warnings in bold letters. I knew she had also been taking out credit cards with different names, as well as all sorts of fucked up tricks and cons. Mum believed that soon our block of flats was to be condemned.

A few of her friends down the pub had already mc
Southend, Harlow and Clacton to Greener pastu
same problems.

Mum's plan had backfired, she had received eviction threats,
and now the bailiffs were coming to remove all the stolen goods
she had obtained with a dodgy credit card. The council were
dragging their feet over the decision of the decrepit building,
and it would appear that the block was to be revamped rather
than flattered.

I walked into a cloud of chaos -Mum had a fag dangling out
of her mouth while she stuffed as many items as possible into
black bags and boxes. "Pack your shit up, Amelia; no time to
dawdle! We have got to get this gear out of here sharpish. They
were going to fucking evict us anyway. I haven't paid the rent
for so long thinking if they tore this block down, then my debts
would be erased with it thank fuck for Ron!".

Mum lovingly looked towards him, making that stupid smile
for men when she wanted something, the practised look of a
manipulative woman using her body to get what she wanted.
You could say Mum had looks, with her home-peroxide blonde
hair and clothes one size too small. But she did have great boobs.
I'll give her that!

I was furious, incredulous even, and there was no way I was
planning on packing up and moving in with loves young dream!
"What! What do you fucking mean?! I'm going nowhere! I don't
like Canning Town - it's a shit hole!

Mum laughed. "Well, we ain't got many choices at the
moment unless you want to end up in some shitty hostel with
bed bugs and rapists at your door all night, fuck that! Now hurry
up; you can't stay here alone, or I'll have the social on my back."
There was no point in me even arguing with her. I just

19

slammed the door to the bathroom, my heart beating fast through rage and fear. Could this day get any worse? School had been shit, and I'd spent the last lesson thinking about the pregnancy test in my bag, so I couldn't even think straight. And I thought I'd come home to sit and do the Pregnancy test in peace, but I'd come home to carnage - typical!

My hands shook as I peed on the stick. Those two minutes felt like hours. If this test was positive, Jerome would have to take me in. I didn't want to go to Canning Town with Scarface Ron in his pokey flat overlooking the market and all the old warehouses. Canning Town was rough, and I was not too fond of it. I didn't even go to school in that area. I sat on the edge of our avocado-coloured bath suite kicking at the broken panelling with my trainers, waiting eagerly for the result to change my life.

Two lines! I rubbed my eyes, closed them, and opened them again to ensure I saw the result correctly. I read the box, and yes, there it was! Two lines meant I was pregnant. I didn't quite know what I felt. I was happy, sad, scared and angry all at the same time.Part of me was hoping it was negative, and then I could have just stomped out of the bathroom and told my Mum to go fuck herself and I wasn't moving. But another part of me was scared, and I needed her.

I know she hadn't been much of a Mum to me, but now she would have to change her ways and at least help me. I was 15 and pregnant, for fucks sake, still a child about to make one of the most important decisions of my life.

I opened the bathroom door to find Mum running around, still bagging up things, and I just held out the stick for her to see. At first, she looked at me and didn't consider what I held. Then it sunk in what it was. "Is that what I think it is?" I nodded my head, still in shock myself. "Yes Mum, it's a pregnancy test, I'm Pregnant." She sat on the chair closest to her and shook her head in disbelief. Then her face started to go red, she began to breathe in and out fast like before she had a fight as if she was working herself up to attack. It was as if she had gone for a run and needed a rest, and now she was hyperventilating. "You've done it now, you stupid little cow!"

Her breath smelt of alcohol and the faint whiff of vinegar. She had been smoking heroin again, I knew the smell. Mum's body was quite animated it could have been crack. Rather than the hug and words of support I hoped for, I was hit with a barrage of abuse. I was a whore, a stupid girl that should have kept her legs closed, I had ruined my life fucked up all chances. Didn't I learn from her?! "Mum, I don't care anymore. You can't tell me what to do when your half pissed and out of it most of the time."

She slapped me so hard round the face, and it was a short sharp shock and one where I didn't know whether to hit her back or cry. Her anger continued to flow. "Don't you dare talk to me about being pissed or stoned child. After all, I do for you! I worked hard to feed and clothe you and this is the thanks I get! Do you realize how hard it was for me to have you back then? Kicked out, all because your dad wasn't white, it's hardly been a walk in the fucking park!"

I smiled, ready to play my trump card "Well, Mum, history repeats itself because this baby isn't going to be white either." She stood back, looking at me, shaking her head, her lip curled in disgust. "And you think it's easy, eh? You wonder why I drink and have a little escape now and then. It's because it's hell, Louisa, seeing your life falling apart and what could have been!! It's fucking hell on earth! You think being a Mum in this environment is easy, always scraping by and trying to make ends meet?!".

The tears fell from my eyes, running silently down my face, I didn't know what to feel anymore. This was so messed up all I wanted was for my Mum to hug me. I was angry at myself for allowing her to upset me like this and my words when they were spoken came out in a sob "I didn't ask to be born, Mum, you kept me! and you remind me every day how much of a mistake that was, how much harder I made your life, well it wasn't easy for me either, you know! Growing up with nobody!".

I spat the words towards her, my hands trembling with anger or fear I couldn't differentiate. Yet she continued her tirade of abuse "You're a stupid girl. You could have done anything, gone anywhere, and what have you done?! You have chucked all your chances away! You see how poor we are - always struggling! It wears you down. It fucking breaks you! And what have you done fucking tied yourself right down."

I shook my head "No, Mum, this is different; he loves me! He has his own place and will look after me. It's not like how it was when you were younger! He's not a boy; he's a man!".

She let out a loud fake laugh, rolling her head back so I could see a mass of fillings and brown-stained teeth. "Oh, he loves you, does he? That's what he said to you, did he? When he was busy getting you into bed and knocking you up! You're a stupid little slut, and you have a lot to learn. You're not even 16 years old yet! What type of man has sex with a child? Because that's what you are in the eyes of the law!! Who is he!? Dirty bastard, every man loves you when you're on your back."

I don't know why I expected anything different from her. What did I want? A cuddle and then a trip to Baby Gap to pick out cute baby clothes? If my Mum couldn't be a Mum to me, then how the fuck did I expect her to be a Nan?.

I wish I had not even told her. "I'm old enough to make my own decisions, and it's not like you have ever really been remotely interested in me, Mum. Your whole life revolves around when you're getting your next fix, drink, or a man, and I don't fit into any of it. Never have and never will".

Mum stood up and threw the packet of black bin liners sacks at me. "Then I suggest you pack your bags and fuck off to whoever has knocked you up! Silly little girl, you think black boys will stick with silly white girls like you?! I don't think so, darling. Trust me, I've been there! You're just the fun; the real one is from his own country. He'll have a ring on her finger before he starts shagging her! And it won't be fun when you're alone with a baby to feed and no fucking money!".

I barged past her and slammed the door to my room. I didn't have much stuff to pack anyway. All my clothes smelt of damp, and of the cigarettes that Mum constantly smoked.

I was leaving but I wasn't going with her and Scarface Ron. She clarified that his part of Canning Town would not welcome a mixed-race baby or me. Ron's social standing was evident from his tattoo of a British Bulldog on his arm and a massive Union Jack with BNP in the middle. That told me all I needed to know about Scarface Ron and his cronies. So here I was, stuffing the nicest of my clothes into a black bin liner that kept ripping. Even the bin liners were cheap! One solitary black bag was all I had at my feet as Mum slammed the door shut in my face.

I only realized as I went to Jerome's house that the next day was my 16th Birthday. Had Mum forgotten? Sweet 16, and nobody knows or cares. It wasn't the first time my Mum had forgotten my Birthday. Many times in my childhood, I only knew when it was because the teacher had a book that listed the whole class's birthdays, so we all got a sing-song of Happy Birthday in

23

the morning. Most kids brought in sweets or cakes to give out and were allowed to wear a Birthday Badge with their age on all day! I would genuinely forget my Birthday and then be shocked when they sang to me. I spent most of the day pretending my Mum was too busy planning my evening out to remember to bring in the cakes and sweets for the class. You may think that is bullshit how can a kid forget their birthday? Maybe it was a coping mechanism but I blanked that date out for a long time.

My Mum had happily abandoned me when I needed her. I wasn't part of her new life or plan. Ironically, my Nan had done the same to Mum, yet here she was doing the same to me. I had never met my Nan or any of Mum's family even though they lived in the same City as us- crazy eh?

Maybe Mum felt disappointed seeing the cycle repeated, or she could have been selfish and only intent on serving her own needs. Scarface Ron would not have had a mixed-race baby in his yard. And there were parts of Canning Town, especially the East End Boozers that Mum and Scarface Ron inhabited, where you could not let it known you had a child that was not white British.

I went to Jerome's house the only other place I could go. My black bin liners bag was falling apart like my life, splitting as I walked in a temper, dropping my clothes all over the dirty streets as I marched to his door.

My stomach went over when Jerome opened the door as I could see a fierce-looking tall black woman standing behind him, already scowling at the inconvenience of the door knocking. I thought he may have had another girl in, but I was relieved when he stepped aside, inviting me in.

This fierce looking woman was his sister Leonie. She looked me up and down like I was something the cat had dragged in.

"What's up with you?" She looked at the black bin liners bag and the face that was swollen from tears.I tried so hard not to burst into tears "My Mum has kicked me out, and I have nowhere to go. Actually Jerome can we talk in private?" Leonie kissed her teeth and sat back to watch some racy R&B video. Suddenly I felt scared, but he stopped rolling his joint on the large coffee table and led me into the kitchen. "What's wrong?" He cupped my face in his hands and started kissing me. "Stop, Jerome. I've got something important to say. Please listen".

He looked at me seriously, and I thought this could go either one way or the other. "I'm pregnant. "It took him a second to respond. "What! Really? Oh my God, that's great!" "Really?" I started to cry, even though I didn't want to but what a day and night!

A complete nightmare. I had an overwhelming feeling of relief, I was wanted somewhere at last. Thank goodness Jerome didn't kick me out. I collapsed into his arms. Grateful, so fucking grateful. I couldn't remember the last time someone hugged me without it being a prelude to sex.

But tonight, I needed comfort, not sex, and I needed to feel that I was safe and not on my own. Because right there and then, at that moment, I genuinely felt like I didn't have anyone. Although I had spent so much time alone, this felt different. It was like freefalling, and I didn't have a parachute.

It turns out Leonie was also Jerome's carer. She came and ensured he was taking his tablets, then helped herself to some of his medications and cash. Leonie was 25, a strong woman in all senses of the word. She had long gelled-back black hair, hoop earrings, and such a solid Jamaican accent when she spoke or shouted that I sometimes couldn't quite understand her.

When Jerome had imparted his news, she shook her head

and kissed her teeth, looking me up and down. "Another baby, mamma! God give me strength and a little pickney at that. Who is this ickle white girl? How old are you, girl?" I tried to make myself stand taller. "I will be 16 tomorrow."

Leonie rolled her eyes. "Lord have mercy! You were underage when he stuck that baby in you! You keeping this pickney or what?" .

Jerome was instantly shouting her down, his Jamaican accent suddenly stronger "Jessum peace, Blood Fyah! Of course, she is keeping my child! What are you, the devil?! Leonie, just because you get rid of babies like pigeons don't mean every other girl is the same." Leonie, sensing it was probably best not to get Jerome riled up, sat down and finished rolling the joint Jerome had previously started. Leonie lit it, and smoked a bit before passing it to Jerome and then staring right at me, her eyes didn't blink. "Listen to me, ickle girl and listen carefully, If they find out, Jerome is the baby's Dad, Jerome, will be in some serious shit you get me? And put on the sex offenders register quicker than you can say paedo. There will be too much social services involvement and even the feds You hear me girl? This ain't a game."

I felt real fear come over me. The word social services conjured up people in suits taking children away, and as for the feds, nobody wanted that shit at their doors. I didn't want to invite any unnecessary hassle into my life. And I knew that getting pregnant by an older man would also create massive problems. Mum had always warned me a hundred times that social workers were bad people. I couldn't let that happen. What would happen to me? This life was not a game. It hit me at that moment that I had nobody, had no real friends to call and help, and this situation here was much more intense than I had anticipated.

26

Leonie threw a £20 note at Jerome. "Go and get some rum - we have a celebration of life to drink to" I could sense immediately she was trying to get him out the way "Yes, man!" Jerome bumped fists with his sister's like it was some secret handshake to say all was OK and left to go to the local corner shop that was open 24/7.

Meanwhile, I was in the interrogation chair with Leonie jumping on me as soon as her brother had left the room. "Let me get one thing straight with you he is unwell, you know that right?" I shook my head, confused. Yes, he could say weird things occasionally and be moody, but I wasn't quite sure how bad things were. I had no experience with mental health. "I'm telling you this now so you can make a decision. Jerome has schizophrenia and has spent much of his youth in and out of Mental Health units. When he is in one of his hallucination or delusional states, you better run, ickle girl, because trust me, it can take three to five police officers to restrain him and believe me when they see a big black guy going crazy, they don't care he is sick, they taser him, lock him up they make him worse. He is always the enemy wherever he goes because of his size and the way he looks. The mentally ill black men are always the punch bag for the racist feds. Trust me, they beat first and ask later." I shook my head, not wanting to hear this. I tried to tell her to stop saying such things because he was all I had, and I needed him. I didn't want to think I had jumped from the frying pan into the fire, but I honestly had. ·

Leonie rubbed her head and continued to swear and call me obscenities, but she had a plan. "Be ready tomorrow at 8.45, I'm going to collect you from here and take you to the Council housing place, and you say you're homeless and pregnant. That way, you get more benefits and grants. You just have to do what

27

I say. Don't go against what I say and get my brother in trouble because then I will be pissed," and Leonie being pissed off is never good. "Do you get me? and Social Services will take your baby away and raise it in another home. Is that what you want?" I shook my head.

I couldn't even speak. I lay back on that sofa choking back tears. What a mess! I'd run from one fuck up to another. That night Jerome had drunk a lot of the rum and smoked a lot of the weed and, luckily, was unconscious on the bed, snoring his head off. I had never stayed the night here before, and I found it hard to switch off and sleep. I mean, what a day! I could hear Jerome mumbling a load of shit in his sleep and twitching like he was having some seizure.

I lay next to him, looking up at the ceiling that looked like it was just about holding up dark, broken and cracked from years of neglect. I hoped that wasn't a sign of the direction of my life another ceiling of decay collapsing inward.

4

Louisa- Bed and Breakfast- Welcome To Benefit City

The council office I had to visit to get a roof over my head was a short walk from the estate where Jerome and I lived in Stratford. The Council Office was a large imposing building on the corner of a main road with so much reflective windows it looked like a greenhouse. It would have made a great Cannabis factory if pot was made legal Newham Council had the perfect spot right here. A Que of unhappy-looking people was already waiting outside, shuffling their feet, chain-smoking cigarettes and some trembling for their methadone or whatever fix they needed. Nobody wanted to be there. The whole place just emanated despair and disillusionment, and you're only there because you fucked up and are desperate. People sit on plastic chairs screwed into the ground to stop people chucking them at staff who scuttle from desk to desk, avoiding eye contact with every soulless inhabitant that graces its doors. Leonie marched into the Que, standing with her arms folded across her chest, scowling at anybody who dared look our way. She always looked ready for a fight and on the defensive. She wasted no

29

time in giving me a dose of reality. "You're not the first; he has a few other pickneys around the place." I wrinkled my nose, a little shocked but pretending I didn't care. "Really? He never said," I was trying to act nonchalant. I was scared to reply to her sometimes, never knowing what reaction she would give or what response was expected. Leonie Smiled. "Well, he won't talk about that, ya know. It wasn't happy times, those girls just like you thought they had a good man, but trust me, when that baby starts screaming, and you can't satisfy him because you have just been split from Vagina to ass, he gonna start going, crazy ickle girl". She blew a bubble gum that went pop almost in my face and continued her tirade against her brother. "He won't be safe to be left with a baby, ya know?? It sets off some jealousy in him that the pickney is taking you away from him, and he starts all these delusional thoughts, and it sends him cuckoo, which happened before. I'm going to give you Wendy's number. That's his last baby mamma. She had to be moved out and now lives in Tottenham near her Mum; he almost killed her, and that pickney, ya know, when he gets like that, you have got to get away from him.".

Reality hit me like jumping into a cold swimming pool on a hot day. I woke up; this was not an escape. This was a fuck up of the highest proportion. Instead of running towards a man that I thought could offer me stability, it was the opposite. I was going to have to do this on my own.

Part of me wanted to think she was bullshitting me, like when you're a kid and you stick your fingers in your ears and hum because you don't want to hear something. But I knew with a sickening dread that it was true. The medication boxes all around the house, the ramblings he would do, the stories he would tell, the moods he would have.

I was fucked in all senses of the word and scared and now had a black bin bag full of shit clothes, no roof over my head and a crazy man as the Dad of my baby.

The smell of those Housing offices, everyone smelling of dampness and despair, and body odour, oh the great unwashed all waiting their turn for handouts, the stink penetrating not only the walls but your soul.

I should have just got an abortion, but I didn't know where to start, even with that option. Things were different back then. There weren't any abortion pills. And I wasn't sure where and who my GP was. As a teenager, I had not been near a Doctors surgery. Not that I was not ill as a child, I was, but Mum permanently cured me with homemade remedies, making it easier to hide how much of a fuck up she was.

I remember Mum having an abortion once. I sat with her while she went to her appointment so they could work out how far along she was. It was in this horrible old hospital called St Andrews. It was like something out of Victorian times, with long corridors, scary noises, and smells. I can remember Mum's relief when she was told she was just under the cutoff date for a surgical termination. I must have been 13 at the time and I remember feeling disappointed that she wouldn't keep the baby so I could have a sibling. That was met with a laugh. "You must be fucking joking; having one is bad enough. The sooner they cut this thing out of me, the better".

So all I knew about abortions was Mum's words about cutting a baby out. I had visions of being held down on a bed while a DR stuck a sharp blade inside me, fuck that; I'd have to keep this baby and hope for the best. I never knew anyone apart from her who had an abortion. All the girls all my estate kept their babies; they were the little passports to the Council flat and benefits.

When it was my turn to be interviewed, shuffling towards a bored-looking council worker who had seen it all before, I showed my documents and told my sob story. I was pregnant and Homeless. I was told I would be going into bed and breakfast. When People say Bed and Breakfast, it conjured up an idea to me of a comfy bed with a warm smiling lady to serve me poached eggs on toast. I had never been on holiday, so I had never stayed in a hotel. I had only seen hotels on TV and in magazines, so the word bed and breakfast was excellent. Would I get a cup of tea in bed? Chintzy flower wallpaper, bed sheets with Roses on the bedspread. Would I even get a newspaper to read while I waited for my eggs and bacon? A hotel sounded exciting and exotic. It would be a step up from where I was. Oh, and remember room service! Hotels would surely have that.

I left that office feeling significantly grown up and optimistic I could do this. I was going to have a Baby that would love me and be the family I never had, and things might just be OK. This might be a good thing. The reality could not have been further from the truth, and I was placed into a rough Bed and Breakfast in Forest Gate along Romford Road.

It was a busy road with many B&Bs, chicken shops, pound shops and brothels. The streets were full of lost, crazy and sad human beings. No matter what time of day, all humanity was there on that road, from devout Muslims in their robes to women covered in headscarves and Nigerians dressed in their finest clothes on their way to church. There were drunks, drug addicts, Romanian street gangs and Chinese women and men with their fake DVDs; it was a busy fucked up place where you had to keep your wits about you.

The B&B I was sent to was a converted house that must have been nice once. As soon as we stepped through that creaky front

32

door and rang the bell, I knew this wasn't what I envisioned. There was music from one room with a heavy bass sound and the noise of kids running around above us. An argument was happening in a room to the side of us, and babies were crying., It was like a madhouse.

This was not a fucking place where I would be having breakfast in bed. All dreams of it being a good move vanished swiftly. The manager, Ali, a short man with a mop of black hair and glasses who smelt of days' old sweat, smiled, showing yellow teeth.

He seemed overjoyed to find me, a young girl placed in one of his rooms. He was a pervert. He had his eye on any female that moved; that was evident. Anything with a pulse was game in his world. His smile as he looked me up and down made me shudder. My radar for perverts was flashing red, and I hoped there was something to barricade against the door like I'd had to do at home.

Would I ever, just once in my life, be able to sleep without expecting trouble? Fucks sake, evidently not. A Chair against a door handle the story of my life. Ali didn't try it on with Leonie, who immediately put him in his place. She wasn't falling for any of his bullshit, and she made it abundantly clear he shouldn't try any of that shit with me, either.

She snatched the key off him, dropped it into the palm of my hand and then departed as she had a manicure and lash appointment. She had to look good, right?.

Ali led me up one flight of stairs letting me go first so he could perve behind me. I could feel his dark beady eyes on me as I made my way up the threadbare stinking, carpeted stairs.

What was it with poverty and piss? The lifts always smelt of it in the block, and now this carpet stunk of piss. Did poor people have more bladder problems or something?

I had a tiny room on the first floor. There was a small dirty-looking single bed, a small wooden wardrobe that looked like a relic from the 1960s, and a small chair that was just the right height to go under the door handle. Thank goodness for that!

Even though breakfast was included with the room, Ali happily told me, "Residents here really prefer to cook their foods in the kitchen, so the money that is supposed to be for your food allowance goes on the gas so you can cook, you can have your Pie n mash whatever you British eat, cereals will be available OK! one word of warning though get in first for the cereals because the kids here are feral and eat them fast. They are like rats and smell like them too".

He then looked me up and down suggestively, licking his lips it was vomit-inducing. "Oh one more thing, no men in your room unless, of course, it's me" he laughed at his joke, but I didn't laugh with him, he now had little dark patches under his arms and a smell of garlic on his breath.

Filthy cunt, if I wasn't so desperate for the room, I may have just kicked him where it hurt and fled, but this would be my home, hopefully for not that long.

A small-looking girl, who I later learned was one of his wives, looked like a deer caught in headlights as she came out of the room opposite that she had been cleaning. Samara, I would learn, was her name, a quiet girl with a headscarf whose English was relatively poor. She bustled around the B&B, cleaning up all kinds of shit, bucket in her hand, clearly playing the dutiful wife, grateful to have this wonderful life in England.

Ali was always yelling at her in their language. His booming voice would make her jump, and she was timid like a mouse. I had known men like Ali all my life, the type to keep their meek women down to make themselves feel more powerful. I decided

34

there, and then Ali was no good. I'd stay out of his way as much as possible because I might be tempted to deck the bastard, and then I would be without a bed.

You could see how a man like Ali loved this setup. The council paid him to take the delinquents, vulnerable and lost and shelter them. He loved that his job exposed him to some of the most vulnerable women in society.

There was always something to be gained out of other's misery, and women who were cast adrift with no family or support were easy prey. There were refugee families crammed into rooms, young Eastern Europeans, all of whom I noticed were females. Two attractive Lithuanian girls who apparently 'Cleaned' for Ali, who looked like models, left every day dressed in tiny short dresses and make-up. Yeah, you really could clean houses in stilettos. It was pretty obvious Ali was their pimp, sick bastard. I was the only British-born person there, and my tiny room was almost like a cell. I could hold both hands out and touch the sides.

The same wood-chip wallpaper from my flat followed me, the council estate's favourite decor. This place must have been one beautiful family home years ago before they were all brought up and made into small rooms for the desperate.

My room smelled of weed even though I didn't smoke it the previous occupant must have been growing it because the smell was so strong.

And my delightful view was out onto Romford Road, which was as busy as the Las Vegas strip day or night. The curtains were so thin they didn't block out the light, and the glass windows were so narrow that the noise of the police sirens and the chaos that was Forest Gate was in my room every night.

The road was a hot spot for prostitution, drug dealing and all

35

sorts of depravity, I may have felt alone, but I was never really alone. All of humanity was right out there staring back in. I didn't need a TV as I had a window; something was always going on.

I stayed for several weeks, hardly venturing out of my room. The other occupants of the B&B eyed me with suspicion. They would talk in their own language and scuttle past me. I'd go to Jerome's to see him for a bit, then head back to my shit box room as he was beginning to seem unwell again, and the new company he had started keeping were not the nicest of people. They were using his house as some drug-cutting den, and strange people always seemed around day and night.

A pregnant girlfriend was no longer fun for him. I had gone off sex, my body was changing, and I had much to think about. I would lay in bed at night, thinking of my Mum and her pregnancy with me. Did she suffer the same heartburn and sickness?

I longed for a woman to confide in, share my fears, or tell me what to do. I tried to call my Mum, but she hung up on me. I had made my bed; I would have to lie in it, besides she wouldn't get Child Benefit now, so I was useless to her.

Four months on, and I was sick of sitting in that tiny room. I was hungry and had been living off noodles in my room because I had a tiny little travel kettle; it was easy to boil the water and eat noodles from a cup and not socialize.

I was now brave enough to use the large communal kitchen; it was time for me to sit somewhere other than my cell as I felt so trapped being stuck in there, and the bigger I got, the more I wanted the space. Being confined to one room was awful. I had to get out because I was starting to feel like a prisoner.

I'd try to get up early to get some cereal before the children of the house consumed the lot. The cereal boxes were the supermarket's cheap brands, and when I looked into the bottom of another cereal box, they were empty. Ali would chase the kids away from the cereal, "Fuck off, you get free school meals, so leave that cereal alone" He would chase them out with a dirty kitchen towel, swiping it like a sword.

Many of the women in the B&B had babies, and it was nice to watch them because they all just seemed to know naturally what to do, how to hold the babies and feed them. They would sit in the kitchen with babies attached to their breasts or tied around their waists as they cooked the most fragrant-smelling food in big pots.

They eyed me with suspicion because I was a local of Newham, and to them, I was white. In their societies, you had to be cautious of local people. Was I a drug addict? a Prostitute? or something worse? If you were told you didn't belong here and to fuck off back to where you came from, you were wary of the native amongst you, always on your guard.

One morning when I was pouring hot water onto my Pot Noodle and sitting in the kitchen reading an old magazine, an older black lady dressed in beautiful clothing appeared looking like she was going to a wedding or something because she looked so dressed up.

She shook her head at me, I thought she was looking down at me because I was pregnant, but it had more to do with the pot noodle I was consuming than my single pregnant status. "What is this thing? I see you eating here every day", She took the plastic pot from my hand, inspected it and turned her nose up at the smell.

She studied the pot noodle like it was from another planet with suspicion, like it would taint her just by touching it. I enlightened her "It's noodles that have flavour, you just pour

37

the water on, and it's cooked. It's straightforward to make its cheap and tastes nice, too" I squeezed the little bit of tomato ketchup out of the small packet that came with it, licking the residue of the powder from the noodles on my hands. She shook her head in dismay, and I held up the fork with the noodles dangling off it like I was some noodle connoisseur. Her face wrinkled in disgust, and she bent forward to smell my noodles immersed in their water cooking. "It smells odd, and the water looks like the dishwater left over in the sink from cleaning the plates. That's not food for a woman growing a baby."

I smiled; she seemed kind. "I don't have anything to cook with, and it's just me, so it hardly seems worth wasting the little money I get".

She held out her hand, and introduced herself. "I'm Glenda. Are you here alone? And What is your name?"I smiled, happy she was talking to me, human contact. "I'm Louisa, but you can call me Lou, and yes, it's just me. I'm on my own, apart from this little one in here" I patted my belly.

Glenda walked towards the industrial-sized fridge and started spooning rice from a large plastic container. It was rice that was orange in colour. I had never seen anything quite like it. She then scooped some yellow thing like a fried banana from another box. I watched her take the food from the fridge, cover it with cling film and put it in the microwave. The smell of the meal reheating was making my mouth water.

I expected Glenda to sit and eat alongside me but when the microwave went ping, she carefully removed the cling film and pushed the plate towards me, indicating it was for me, and I should eat. "You like Jollof Rice and Plantain? And here, try some pepper soup. I'll leave the soup in this tub, but it's yours, OK? You eat it, and here you have some sweet potatoes. You

38

can't eat these dishwasher noodles when growing a baby."

I then noticed that she hadn't even heated anything for herself. She had come into the kitchen for water, saw me eating my shit food, and decided to share her more nutritious food with me. She grabbed her bottle of water from the fridge, instructed me to heat the soup and left for church.

My goodness, the taste was terrific; after surviving on Pot noodles, the flavours of proper food made me instantly crave more. This lady didn't know me but was willing to share what little she had with me, making me want to cry. It must be the hormones!

That meeting with Glenda changed my life because she told the others I was OK; others then started to smile and chat with me. The older ladies liked to congregate in the kitchens, and most couldn't speak English, so we would communicate with smiles and gestures. Fatima, another angel put on this earth to support me, was a petite Somalian lady, softly spoken with so many children it was hard to know who was who.

All these women had one thing in common: no husbands or men were in their lives apart from their sons. They were all escaping some terrible pasts that were evident.

When you're a woman that has trod a hard path in life, you can sense it in others. It's just an instinct. Even if you don't speak the same language, you know the score; you can see it in their eyes.

Glenda had a one-year-old baby boy and two other boys, and her oldest was a girl called Adeola, who was studying during the evening and looking after her siblings during the day. That way, Glenda could do her cleaning job at the local hospital.

All the children slept in these tiny rooms with their mothers and siblings, crammed like sardines in a tin. It was claustrophobic, sleeping top to tail in bed bug-ridden beds. From one to another, life was shared, including disease and illness.

They always had second-hand clothes and shoes passed down from older child to younger one, they spent their whole lives never having something outright of their own, well hardly, the only time they didn't need to share was when they were on the toilet. Soon Glenda and Fatima looked after me like I was one of their broods. I had that look like Bambi caught in the headlights. I needed some nurturing and motherly love, as I was severely lacking.

Glenda took a small tin of mackerel from her bag and pushed it towards me. "These cost 60p for Skinless and Boneless Mackerel. Now listen, this is probably cheaper than what you are buying with those noodle things, and the mackerel is good for your baby's brain, so swap this noodle thing for this mackerel.".

I had never met women like this before and they made everything look easy. They could cook, clean, and sew the lovely thing was they never made me feel inferior because I had never learned such skills.

I often froze like an idiot if they asked me to peel a potato, as I was not raised around any women that cooked. Sure, my Mum fed me, but it was always microwave meals or foods chucked in the deep-fat fryer. I had not experienced the chopping of vegetables and fruits. They welcomed me as if I was one of their own, which was quite something considering all the racist abuse they suffered along the way. To take a lost little English girl who was slightly more tanned than ordinary white girls under their wing was lucky for me.

Ironically, my Savior was the immigrant community because, by now, I was starting to miss my own Mum. I wasn't sure what I missed but it was something. Even though she was chaotic and hard work at times, she was still my Mum, I tried calling her mobile again to try and reconcile, but the line was dead. She had cut me off entirely, and I wasn't sure how I could ever find her again or what the point would be.

I could go to Canning Town and ask around the pubs, but what would be the point? Some of those working man pubs were scary places. Funny, isn't it, how I was accepted and made to feel more at home by strangers to this country than those who had always lived there?

I met many women during my time in that B&B, and new people were always coming, others being moved on or running away. Some Women were ferocious, like tigers protecting their cubs, and I could see how being a Mother could go either way or the other. You could prioritize men and yourself or prioritize your children. I knew which category my Mother had fallen into, and the women I stuck with were not the cheap alcohol drinking go out and get laid types, anything to escape the monotony of their fucked up lives.

I stuck with those fighting for better because I still believed deep in my heart that I might survive this poverty-stricken life and eventually have a better one. I had to have that hope for my baby, and I wanted to give it a chance away from here; it's incredible how some of us are running from war zones to this land full of promise, but I'm in the promised land legally but with no hope.

I'm safe, but I'm not safe because despite having nothing, most of these families have each other, and that love and devotion are priceless. I don't have that. It's like jumping out of a plane without a parachute. I know nobody would catch me if I fell. I have no safety net.

As my pregnancy advanced, Glenda became the Mother I

41

needed, and Leonie stepped up into her aunty role by taking me under her wing and demanding everything for me. I had a midwife and a support worker from the young pregnancy team, and Leonie came to all my hospital appointments. She would yell about my rights and what I needed regarding benefits and grants. Or Leonie could have just been making sure I didn't divulge that the Dad of this baby was older and had a severe mental illness.

In the eyes of the law, it was Statutory rape. They would have stuck my unborn on a child in need plan before they even entered the world. Leonie told me it was all about looking like you were supported by family to the authorities, and that way, we didn't invite unnecessary attention.

She sounded just like my Mum, the functioning addict that could sit and smile at the teachers like butter wouldn't melt, then meet her dealer on the corner of our road on the way home. Functioning addicts, yes, not all drug addicts are scum bags on the street begging for cash. They are the people you see in suits on their way to jobs in the city with Charlie in their pocket, the lawyer with the see-through bag of brown to relax after a hard day.

Drug addicts are from all walks of life; some are clever or have an income to hide it. My Mother had taught me well; Leonie didn't need to school me on avoiding local authority involvement; I was the birth child of it.

I avoided the parent groups for young Mums my midwife recommended and didn't go to any Sure Start centres as Leonie told me the workers there were spies for Social Service. They would report you to Social services if they thought you looked like you were struggling.

Without Leonie's benefit and grant knowledge, I would have

been screwed. She was part of a group of women on the E15 estate who demanded better housing and services for single parents, the poor and the helpless. And boy, did she know how to use her voice. The only reason I got housed so quickly was her ranting.

When the housing officers saw her enter the building, they ran for cover. She often made appointments with the local MP and took a portable megaphone with her to ensure the voice of the young mothers was heard loud and clear.

Leonie worked hard to make changes in East London; it was like Leonie always needed a battle to fight. It allowed her to vent her rage because she always seemed angry. Without a battle to fight, what would she do? Her life would be boring.

Soon I became tired; my petite body was feeling the strain of my baby, and I stopped seeing Jerome. I think he had moved on anyway, and the rumour was he was now screwing around with a young girl who thought she ruled the area.

I was pretty happy that she was keeping him occupied because it meant he kept away from me and my baby. I spent each day seeing my body change and soaking up the warmth from the communal kitchen. I would go to Forest Gate Library to get books on Pregnancy and Motherhood, spend my days reading about what to expect, and then sit with the Families in the B&B every evening chatting.

This was the closest I have ever come to having a family. It was the most peaceful my life had ever been. When you live with a chaotic parent with arguments and violent men in the home, you are always on your guard, and you know, after a while, it's exhausting. This was my time when I could shut my tiny plasterboard government-funded door and just be me on my own with a tiny baby kicking in my belly.

43

Everyone had their take on my pregnancy and Motherhood; with so many different traditions and home remedies, it was a melting pot of advice.

We all had very little but ate together, sharing Lentil curries with beautiful flatbreads, incredible soups, stews, and rice. All from different countries but all with the same determination to give our children the very best and to live lives full of hope, happiness and, most importantly, love.

It didn't matter if you came from Yemen, Somalia, Ghana or Nigeria; we were all in the same boat. We were vulnerable and isolated but had to be strong for the children we had brought into this cold world. Every woman in that B&B provided me with Babygro's, bottles, and everything I would need for my tiny baby when he or she arrived.

Meanwhile, Jerome was in crisis, being tasered outside his house less than a mile away after creating carnage on the block. He had head-butted one police officer in his delusional state and tried to bite the nose of another. Rather than treat him like the mental health patient he was, the Police had beat him senselessly in the back of the police van, if Leonie was to be believed. Sometimes I felt she overplayed the police interaction with him, to have something to be angry about. Consequently, he was sectioned and detained in a mental health unit; he had been doing much more than weed and drinking. Jerome had not been taking his medication, spiralled out of control, and almost strangled his new beau.

I was so glad that I wasn't part of his life. Having his baby, I knew, unfortunately, meant we would always be linked, but I would always try to keep him at arm's length. But from the moment I felt my baby kick, I knew it was just me and this tiny baby that depended on me. I felt strongly I would never let this baby down. Everyone around us may have failed us, but I would not do the same to this life I was growing inside me. It was a gift, and I was looking at it now from a different viewpoint.

I felt this baby had changed me directly for the better, and it gave me something to live for. My life wasn't just about me. Motherhood had previously been sold to me as something complex and demanding, something that ensured those who had delivered you turned their back on you. I looked around at the families I was now living alongside, they did not have much, and some were new to this country. But one thing that was in abundance was love and togetherness for their children.

This was Motherhood, and it was all about love and devotion and being there for one another when times get tough. I rubbed my hand against my swollen belly and knew I had to change the narrative. Mine and my Baby's life and bloodline would not dictate who we became or our lives. I would be a Mum who cared, and I would be a Mum that ensured she did everything she could for her baby.

I would be breaking that continuous cycle of being let down. I had to be strong for my baby now because, let's face it. I had no other fucking choice.

5

Louisa- Tower Blocks Castles In The Sky

On a warm July morning, there was a hive of activity, the
hoover had been going earlier than usual and the smell of
bleach filled the air. Cleaning was never a priority in this place,
so we knew something was up because it was a Saturday and
there was so much action. Ali wore a formal shirt, and his usual
body odour was replaced with Lynx Africa's scent. Someone
from the Council is visiting us all at 11 am to update us on our
temporary accommodation. Most of us had the letter to inform
us of this pushed through our door late last night. I was too
tired to be up all night, worrying about what it could mean.

There was an air of intrigue and unrest amongst the other
families. The government had moved many of them around the
country over the years. The same land, always a different city,
another place, same problems. Just when you started to feel at
home, it was time to be uprooted again to new schools, the bull
ache of registering with a new GP again- never-ending forms
and starting your life all over.

I was rubbing my enormous belly, drinking tea with so much

sugar the spoon could stand in it, praying and hoping they wouldn't move me out of East London. I knew my area, my domain, and I prayed hard to whoever was listening, be it Allah or Jesus, not to take Glenda, the Nigerian lady or Fatima, the Somali lady, away from me. We were poverty-trauma bonded, our friendship had blossomed and I wanted to be wherever they went.

The council officer who stood in the dining area of the B&B was a short English man with ginger balding hair. He gave off the vibe of someone who didn't want to be here on a Saturday and in our company. He had a stain on his tie, which looked like a dried egg had dripped down onto it, and damp patches under his arms, the day was hot, and he was already flustered. You could tell he felt uncomfortable being here.

Whatever customer service course they put him on, he needed a refresher. We were a sea of women with children looking to him for our fate, which made him sweat. I could see him blush, the pink creeping from his neck to his jawline and then onto his cheeks like he was having a hot flush. Our untrusting eyes were on him now, the sweat beading on his forehead. We were tigers protecting our cubs. No man in a cheap suit would come in here, split us up, and move us about. We were a tribe, and we wanted to stay together. These families were sick of being moved about with not much notice. They never had a say in what shit hole they were moved on to next, and there was safety in numbers.

So we all looked at him like he was Satan come to tell us we were moving to hell. There were so many voices speaking at once, Women worrying if this White man was an immigration officer, all different languages being spoken fast. Still, all with the same underlying tone, one of fear and uncertainty.

Ali had to clap his hands together for calm before the man

47

could even begin to speak, and when he spoke, his voice sounded posh and shaky, like he was afraid of us. "I know many of you have been in temporary accommodation far longer than anticipated, and I bring good news. As many have requested, we are still keeping you in Stratford. These places might need a bit of work, but I'm afraid that's the price you pay for staying in London. We will be moving you to an estate ten minutes from here in such a vibrant and up-and-coming part of Stratford where regeneration is key,".

He finished with a smile as if he was gifting us a three-bedroom semi-detached house in Chigwell with a swimming pool. "Congratulations, I am sure you will all be so happy in your new homes, and remember now, Newham is a place to Live, work and stay! And We have some kind council officers here to help you fill out your Housing Benefit and Council tax forms and to complete your Tenancy agreements. Thank you for your time, and I wish you all the happiness in your new homes" his smile didn't quite reach his eyes. It was almost like a grimace, and before we could bombard him with questions, he left, with the sweat patches under his arm now circling the side of his shirt.

It's OK, Mr Council Representative, we are still humans, we don't bite, and you can't catch fleas off us, or maybe you can... stupid man. He can fuck off in his Volvo car, taking a high salary from the borough that keeps refugees and vulnerable women like farm cattle. It certainly wasn't a place to live, work and stay for him clearly because he couldn't get out of that room quick enough, stupid twatt.

There was excited energy in the building, new homes, and new beginnings; council officials produced housing benefits and Council tax relief forms. It suddenly felt like the last shopping day before Christmas, and everyone was excited about what was to come.

For some of us, this was our first chance to have our front doors and spaces. Many of us were escaping violent men and unstable homes. This was the first time to breathe peacefully, knowing they were safe; this was our new kingdoms.

I was busy filling in all sorts of forms and signing my name, and then I spotted the address of where we were going, and my stomach dropped. It was my previous address, and I initially believed it must have been an error.

My old address was in the new address box. I tried to correct one of the council officials, and she looked me up and down and shook her head. How dare I even question where I was going? This council officer was a typical Essex girl with straightened blond hair, the orange foundation that didn't match her skin tone, and Gel red nails. She spoke to me in such a detrimental tone, already bored with having to talk to me and acknowledge what I was asking. "That is where you are going. Carpenters Estate, Brightling Point. It is not like you have much choice, luv is there".

She looked me and my belly up and down as if I was diseased, moving her fake Chinese Louis Vuitton bag closer towards her as if me breathing near it would taint it.

She then moved on to the next person waiting anxiously with a form in their hands. How powerful she must have felt doing her silly job feeling important. Girls like that who had easy lives and then looked down on others with disdain made me angry. Well, what are you lacking in your life if you have to have a designer bag and a nice car to make you feel that you are something? Cunt.

I was poor and a single mother, so I had no right to decide where I lay my head. I felt like one of those animals shipped to the slaughter in a pen, worthless and having to be led to the destination with no choice. We are not worthy of anything, but it takes a lot of strength to survive as Single Mothers. Yet we are cast as the underclass who have disgraced ourselves by bringing our bastards into society. You're paying for my flat right? So why should I get a say on where I live?

Oh, the irony, I was returning to Brightling Point. The very same tower block my teenage Mother had dragged me up in. The one where my Mother slammed the door on me not so long ago, leaving me with a black bin bag and a cheap pregnancy test in my hand. Here we return to shared bins, shared lifts and stairwells, same clothes, still smelling mouldy, to where I thought I'd escaped.

The only godsend was Glenda and Fatima were also moving to the same block, so thankfully, my support network was going with me. The feeling that I could be moved at a moment's notice away from these incredible women and the area I knew so well it petrified me.

I only had 10p credit on my mobile, just enough to drop a missed call to Leonie or Glenda, who would call me back., I never had money to connect calls. So many families were bustling around taking toilet rolls from the bathrooms and the soaps from the showers in the B&B, so we had something to bring to our new abode, not just the black bin bags that contained our worldly possessions. Some families had suitcases that had travelled around with them and looked battered and worn, just like us.

We looked like a dysfunctional family going on holiday, yet our destination was bleak. There certainly wasn't any shiny new build flat we were going to.

The block that should have been demolished years ago loomed

ahead. These were cheap prefabricated housing built in the 60s to deal with the number of homes needed due to Newham's increased population. The block had been earmarked for demolition so many times, but with council cuts and considerable changes to the landscape in the East End, they had painted it on the outside and deemed it habitable for us.

I mean, where else were they going to chuck us? Some of these immigrant families had lived in camps. They had lived in absolute squalor, some not knowing if they would be raped while they slept in tents, freezing, wrapping their children in the clothes on their backs while they stayed cold. So for them, at least it was a safe space; they weren't like the Leonie's of the world, knowing their rights and shouting for them.

Some of these women had immigration issues, and some had Children that belonged to their sisters back home, so they lived with them for safety. They were tuned to keep their lives low-key. Like me, I never wanted to draw attention to myself; always told to keep quiet and put up with everything and never attract the attention of the authorities. We were grateful for what we were given because how could we expect anything more? The government viewed us as a stain on society, and the people paid to help us see us as dog shit on their shoes, so why would we ever open our mouths and complain? Nobody would listen.

Our voices were unheard because wherever we turned without money, we had no power, so we found support in each other. I had never seen Fatima so animated, packing all her belongings in a battered old suitcase. I hated to burst her bubble and be the bearer of bad news.

I had lived there long enough to know where we were going was nothing to get excited about. "Fatima, it's a shit hole, like honestly, I grew up here, and it was terrible then, full of

51

dampness and rats, so don't expect a palace or anything like those nice tower blocks that you see in Stratford, those nice new builds because this will be the exact opposite.

Fatima just shook her head; nothing was going to diminish the happiness she was feeling. Fozia, her daughter, beamed as she spoke, "If you had lived in some of the refugee camps we stayed in, you'd know that this is paradise; we can close our doors and not worry if we will be raped; I've had to sleep with one eye open all my life, always on the alert. My Mother can, for the first time in her life, have her own front door; when she closes it, it's just her and our family. We will never complain. We will be forever grateful for that small mercy alone" She kissed me on the top of my forehead, a small gesture that made me so happy, then carried on packing her bags, saying "Alhamdulillah" under her breath over and over.

We suddenly had our front doors and balconies; even though it was a concrete jungle we could start putting down roots. We would make it work one way or the other. No matter the state of the buildings we lived in, we would have each other, which was something money could not buy.

I began feeling all sorts of emotions as I knew I would be returning home but just on another floor. But I was returning with friends and people with a similar outlook. I wouldn't be rushing back to Mum's so-called friends, the women who drink and fight and bitch about each other.

Leonie was disgusted they were moving us to Brightling Point, saying that the others that lived there before us had complained so much they moved them out to Harlow and Birmingham, but now we were being forced to live in the shit-holes that the British-born people didn't want. Still, ultimately, the new inhabitants wouldn't use their voices to complain, whether

52

through ignorance, fear or just like Fatima being grateful to have their own space for the first time.

I would never complain because I wanted to stay where I knew everything. I didn't want to move out of the borough. The thought of that scared me shitless. I may not have had much, but I knew East London. I couldn't have coped with a new area; it would have been like pulling a rug from underneath my feet. Glenda was also overjoyed as she explained that she had prayed for a space for her and her Children. We were taken to the block in a coach while Eastern European cleaners looked at us with disdain, waiting to clean the B&B and the mess we were leaving. Ali had arranged the coach; he wanted us all out as quickly as possible. Later I learned the reason why it was because the B&B had been sold and planning permission had been granted to build upwards, and it would become a small block of flats. To pack more people into an overpopulated area, it would seem every little space was being built on lately.

I remember a few women looking afraid, thinking we were being tricked and going to an immigration center, but no, we were going into the bright lights of Stratford. But there were no bright lights and warmth where we were going. It may have been called Brightling Point, but nothing was bright and sparkly in that environment apart from all the fake jewellery on the women.

When we bundled off the coach, the children dispersed like excited holidaymakers. I noticed a few changes right away. The Council had made the exterior outside look relatively pleasant. I learned all gas appliances had been removed from when I lived there due to the Ronan Point tragedy, where a gas explosion had caused one whole block to collapse. It had taken them years to get around to doing this. They may have been structurally sound, but they still had open wooden window frames.

You won't die from a gas explosion, but your kid might fall to their death. But then again, as a single mother, that would be your fault for not watching your Child. The Council had created a play area for the children, with a caged area for football and goalposts sprayed onto the floor and a basketball net at each end. New swings with tires at the bottom chained to a metal pole. We can call it the Ghetto swing, only worthy of old tires—a small car park littered with old cars and a small community centre that was newly built that ran English classes and Baby massages and other events.

And to most of these women, the block seemed to signal freedom, but I only felt despair. It was all dressed up on the outside to look attractive to the eye, but the reality was inside, it was rotting, all fur coat and no knickers. I looked up at the tower block and felt that sinking feeling of being alone again.

Tears stung my eyes as I looked around me; everyone was so happy to have their front doors, but I wasn't one of them. When my door shut, it would signify it was just my bump and me. I wouldn't have a warm communal kitchen where people gathered to unload their woes from the day, I would have to cook for myself, and I wasn't sure how I could replicate all the wonderful foods I had tried when I was in bed and breakfast.

I didn't want my closed door to make me feel shut out and alone again. My due date was approaching, and soon I would have another human being that depended on me, and I didn't know where the fuck to start.

I was placed on the highest floor because I was more mobile than some others, and if the lift wasn't working, a 16-year-old girl could walk it, right? Even if the lifts were operational, you wouldn't want to step into the piss-smelling coffin; it made me feel claustrophobic, just glimpsing. I held the key with a bit of string around it that had my door number on number 276, holding it with shaking hands.

As I was about to descend into hell up the concrete stairs, I saw a man who looked as if he had learning difficulties pacing up and down, looking confused either that or he was a crack addict, but he looked too clean. No, he had learning difficulties. I had an instinct for these things. He wasn't on our coach, so I wondered where he had appeared from.

It looked like a few people were moving in here today. I felt for him as I felt the same; without family, it was only me and him alone, so I decided to make a friend. "Are you OK?" I asked, trying to appear kind. He stopped pacing and looked at me, confused that someone was talking to him. "I'm not sure what to do, this is my number on this key, but I've lost Cheryl, My Carer; she is taking me up to see my new flat."

Before I could take the key to look at the number and help him to his new abode, a young black girl with long dreads came running round the corner breathless, looking relieved to see him. "Oh jeez, Peter, why didn't you do as I say for once! You should have waited outside that shop, for Christ's sake! You can follow instructions, can't you? You bloody spastic, that's what you are! Now you listen to me or you won't be able to live alone".

She took a packet of cigarettes out of the blue plastic carrier bag, stuffing the fags into her coat. She thrust the bag towards him, which contained a few frozen ready meals, the cheap 99p ones, some tea bags, a fizzy drink and some chocolate, a corner shop special.

I looked at them both, confused and taken aback because this girl looked as young as me, and she didn't look like she could be trusted with a pet, let alone a vulnerable man. Her hair was gelled back tight to her head and she had long acrylic nails. She looked a bit like a younger version of Leonie and equally had as much attitude.

She must have picked up on my thoughts as I looked between them. "I'm his Carer, no need to look at me like that; come on, Peter, let's go. Let's get you settled into this shit hole so I can continue my day. I got places to be, ya know" I looked at his key, clocking the door number. "You're the floor above me, and this lift isn't working, so we must walk." Cheryl spun around. "What! Your joking, right? Do you mean we have to climb all these dog shit stairs? I've already done a workout chasing him today:" Of course, they weren't dog-shit-stained stairs. We couldn't afford to feed ourselves, let alone dogs.

Peter started getting agitated. "Cheryl, please don't swear it upsets me. You know these things. And I'm going to have to go slow because of my breathing" he looked like he was going to cry.

I stepped forward. "It's OK, you can walk with me", I pointed towards my belly. "I will be slow going up the stairs too, so just follow behind me" Peter seemed happy with that idea, and we made our way up the concrete stairwells; each block seemed to have its aroma. One smelled of onions and Garlic frying, and the next smelt of weed. I almost had the instinct to go and see who was in my old flat, but I couldn't bear to step foot on that landing in case my Mum would be standing there laughing at m; look how far I had come right back to where I had started but now on my own with a belly full of arms and legs.

Cheryl went on in front of us, connecting to whoever was on the phone, telling them she had the fags and would set this spastic pussy hole up in his new yard and then be with them in

20 minutes. This so-called Carer made me angry with her words because anybody could see that Peter was a kind soul by the way he smiled and helped me up the stairs, I decided there and then he would have a good neighbour in me. I would repay some of the love Glenda and Fatima had showered on me by being nice to him. I knew how it felt to be alone and helpless, so I made it my prerogative to make this man feel welcome and perhaps share a meal with him occasionally.

I will never forget how grateful Peter was as we made our way up the stairs, stopping at intervals to catch our breath and laughing at how unfit we were. He told me he had lived in a care home for several years, but the Council had sold it and turned them all into flats. He was deemed safe enough to live alone. He took pleasure in telling me he knew how to reheat his food in the microwave and how Cheryl would be coming daily to ensure he took his medicines, kept clean with a wash, and got his shopping for him because money was not his strong point. No shit Sherlock, it looked like Cheryl had spent most of his money on her fags.

We made our way up the stairs slowly together, and I told Peter to give me a knock if he ever needed anything. He was going to live above my flat, and I knew from past experiences how the person who lived above you could either make your flat heaven or hell with their noise that would reverberate down the thin walls. Extending that small hand of friendship meant so much to him. His face lit up, and he kept saying thank you as he walked up the stairs to Cheryl, who had the door open already inside, weighing up what she could steal.

I was tired already after heaving my pregnant belly up the stairwell. Then I counted along until I saw my door, painted blue and already peeling like an onion, revealing layers of life it had seen before. I opened the door with trepidation, unsure of what I would find inside. What was I expecting? A furnished flat and a welcome home mat? No, there was just a shell of a flat with bare walls and flooring that had been ripped out, leaving glue marks from the previous tenant's floor. Coldness and the overwhelming smell of dampness assailed my nostrils; here was my canvas; it was time to start painting my picture.

But that fucking smell followed me. Poverty, it fucking stinks. Every room was freezing, even though it was a warm day; the rooms thankfully had electricity as I walked around, illuminating each room to look at the space I had. Naked light bulbs hanging down on long nicotine-stained yellow wires from the previous tenants smoking. Cigarettes and Chip Fat, the poverty plug-in scent penetrated the air it clung to the walls. You could see where the skirting boards were supposed to be white but had also turned yellow from the smoke. The kitchen cupboards were still the same cheap white MDF board with a silver strip at the top. The windows had black mould on them and opened outwards. No way were they safe. They looked designed to be suicidal-friendly and easy to jump from. I did wonder if that was purposely designed that way.

I had a small kitchen, a bathroom and toilet combined, a living room, and one bedroom; the landscape and layout of this home were the same as my old flat, just with one less bedroom and a different smell.

This was mine and all mine alone, I could spray paint the walls Pink if I wanted, but as I closed the door, it suddenly made me feel grown up. This was what being an adult was about. Many Families were huddled on their new floors sleeping in their jackets as the flats came unfurnished, with no white goods or beds.

The flats were essentially empty shells and it was up to us to furnish and decorate. Leonie was on the case, advising us to apply for grants, and the local churches and mosques helped us. Because when you get a council property it is just the shell; remember, you're already poor but it's up to you to furnish it, and when you are just about surviving, it's tough to get those extra things you need like a bed or a cooker. Clothes and furniture began to arrive, with charities helping us by giving us all they could.

The community centre was suddenly a hive of activity. It reminded me of something that gets set up amid a tragedy, like if there had been a flood or fire. That night I ate chicken Biryani out of a foil tin container delivered by the ladies from the local mosque with a plastic fork where the prongs kept snapping frustratingly as we tried to spear the meat.

I sat with Fatima and Glenda cross-legged on Glenda's floor while I sat on an air mattress which someone had blown up for me to sleep on. All by candlelight, you might be forgiven for thinking I was in Syria in a faraway land, but no, this was London with the bright lights of Canary Wharf shining her beacon of hope upon us. I was hungry, tired and fed up, but happy we had our own front doors.

Glenda's beautiful material that she planned to turn into dresses was quickly transformed into makeshift curtains. The next day it was all systems go, with families running up and down the block to see who was living where and what items they needed. I was given a massive table, and I said no, send it down to Glenda; she had more use for it than me.

I was happy with the breakfast bar in my kitchen that was just about standing up. I wouldn't be entertaining guests for dinner, that was for sure! The women of the block were like worker

ʂ; nobody just went and shut their doors, and everyone was
ʃuded in helping the other. Poor people seemed the most
generous, with the biggest hearts and much to give.

Not only had some of these sold their bodies but their souls to
get their children to the UK, so this tower block was a palace for
them. Even though me who was British born, I knew we were
being cheated. But I was just like a ship sailing in rough seas. I
would cling to any port in a storm. Sometimes it was about the
people you were with, not what you had.

I looked across East London from my tiny balcony; too much
bird shit. I didn't know they came up this high. I'd have to ensure
I got some old CDs on a string and hung them up to deter the
birds. I knew my landscape, and that was my comfort. The flat
might be cold and smelly the area may be increasingly becoming
more dangerous, but it was mine. I knew where not to walk
after dark, I knew which families were best to be avoided, and I
knew all the schools, shopkeepers and people around that estate,
including my Baby's Dad mentally ill and deranged most of the
time, at least up here I could keep an eye on him.

It may have been some crazy fucked up place, but it was home.
The same issues that prevailed over me as a child in the block
were the same all those years on. Drainage issues, toilets that
blocked quickly, yellow water that looked like sewage coming
up through the bathtub, black mould around the walls, windows
that had gaps that were a blessing in the summer but in the
winter let the coldest wind blow in.

I ended up in the Hospital one year. I remember it vividly. I
was 5, so it was 1985 marched to Hackney Hospital for Children. I
was frozen and had got a nasty throat infection. My temperature
kept me warm, but I was hospitalised so poorly from sleeping
next to a window that had a draught. I remember my Mother

asking for a letter from the doctor to take to the council offices as I was constantly ill, but they could see a junkie with a snot nose encrusted Child.

They took the letter from her and said they would look into it. I know the housing officer dropped that letter straight into the bin, shook her head and walked away. My Mum never did see what the housing lady had done, but I did, and I knew then that there was no point they would never listen or take our views seriously.

It's tough to polish a turd into a diamond. That's exactly what our homes were like. I felt like a child playing at being a grown-up. I had to buy toilet paper and toothpaste since I was an adult nobody else would be buying it for me. There was only one bedroom, and I had already decided that the bedroom would belong to my Baby, and I would sleep in the living room. My impending motherhood status was scary. Part of me wanted to run downstairs to Glenda or Fatima and be a child with them, sneak in and sit with their own children being fed and cared for. I'm not ready for you, Baby. Even though you are kicking me every day to let me know you are coming, part of me wants to run into another woman's arms and be a child again. I'm scared I won't be able to cope if I don't know what to do when you come into the world which I guess is normal as a first time Mum.

When some money was credited to me, thanks to Leonie who did most of my benefit forms and set me up with a bank account. I felt at a loss and unsure of what needed to do. Food first or electricity? I mean, what did I do with the little blue electricity key? I dropped a call to Leonie, who called me right back and then turned up angry and vexed.

She taught me how to do the basics like top up my electric key, pay my rent on the pre-pay card, and what little money I had left was for food. Everything I had to buy had to be the cheapest, and I would scour the supermarket for yellow sticker reductions and the Value branded items, the most non-nondescript scrap-the-barrel shit you could eat.

Crazy how somewhere in this crazy city, pets would eat better meat than I was. The church Glenda went to had a scheme where they had something called a baby bank which helped mothers in need, and by the end of the week, I had a bed, fridge and cot and some secondhand baby clothes that looked brand new.

I had a scan and knew by now I was having a Girl. I loved going through all the second-hand bags of clothes at the church, looking for Pink baby dresses and blankets. Somehow having a little girl felt special like I would have a friend for life, which is the bond I see other Mothers and Daughters have. I know I didn't have that with my mum but I was determined to do things differently.

Leonie was on the case for the other items for the flat, and one night she came banging on my door with two strong men carrying a second-hand sofa. Then the next night came the oven and a man to wire it in. I was told not to ask questions, so I didn't. I happily let her help me furnish the flat.

Despite her hard stance, she never let me down. My Baby kicked me daily as if to say don't give up Mum, I need you as much as you need me. I was nesting now and cleaning up the flat on my hands on knees with bleach trying to make it homely and clean for the baby.

I couldn't understand how my Mum could have turned on me and hurt me the way she did. There is nothing like impending motherhood, and my maternal instincts made me question how my one caregiver could get it so cruelly wrong.

How could she blame me for ruining her life? I didn't ask to be born. I was never a bad child; I couldn't help being different from her white racist family. My own mum couldn't have resented me just for my skin colour? It's sad, and I had known more love in those six months away from her than I ever knew in my entire life with her.

My neighbour directly next door was Fatima, the older Somalian lady from the B&B. Her flat was always full of children and babies. It was hard to know who was who; she had several sons and an older daughter who had recently given birth to her 5th Child. There was always laughter, the ambience of togetherness, and the most amazing smells from her cooking.

Fatima is still, to this day, one of the kindest Women I have ever met. She would give you the last morsel of food off her plate if you were hungry, and she was always there for me whenever I needed her. Fatima's English could have been better, but she helped me immensely, bringing me mint tea meals with rice and meat; the women always cooked in bulk and helped keep our tummies full on a budget.

More bags of clothes for my baby girl started appearing, and also maternity clothes for me. Fatima's daughter also shared her Mother's kind and caring nature. She helped me pack a few things I would need for the hospital in a plastic bag and sat with me many evenings, telling me what to expect when my Baby finally arrived. She even volunteered to be my birthing partner, but I had already decided I wanted Glenda or Leonie.

It struck me that the immigrant communities helped each other more than the natives. The women would give advice, even in languages I wouldn't always understand, but they were passed on to me with knowledge and wisdom, having been there. We sat in flats full of absolute shit and squalor, but we had won the lottery regarding friendship and tight bonds. I mean, there were still some people in that block, older women that had known my Mum and me, but they never even glanced my way. I'd rather be sitting here on the floor, crossed-legged, eating rice with the faces of genuinely caring people than sitting in designer labels in a posh home surrounded by cold-hearted white bastards.

Glenda's flat was below mine, and I felt safe having these women around me; it was like a cocoon. Glenda always cooked massive batches of Puff Puff which I had become addicted to during my pregnancy, Pepper soup, jollof rice and my favourite, Plantain. Glenda joked my Baby would be born expecting Nigerian cuisine. If it weren't for the generosity of this community, I would have gone through my pregnancy eating cheap rubbish. It was another culinary world I was discovering with my new neighbours.

I was shocked to learn these women had jobs and were going out to work and raising families. They got jobs as cleaners at the local hospital; they worked long hours and for very little pay but they all had a strong work ethic.

These women didn't just sit back and take government hand-outs; they worked hard, leaving their homes at 6.30 am to break their backs, cleaning up the shit none of us wanted to do to support themselves in a country that did not welcome them.

Think of that the next time you talk about immigrants because not many British people are cleaning those floors. Thank goodness for their generosity because I was penniless.

After paying my electricity on the key meter and getting the basics, I didn't have much. I didn't even have a TV license. I remember when the inspectors knocked, convinced I was hiding a TV; sorry, Sir, I can't afford a TV. Getting a stolen TV came many months later.

The day my waters broke, I crawled next door to Fatima. She

had just returned home from her shift at the hospital; it was 8 pm, and I heard her footsteps as she made her way to her flat.

I had been in pain intermittently for most of the day, not wanting to believe this was finally it. Then I decided I would go to the hospital as the pain wouldn't stop, and it was worsening. Again I was living life with the mindset that if I blocked it out, it wasn't happening such a foolish idea when a baby was boring down on my vagina and my contractions were becoming stronger.

As soon as I saw Fatima, I fell to her feet in relief at seeing another adult; the cold night air made me suddenly terrified, the pain was worsening, and I genuinely felt I would die.

Fatima's daughter Fozia heard the commotion and gently led me back into my flat, explaining that she had done this four times before and everything would be fine. She didn't seem much older than me, yet she had an air of confidence.

She called Leonie, who arrived 24 minutes later, kissing her teeth and telling me she had been on a date with a hot man before I disturbed her. I can't remember much more, but Fozia asked me where was my hospital bag. My what? I didn't have a hospital bag or even own an everyday bag. What was a hospital one? I had a plastic carrier bag with a few bits in- A bag for life, ironically for a new life, as it turns out.

I was bundled into a car god knows whose and driven at speed to the Hospital. The rest is a blur of Nurses and people in scrubs and then me being told to push, and the rest feels like a dream gas and air and I was flying.

My beautiful Amelia Louise Doherty was born on the 1st of September at Newham General Hospital. My life was changed forever after seven hours of labour and a third-degree tear. I was officially a Mum! I gave birth alone, just me and the midwives, who kept asking if there was anyone they could call for me.

Luckily Glenda and Fatima worked in the same hospital and could swipe their work ID badges and come in and see me. That's the lucky thing about being a cleaner in the NHS you can walk anywhere in the hospital undetected. Something clicked when Amelia's angry little face looked into mine. She looked furious with a scrunched-up little face as if to say how dare I bring such a beautiful soul into such an awful environment. I couldn't believe someone so perfect as my Baby would be returning to live in such a horrendous block. I kissed her button nose and curly black hair and made her a promise I would never repeat the mistakes that my Mother had made.

I lay in that hospital bed, all pain forgotten, smelling her new baby smell, marvelling at how beautiful she was. I counted her little fingers and toes and when she curled her tiny little hand around my finger I felt the love for her flow through me.

It was hard to believe that me and Jerome could have created someone so perfect. I was adamant I would get us out of that block and try my hardest to give her the life she deserved. Whatever happened, she was my little girl, and I would always protect her and love her. The feeling of protectiveness I felt for this tiny human being, I couldn't put it into words it was ethereal.

Glenda and Fatima brought me everything a new mother would need, large sanitary towels, Babygro's, and bottles for the milk I was expressing, and it was like a cover-up bundle. I would have looked wholesomely unprepared and not ready to be a mother. I think the staff assumed that Glenda was the Grandmother as she was black and my baby was mixed race.

The way Glenda picked up Amelia so lovingly you would have thought that too, the look of love and adoration she had for her, marvelling at her tiny body, my biological mother god knows where. I was visited by the young Pregnancy team and given some leaflets for Mother and Baby groups. I smiled politely, then chucked them in the bin. I knew how to play the game to keep the professionals happy and smile; everything was ok.

Jerome came to see us the same night I delivered Amelia as he had just been discharged from the mental health unit, or maybe he had escaped. He had the cannula in his hand where they had given his medicines through the drip. Leonie just kissed her teeth and whipped the cannula out of his hand as if this was something every day that she did.

I was terrified as I watched the trickle of blood trail down his hand and his crazy eyes asking to hold his Baby girl. Jerome held Amelia in his arms, and I suddenly felt the need to get him as far away as possible, as if he could taint her just by breathing near her. I couldn't wait for them both to leave so Amelia and I would be in our little bubble that didn't involve a mentally unstable Dad. Leonie must have sensed my unease as she made some excuse about me looking tired, and then thankfully, they both left. I knew there and then I had to get Jerome out of our life some way, but that would be easier said than done. I would have to keep on the low and hope I just became another one of his Baby Mamma's. The only good thing was I had delivered a girl, and I knew that Jerome liked the idea of a mini him, a son to carry on his name. Motherhood, how you changed me; I was a tiger protecting her little cub; things were different now; I had to grow up fast. It wasn't just about me anymore, this tiny precious bundle. Amelia only had me, just like I only had her. It was time to put my big knickers on, fix my smile step up to this game called life.

6

Louisa- Stolen NHS Blankets

The day I brought Amelia home, the weather was humid and the air heavy, the type of weather that created the type of pressure that could give you a headache. People fanning themselves with newspapers waiting for the storm to clear the air and for the heat to dissipate.

As I stepped outside for the first time since becoming a Mum, I cradled my bundle as close to my chest as possible. I didn't want her to breathe the polluted air or hear the drunk man swearing obscenities at the hospital security guard as he was being marched out of the hospital. I tried to shield my baby, I wanted nice sounds, sunny weather and flowers to welcome her when she took her first breath of the big world outside.

To the right of us were blue skies and sunshine, and then to the left was a grey rain cloud heavy with rain, complete contrasts. I could sense a storm was coming; the weather was replicating my life. There may be sunshine, but we have a storm ahead to march through.

This shit hole area was not suitable for this beautiful baby, with her perfect little hands and toes having to be swaddled in stolen blankets to return to that awful flat. It didn't sit well with me. It was like growing a rose in a bed full of weeds. She was just too beautiful to be tainted by that life, but what choice did I have?

Leonie had arranged for a taxi to take us home. I was still sore and had a cheap car seat Leonie had found, which I reluctantly placed Amelia in. I had a bag full of tins and breakfast cereal packets, which Leonie told me I was to leave in my cupboards on display so that when the health visitor visited, I would look stocked up, and prepared like I had this all sussed out I knew how to be a Mum, I had my shit together.

Welcome home, Amelia; our welcome committee was the immigrant older mums that picked you up like experts, Kissing and showering you with so much love. Glenda's youngest was Leon, who was one-year-old by now, and we would lay you both side by side while Glenda and Fatima imparted their pearls of wisdom about raising babies.

I felt so at home with my baby attached to my breast and women sitting cross-legged on my floor. The women all brought me so much food parceled up, and I had never seen my fridge that full in my life. I was finally one of them, the mother-hood tribe, I had joined the club. I had membership; I was somebody at last. I had an identity.

Adeola, Glenda's eldest, would bring little Leon in to sit with me while she did her Uni work and Glenda was at the hospital cleaning. I thought she was amazing how she managed to study and work just a year older than me. I was in awe of her. "You can do this too; you know" She always encouraged me. "I don't think so, Ade. I mean, I left school with nothing because of my pregnancy. I chose the Motherhood path, not the academic one." Adeloa shook her head. "But that doesn't mean you just chuck your life away. I mean, I'm with the Open University doing my degree. I also came here with nothing because we were in

69

refugee camps for most of my childhood. If you want something, you have to make it happen". She left me a little booklet on the study options, but I chucked it in the bin.

The University of Life was the one for me, not anything academic, even though I wished it could have been. I couldn't do anything now that Amelia needed me, and it would take all my strength to get us through the day without putting study into the mix. Girls like me from council estates with teenage pregnancies didn't go to University which was a fact! We knew things, like what benefits you were entitled to, what flat sold crack, or where to go to get knock off goods, but any other knowledge was way over our heads.

The good thing with the block was there was no pretense, and people were what they seemed, down to earth and willing to help. I didn't need to be embarrassed that all my baby products were hand me-downs or from the basics range of the supermarkets, nappies so cheap they caused my baby's skin to turn her bum red. They showed me what genuine kindness was. I only found true kinship in people suffering or had been there themselves struggling every day to survive they gave what little they had. Glenda and I had such a bond. She taught me so much about being a mum to Amelia; I wouldn't have survived those early days without her. Glenda taught me how to latch Amelia onto the breast. If I was tired, she let me sleep, looked over my baby when she came home from her work, and gave me nutritious food. They say it takes a village to raise a child, which is so true. I will never forget those first days and nights at home with Amelia when all my well-wishing visitors had gone home. I breastfed her and kept looking at her in the middle of the night, not quite believing she was mine. I kept expecting a social worker to knock on the door to say give her up. She needs better than you can give her, you really don't deserve this precious life.But that knock on the door never came, and I know I had

70

been warned about the dangers of co-sleeping. But I couldn't bear to put Amelia into the cot on her own in such a cold room, so I slept beside her.

I used the stolen baby blankets from the Hospital to pad out the windows and stop the cold draft from blowing in. And we slept together in that small single bed with second-hand quilts and pillows as flat as pancakes, and I would kiss the top of her little head and sleep the most peacefully I had in years, feeling her little heart beating next to mine her smell had the same effect as Lavender it soothed me and made me calm. I must have been the only Mother coming out of the Hospital with bags heavier than when she went in. I kept hiding the blankets and towels they gave me so I would have extras when I went home. The white towels in my flat all had Property of the NHS written in blue, a perfect reminder that I had to take what I could. I did try to steal the toilet rolls, but do you know they are locked into their dispensers with a key, so that was a no-go.

Those early years with Amelia were hard, there was no mis-taking that, we had little money but they were also some of the best years of my life. I know I was still a child myself. I still had the word teen in my age, but I changed so much as a person. I wanted more, I began to visualise a better way to live, and I wasn't going to get it by staring at four walls daily. I certainly had no interest in taking on a man, I wanted it to be just me and Amelia. I sat looking through the Newham Recorder newspaper job section. Now this was when shit got real, I needed a job that would work around school hours, and I needed one that didn't require qualifications. I also needed a job that didn't pay that much so I could get my rent and Council tax topped up. There were plenty of 9-5 positions, but I would need something else.

I needed something where I wouldn't have to pay out for childcare as that would defeat the whole object of getting a job, paying someone else to be a mother to my baby.

When Amelia started school and was in reception full-time, Glenda convinced me to come and interview for a cleaning job at the Hospital. There were always vacancies, and the hours were 7am-3 pm and overtime if and when I wanted it.

 Glenda had it all worked out. I could drop Amelia off to her in the morning, and Adeola or Fatima's daughter Fozia would walk all the children to school. I would be home by 3.30 pm to collect Amelia, so everything worked perfectly. And for my mental health and sanity, I was escaping the four walls that seemed to be closing in on me more and more every day, and it wasn't like I had money to spend. My life was depressing enough as it was. I had always wanted to do Nursing since I was a kid. I know it was only cleaning, but Glenda said if I worked hard and got my face known around the wards, it could lead to other opportunities. If I worked hard, I could become a healthcare assistant, potentially leading to doing some NVQ training and then Nursing.

I remember visiting one of Mum's friends in the hospital years ago and being amazed at this tall black lady in her starched Uniform making everything better. It was like she was an angel, it always stayed with me, and I remember telling Mum I wanted to be a nurse, to which she replied, "You need brains to do a job like that, and you ain't got any". Thanks for the vote of confidence, Mum. I was eight at the time. Ain't nothing like your role models to build up your confidence.

So I went with Glenda to her place of work at the big local Hospital the last time I visited the imposing building I was delivering Amelia. I chatted with her supervisor and was told I could start on Monday. That was an informal interview, thank goodness. They were desperate for staff and gave me the early

72

shift, 7 am to 3 pm, perfect. The woman who interviewed me was Diane, a lovely old East End lady who joked it was nice to have someone who could understand English on the team. She was a down-to-earth woman with a heart of gold; little did I know further down the line; she would be one of my greatest allies. So I was up early Monday morning with anxiety running through my veins. I made myself a coffee and drank only a tiny sip before

I had to go running to the bathroom, where I had an upset tummy. I was analysing everything; would I know what to do? I know it was just cleaning, but this was a big deal. It was my first job, and suddenly I felt afraid. I didn't want to let Glenda down as she had recommended me, I wanted to do her proud. Luckily I was shadowing a lovely lady called Svetlana (Lana) for short; she was 60 and a charming lady. She was blunt and to the point. She showed me how to unblock toilets with hot soapy water because waiting for the maintenance team took forever. She showed me what mop to use and what all the different signs meant on the cubicle doors. It was a shock at first to enter a room where someone was sick, as I had never seen this before, people with tubes coming out of their bodies. Me mopping around them as they fought all kinds of diseases, and we didn't just go in with our mops; we got to know them. We said Good morning and chatted with the long-term patients, it was nice to talk with them, but the work was backbreaking on your feet all day bending and pushing mops and buckets.

73

Amelia liked getting up early and running downstairs to Glenda or Fatima's flat next door, I forgot how being an only child with just me and a crazy Dad would be so isolating. In Glenda's or Fatima's, homes there were always so many Children running around playing together, sometimes there was tears from spats but there was so much fun. I could see how she liked the togetherness of family. I felt guilty at times I couldn't give her that. Walking to the Bus stop, there was a whole tribe of us going to work at the Hospital. We were like one big messy, happy family muddling through life together. That bus was full of different languages and various cooking smells on people's clothes, we worked hard, but I was happy. A block full of kids and adults helping each other out.

We shared food, clothes, and birthdays, just balcony after balcony of supporting each other. Now at that time, there were two different camps of women that I was around. At the school gates, some women thought it absurd to work. Most of these girls were the ones I knew from years in the block or had gone to school with. For some women, it was far better to live off the state, get everything paid for and spend your days sipping cheap wine and chatting up men. Cheap fags, tracksuits, chicken and chips and estate bred men were the order of the day. They got their Greggs sausage rolls on the way home from the school drop-off. The all wore the big gold hoop earrings and gold clown necklace dangling in-between their cleavage and gold necklaces with their names on 'Tracy, Debbie, Sandra, Karen' just in case they forget their names or needed reminding, it made them all look identical, the chav uniform. Every council estate in London had the same women that looked like that, whether it was East, North, South or West.

Amelia and me would lay together every night telling each

other about what we had done during the day. Ame would be full of painting and playing with Lego and I would tell her all the funny people I met and how some nurses had big bums, that made her giggle. My life had opened up, what would I have told her if I had stayed home all day? Well watched Jeremy Kyle, then Good Morning TV, had a cheeky wine at lunchtime, and then napped before I collected you from school boring and non-descript. I no longer felt claustrophobic with walls closing in around me, and I loved a routine, or else I would have gone mad like a prisoner trapped in a tower block with no money.

What could you do – walk in the local park with the drunks and junkies? No way- walk and do window shopping in Westfield to look at everything you can never afford. Hello Waitrose and shiny shops, how you taunt me.

The ironic thing was Glenda told me once on the way to work that she had been a Midwife in Nigeria, but those qualifications didn't count here. So she mopped the floors for a pittance and had ten times more knowledge and experience than the white, educated University all paid for middleclass midwives that had a salary triple her amount here in the UK. It was more important to Glenda that her Children study and achieve than herself, and it got me thinking about Amelia's future.

I hoped that Amelia would want to go to Uni or make some-thing of her life. I had never grown up around people that did anything more than drink and reproduce, and suddenly I saw there was more out there. I felt it was too late for me, but for Amelia, I hoped there would be a way. I can't say that financially I was better off working, but I did relish the routine as an adult more than I did when I was young. I loved setting my alarm, getting my Uniform ready, and conversing with other adults and people like me who were trying to make a living. I was proud of

75

my Uniform, which I ironed every night, the Iron brought £2 from a charity shop.

I made new friends, and I chatted with patients. I felt more like a human being, not just singing baby songs to my child I was someone, I was an employee. I was a Mother and a Worker rather than just a single parent, I always had negative statuses attached to my name- Unemployed, Homeless, teenager mum but not now though I was a worker I paid National Insurance contributions. The little wins! And I was asked by another human being, "How are you?"; I had an identity because, for years, I felt like I had no positive identity.

I still belonged to a city of Food Banks and cast-offs. I began to rely on the women in my work circle to top me up with the essentials like deodorant, sanitary towels, tea, and coffee, which were necessities but a little expensive. Anyway, our lives went on like that for a few years. When Amelia was in primary school, life was easy, we got free school meals, and she had a lovely upbringing in the block. On summer nights, I would sit on my balcony out the front on my plastic chair with all the other mums chatting to escape the city's humidity. We were such a tight-knit community.

If it were a kid's birthday, we would all come together to make sure someone baked the cake and someone cooked the rice; we were all one and together. Don't get me wrong, we still had the crime and the poverty, but things started to change the older the children got. It seemed people experiencing poverty were rising and wanting better, there had been riots all over London. A black man had been shot dead in Tottenham and it sparked great unrest. people started looting and people were angry at the Police, people had enough of being held down held back just because of where they were from and the color of the skin.

76

I remember Jerome becoming increasingly out ⟨
during this time all his pent up frustrations at the police came ⟨
the fore he was a dangerous man to be around at this point.
Then in time coronavirus struck, and things got mad again.
For us working in the NHS, there was no lockdown, the whole
country lost their minds and stayed home, but we had to wear
our uniforms and go to work. We were treated so good for the
first time in years, I can remember we had allocated shopping
time at the supermarkets as long as you had the NHS ID you
could jump the que.

But even though people applauded us it was still scary going
off to work and into an environment others were scared of. I
had to clean room after room dressed up in a white gown like
space suit to protect me and a plastic shield over my face that
nobody ever taught me how to use. Nursing and Medical staff
got the low down and the testing to see what masks they were
compatible with, but not us. We were cleaners; we were unseen.
We had the personal protective gear chucked at us and had to
get on with it. I just put my scrubs and mask on and went to
the ward, where there was a room full of personal protective
equipment. I stumbled about for the first half of my shift before
I saw somebody peel off the plastic film on the face shield. I had
been working with the film on my face shield, meaning I could
hardly see. Nobody ever taught me the correct way to gown up
and take off the stuff or even how to put it on right.

Cleaning in such an environment with all that protective gear
on was unbearable. It was so hot the mask would make my
skin sore from sweating and rubbing. So at first, we wore all
the equipment they could chuck at us, and then within a few
weeks, when the personal protective stuff started running out,
the rules began changing. We only had to wear masks and gloves

in certain areas and save the whole kit for aerosol-generating procedure rooms and Nursing staff were prioritised.

We would turn up at work and hope for the best, and it was unfortunate because one of our colleagues did pass away from Covid. It was quite a shock to the system; it could have been any of us. We see so much pain, suffering and death, loved ones dying without their nearest to them close by.

I never forget one woman, Grace, who was an elderly lady dying in the corner of the ward, unable to tolerate the invasive Oxygen machines. She was begging me to give her a little sip of water. I spent most of that shift sweeping up and mopping by her bed just so I could comfort her. The nurses were so busy that the older ones who wouldn't make it were pushed to the side, left to die quietly in side rooms and corners of the hospital bay. It was the younger ones that took a lot more work.

I never forget just before my shift ended, walking over to her bedside to say goodnight and noticing her eyes were open, but a film had clouded over them, and she wasn't blinking; her mouth was open, gaping like she was in shock, she was dead. I had never seen a dead body before, but I knew she had gone. I broke all rules. It didn't even enter my head; I could have caught Covid myself.

I was being stupid, but human instinct just took over. I put my mop down, and I kissed her goodbye. I prayed that my kiss on her cold head would be of some comfort to her before she was shoved into the blue tarpaulin-covered gurney the porters used to take the bodies down into the mortuary such a horrible-looking thing. I always wondered why there wasn't something nicer.

But I guess you couldn't have anything that looked like a coffin being pushed around a hospital it would be pretty bad for

78

business. Just another body, another one to go to the mor but I knew this woman must have been part of so much more. It saddened me to think she had her final breath alone, in a hospital overrun with madness with no loved one by her side except me, a stranger in a mask smiling down at her, to kiss her goodbye. She never did see my real smile it was hidden behind the mask. It fucked my head up for a bit that this woman's last moments on this earth were alone, gasping for breath, surrounded by nothing but strangers looking like they were in space suits.

How scary and sad that must have been. She probably survived the blitz world war two shit and yet she died alone surrounded by strangers whose faces she couldn't even see. It was a crazy time when we had respect, and people put banners in their windows for the NHS workers. They clapped. They appreciated us. We were doing everything the regular working people were afraid to do; finally, we were noticed.

Amelia was in year six at this time, her primary school prom was cancelled, it sounds terrible but I was secretly relieved as I was dreading finding the money for the prom dress. I was lucky as a key worker that Amelia could go to school but it wasn't the same, and it was easier for me to pretend she had someone looking after her at home than get her to go into school.

The real world started to open up after the lockdown when you could shut your kid alone all day and avoid social interactions. People were like butterflies coming out of their cocoons, ready to show themselves to the world again and what a world it was. Going from primary to secondary school was like cotton wool to barbed wire.

When Amelia hit secondary school, she changed overnight. Amelia hated secondary school; it was like the safety and comfort of her primary school was long gone. secondary school was a tough place on the estate, things really did change drastically. Suddenly Amelia hit puberty like a small bird crashing into a wall. She changed from a compliant baby robin to a machine-chattering Magpie always on the defense, grunting her replies to me and answering back. Suddenly she didn't want to help around the flat, and she didn't want to be seen with me or around me.

I became the moaning Mum, everything that I said or did was wrong. Jerome suddenly became the fun parent, the one to allow her whatever she wanted and if I tried to instill discipline I was the bad one. Good cop ,bad cop and I was definitely the bad cop. Suddenly Amelia had new trainers and a new phone and cash which she said Jerome had given her. He was up and down with his mental health at this point so I never made contact with him to see if it was true that he was funding Amelia's new lifestyle.

After one of my shifts, at the hospital I returned home to find Amelia distraught with Leon, Glenda's youngest boy trying to calm her down. In between sobs, she told me what had happened. "Mum, they tasered him, I tried to tell them to stop, but they wouldn't listen. They kept saying he was aggressive and violent, but he wasn't. He was just unwell." My stomach went over. I had tried for so long to protect Amelia from ever witnessing something like this. I had seen it before and I knew how scary it was to watch. The story unfolded, "the Police have taken him away. He was shouting and causing problems. I saw him on the way home from school. I think the shopkeeper had called the Police, Dad had no shirt on and was swearing and wouldn't listen to me. It was as if he didn't know who I was." Leon looked towards me, and momentarily it was like a stranger in our flat, he had grown up so quickly and the boy who he once was had gone, he was turning into a man, but I could only just see him

80

as a little boy. His voice had broken and he sounded so different "Aunty, I told her, Police ain't going to sit and talk with a black man in a mental health crisis; they go in all guns blazing. It's always the same if you are black; there is no talking you down. The feds do not give a shit" I was just about to start telling him that wasn't true, but what did I know? He was the one who had been stopped and searched most of his life just because of his colour. He moved off the sofa, sensing I needed time alone with my baby.

I got up and walked him to the door. "Thanks for sitting with Amelia I appreciate it. Listen, Leon, I appreciate what you did today bringing Amelia home and ensuring she was ok. You're a good boy. Keep on the right track. Don't let anything change that." He smiled at me, I could still see that little boy of Glenda's still in there somewhere but he looked older and somehow more streetwise. Leon's eyes looked as if he had already seen too much of the world, and since when did he topple over me in size? I know Glenda worried about him.

He certainly was nothing like her other children who went with her to church and studied. I could see on his face he was already lost to some unknown lifestyle. Suddenly it occurred to me that they may have been more than friends but I dismissed it, they were more like brother and sister growing up together. I always worried about boys on the estate and I was thankful that Leon and a few of the others like Fatima's older boys would look out for Amelia. Not a week would go by without knife crime hitting the headlines the inner cities were becoming awash with gangs peddling drugs. The crazy thing is I had grown up around an addict. I knew the signs, and none of these kids were doing drugs. I was pretty sure of that. They were too clean, too concerned with making money. These kids had designer probably fakes, but they all looked fresh, and that .. . .ne stance of addicts. In some ways it was harder to have a Son on the estate because it always seemed to be young boys that were being stabbed. We never heard of any Girls being caught up in Gangs.

I think because a lot of us parents didn't understand it we never really knew what was going on under our noses. SnapChat, WhatsApp the world was changing incredibly fast and for us parents we were just about managing to get by with what we had. Amelia wouldn't settle until she knew her Dad was ok, so we sat up until 11pm then Leonie called to update us. Jerome was now sitting in Newham A&E with a cut to his head and was going to be sectioned and taken to a mental health unit.

That night I lay with Amelia in her bed it was nice to be close to her for a change. We hadn't chatted like this in ages, she was full of anger, this was her first experience of police and mental health. I held her while she sobbed at the injustice of it all. "Mum it makes me so angry. Mental health is not something you can see like a physical ailment, I was trying to tell them that my Dad was ill but they just piled in on him like animals, they didn't even care they were hurting him, they just went at him like a pack of wolves" What could I say to that? It would never change, when Jerome let loose he was out of control, the police were never going to take him any other way. I tried to calm her down "I know, my lovely, but it's just how it is... When you Dad gets unwell people don't stop to look at the bigger picture its always going to be that way. I'm glad Leon brought you back home you and him seem close?" Amelia rolled her eyes, I had said the wrong thing, the nice moment was over I was back to being the interfering Mum, seriously it was like skating on Ice with teenagers, one minute your talking fine and the next crack-you say a wrong word and then you're out. "Mum, please. If you're going to start with a lecture, you can go. I've had enough for one night...my head is pounding and I want to chill" I exhaled I had to say it... "I just want to make sure you are safe; I know what it was like to be a teenager with an empty flat. And how boys can pressure you into things you might not want to do. Are you having sex? you have to be careful." Amelia put her hands over her ears. "Ugh, Mum, you're so embarrassing...No, I'm not having sex. Can you go now? I want to relax" She turned her back to me stuck her ear pods in her ears listening to music our conversation over and we had been chatting so nicely.I fucked up again by saying the wrong thing I didn't feel I could do anything right by her lately.

I needed to work extra hours to get more money because things suddenly became more expensive. I didn't have to rush home to collect Amelia from school at 3.30pm. She had the freedom of walking to and from school on her own which secondary school brings. Our Electricity bills all went up, food prices suddenly shot up. War was being raged between Ukraine and Russia and that's why life was more expensive or so they said? Covid fall out well whatever it was, life was suddenly harder for everyone. Amelia's secondary school uniform was double the price of the cheap supermarket ones you could pick up for primary school. The Uniform all had to be branded with the school's logo, I went along to a Second-hand clothing bank, much to Amelia's embarrassment, but she wanted Kickers shoes too, so I said it's one or the other that's brand new, the blazer or the shoes I can't afford both. She opted for the second-hand Uniform as wearing Someone else shoes to her were abhorrent. So I took the extra hours at work to compensate for Amelia having a shit life and to keep our heads above water. If Amelia wanted branded trainers,

I would ensure she had the trainers, I wanted her to eat food that was good after spending so many years myself eating utter shit. It didn't matter that I was taking meals out of bins at work to eat for lunch to save money. I had to ensure my Amelia was happy, and as a good parent making sacrifices for your child was something you just had to do.

I was broke as soon as I got paid the money went in and back out just as fast. Everyone I worked with was in the same position I wondered if this was the better life that people came here for? Could we still dare to dream that we might one day work our way up to something better? What would break first our backs or our dreams? But was this it? Stealing food off of the leftovers on the Hospital catering trolley? The food was bad. We were eating slops, the same meals ironically fed to prisoners, from the same outsourced company that supplied cleaners and catering to the NHS. I can't tell you how stealing little sugary biscuits from the patient's afternoon tea trolley stopped me from fainting on the hot wards, as sometimes that was my only food for the day. It kept me going.

This same outsourced company raked in millions but the workers never benefited from it. I worked with Nigerians, Ghanaians, and Eastern Europeans. I was the only English-born worker in that cleaning group, but they were like family to me, an oversized mixed-up family with everyone helping the other. You would have Svetlana from Lithuania cooking Beetroot soup for Glenda from Nigeria because she liked that soup. Glenda reciprocated with Nigerian delicacies for Svetlana, and they took it in turns to boil each other an egg for their breakfasts so cute. We became the working poor as the cost of living began to bite, and many of us went to food banks, let me tell you, some of the hardest NHS workers, your cleaners, your healthcare assistants that did the genuine primary care like washing and feeding your mothers and Dads in Hospital they were the lowest paid. A Band 2 salary was the lowest in the NHS. In 2022 it was £20,758. It hardly stretched anywhere. It was the minimum wage, By the time you paid all your bills, you were left with pennies, especially in London, one of the most expensive cities in the world.

I would come home at 8 pm, absolutely exhausted after being on my feet all day, Amelia would be home, but I could tell at times that she had just got in. Sometimes I thought I could smell weed or alcohol on her, but if I ever mentioned it to Amelia, all I got was backchat and pushed her further away. So some nights just to have peace and not an argument I let things slide.

That is the problem when you're a single parent, and everything falls on you. You have to work but also provide the emotional stuff, the material items your child wants so badly. You have to split yourself into a thousand different people in one day as a woman, you are labelled with many different roles and judged for all of them. Woman, Housekeeper, Worker and Mother, and quite frankly, it's impossible to flourish in all roles. But I didn't want Amelia to have the relationship that me and my Mum had. I didn't want to have that atmosphere in the home where you were always waiting for the next argument and fight and the silliest of things could blow everything out of proportion.

I'm embarrassed to admit that, at times, I preferred being at work rather than being at home with a moody teenager. As a child of a broken home, it was strange how women like me built homes with unsuitable men. I often wondered, was this out of desperation for stability a loving family? One thing I knew when I was younger and with Jerome, I did love him and dream of the perfect family setup. I just inadvertently brought all the

85

trauma of my childhood with me. It was like I packed up all the chaos of my early life in a suitcase, and it came with me into my adulthood.

I tried to be the opposite of my Mother but felt I was still doing it all wrong. Those early years were so easy compared to the teenage years when I would know Amelia had gone to school and then played outside on the block, always in my sight. I always knew the friends she kept and how her day had been. Teenage years are just full of angst and mood swings; they were indeed the most challenging times of Motherhood. You had a child that started to look like an adult, but was still your baby. You wanted to protect them but equally you knew this was a time of allowing independence.

Our block suddenly felt unsafe to me, I started to notice groups of teenagers more and when I passed them I would cast my eyes wondering who I recognized. When the local news came on I had to turn it off, I couldn't change my landscape so what was the point in getting myself wound up and scared about all the things that could happen? Parenting a docile child to a teenager was like putting your hand into a lucky dip you just never knew what you would get, you just had to close your eyes and hope for the best

7

Louisa- School Days, Coffee Breath And Insecurities

When Amelia hit year 10 of Secondary School, things changed massively. Suddenly there were more shoes, clothes and items around the flat. Amelia suddenly had perfume and make-up as if she worked full time in Superdrug. She had three mobile phones and her trainers were all box fresh.

Now this is when I got the worst parent of the year award, I had a slight debt that I owed. It was for the Oven that I had to buy off the catalogue because ours had stopped working. Now when you go on those catalogue websites, and suddenly you're accepted for a credit limit for all these nice things. Well, it's like Christmas. I could order my Oven and I chose the cheapest one and a new Microwave. Getting it on credit meant I was going to pay way over the odds, probably five times over. I mean how the fuck did I even pass a credit check I don't know? But I did. I thought it would be OK, and I would do some overtime, etc.

It doesn't seem a lot when you're choosing the twenty then thirty pounds a month payback over five years. It all seems manageable until it isn't. And that's the funny thing with debt, the more you owe the more interest you pay and soon you are fucked with mountains of debt to pay.

So I was defaulting on the money for the Oven and microwave and had the threat of Bailiffs at my door.That's when Amelia left a chicken Box on the table one night but there was money inside of it. Now I know what you're thinking. Why would you think this is right? What an awful parent I must be, to take cash from my daughter?

Firstly, she said she got the money from Jerome, she said he had been awarded higher level disability money due to his mental illness. Deep down I had a feeling that it wasn't true, he wouldn't have shared any extra money with us, but you never know a leopard might change his spots.

You may all judge me, but it was nice to feel I could breathe for a bit. I'd hate for Bailiffs to take the items we needed to survive. I'm embarrassed to say Amelia was helping pay the rent. I always said a bit of extra money and next month I won't take it, but then something would come up.

One week I cracked my tooth and needed root canal work I had to pay for it because I was working, something was always needed, and the envelopes would appear again with the cash.Housing benefit only went so far and I was enjoying this welcome reprieve. Judge me when you have gone without meals and had a stomach growling with hunger pains.

Please sit in my seat where I've had to use toilet roll as a sanitary towel because the £1 for them could be £1 towards pasta that could be boiled and used as food. Period poverty, hey, it's real, to be a woman and bleed is expensive.

I'm already feeling like I'm living on edge for taking the money from Amelia. So when I'm sitting outside on the grass outside the hospital in work enjoying my half an hour break when the

School rings me it turns my stomach over what has happened?. Secondary school telephone calls are different to Primary school ones if your kid pukes or falls they call you, secondary school calls are for serious shit. It took me a while to realise it was my own phone ringing, usually Amelia would txt I had an old phone an old Nokia. The drug dealers loved them; apparently the pay-as-you-go sims as they were untraceable. But I'd just had the same one for years, a leftover from one of Mum's blokes. I had never wanted an iPhone or anything snazzy because I liked living on the low -key.

I never really knew any of Amelia's Secondary School teachers. They were just voices on the phone, Unlike Primary where I knew them all by name. So the call is about Amelia's attendance or lack thereof and how they have asked Jerome to provide medical letters and doctor's appointment confirmations for her absences. They must have known by my stuttering and confusion that I had no clue Amelia was absent so often from school.

I was clearly none the wiser. I was really showing myself to be a real mother of the year here wasn't I? Not even aware that my Child has been missing school, often taken out of class for appointments by Jerome. I was actually gob-smacked when I heard that and part of me wanted to hang up the phone and call Jerome and ask him just what the fuck he thought he was playing at.

But I knew that would be like a red rag to a bull and would have been an absolute disaster. He could come to our flat and cause us so much drama, I didn't want Amelia to see that again. I knew to choose my battles wisely with Jerome.

The teacher asked me if everything was OK at home, and I said of course, even though I was only home to sleep and then get back to work, fuck! more guilt single parenthood sucks. See the dilemma? You need money, but you need time at home I was caught between a rock and a hard place I couldn't win. Oh, there was more -Amelia had changed they said, she was more disengaged and getting into more trouble by answering her teacher's back and not being the good student she once was. This all hit me like a fucking thunderbolt, I was stunned and knew I had to keep it together and act in control. It was as if they were describing somebody else; this was not my daughter. I almost wanted to double check they were talking about the same girl.

Now I hate schools and teachers, actually, let me rephrase that, I hate secondary schools, those large imposing buildings full of boisterous kids. Schools still made me feel anxious and put me on edge, just as they did when I was growing up.

The smell of the paint and the reception areas full of happy colourful displays and School Offices always seemed to have a nice glass fish tank.

Those feelings of inadequacy all stem from my own Childhood, where living on edge wondering what was going to happen next created such a heightened state of alertness. It created an adult with low self-esteem and fear of authority. That now would have manifested itself as a feeling pretty worthless and that everyone was looking down on me and waiting for me to fail.

I thought back to the girl who helped me fill out my forms when I was in the B&B from the council office. She was my age but had a layer of confidence, and she had nice clothes and makeup and a designer bag, was it easier to feel more confident when you had a mask to hide behind? Or was it because she had a Mum and a Dad who instilled confidence and the ability to feel like she could go and take life by the balls because she was worth it. Girls like that, shone in their loving families with their freshly shampooed hair with their adult caregivers buoying their confidence so they could step out and be fully functioning adults, without a single drop of self-doubt.

My low self-esteem made me feel fucking bad at the best times, I was constantly worrying about things that had not happened yet it was just in my DNA. I was running through worst-case scenarios. I rushed to my work supervisor's door and had verbal diarrhoea. Diane told me to stop and go and sort out whatever was needed, but she would be grateful if I could come back to work and finish my shift because it was Eid, and a lot of the staff was off celebrating.

Diane didn't know I was scared because I had taken money off Amelia. I didn't know what can of worms the school had opened, I was actually afraid to consider that Amelia was involved in bad things. I felt scared what would they do to me if they realised I was not a good enough Mum which is something I had always felt?

My teenage years were spent sitting in an office just like the one I was in now, and I used to play truant a lot, so was eventually excluded. I ended up in a PRU that's a Pupil Referral Unit because I couldn't handle School.

So the school smell and the children's running around, immediately made me feel sick, even here now as an adult I felt like I needed to run. I got labelled a delinquent because I couldn't cope with mainstream School but I was incredibly misunderstood. Nobody ever asked me what was behind my delinquency, and to be honest with you, it was a vicious cycle because my evenings were always disturbed with fights or drunken drug feud brawls at home, or occasionally my Mum having a meltdown at the state of her life.

So I was tired when I got to School, which meant I couldn't concentrate and fell behind on my studies, and then I was teased for being a tramp, so I just hated that toxic environment. Now I felt scared that Amelia might be going through the same without me even knowing.

The stress of Jerome might be affecting her more than I realised. So I made my way to the School and this was the first time I had ever been inside Amelia's Secondary school. I signed into the School Office which had as I predicted Prim and proper office staff looking at me with sympathetic smiles. I already knew what they must be thinking of me, in my black jeans and cheap T-shirt, I was about 20 minutes too early for the meeting, but I didn't want to be late. I sat in the waiting area on display flicking through a Metro paper that was left there. Yes, I can fucking read I felt like saying to them I'm not illiterate, I may have fucked up at being a good Mum but I can read.

Those type of women are just like Dr's receptionists, and they sit at their desks looking across at the fallen that grace their reception areas. And you may wonder why Jerome had not been requested to join the meeting. No way, he was a liability and if the School knew what he was really like, then Social services would have been involved, and god help us with the consequences.

Jerome was stoned a lot of the time or psychotic, and mostly both. It was getting to the point where people would stop me on the stairwell to tell me some of the things he had done. He was a massive liability and was the reason I was sitting here in the first fucking place.

Mrs. Oxford a white middle-class woman dressed like an old hippie came to greet me and welcome me inside the school. I jumped up like I had been burned then immediately regretted looking so foolish and eager to please. Mrs. Oxford was in her 50s She gave the air of a woman still trying to look young. Another lady was in the small room I was led to, she was the deputy head, Mrs Knight, another white woman trying to be something she was not. She even had on an African-shaped necklace and weird-coloured beads all up her arm. OK, we are in multi-cultural Newham, so I'll give her the benefit of the doubt. And last but most certainly not least, diminutive Mrs Douglas, the welsh safeguarding lead with a face that immediately made you feel like you had done something significantly wrong.

They all sat round a large white desk, and I felt like I was the Child back at School waiting to be reprimanded and not the parent of a teenager. I felt like if I didn't give the correct answers, I'd be told I was staying behind for detention. It was that kind of vibe that they were the ones in power and would be telling me what do and highlighting all where I had gone wrong. It was like I was a Kid again, teachers with coffee breath and disdain for the kids who were misbehaving but little did they realise the kids rebelling and misbehaving were the ones who needed them the most.

I feel as though I zoned out, I was suddenly remembering when I was younger in an office like this being shouted at and wishing that I could have chucked the desk in the air and shown the teacher the bruise that I got from the night before from fighting with my Mum. I was having a flashback of that time, and Mrs Oxfords's voice calling my name finally snapped me out of it. "Louisa? Are you ok? You seem to have gone a little pale".

I nodded that I was ok and let them continue talking; if I'm being frank with you, I felt petrified. All sorts of words were being used, and I needed clarification on their meaning. The

School had a behavioural tariff system where if your Child reached 13 points, that meant they were excluded. Coupled with Amelia's continued absences from School, they were worried it was heading in this direction. They even knew about Jerome's mental illness. Multi-agency working got to love it, professionals gossiping about how shit our lives had become. They share information with other professionals to help safeguard the children.

Apparently, Jerome's social worker had alerted the authorities that they had spotted her in his home during school time. Which altogether was not a crime but had raised some concerns. Jerome's neighbours had alerted the local authority that Jerome was out of control, he had teenagers in and out day and night and they were worried that drug dealing was taking place from the property. Do you see how these sneaky bastards operate? I didn't even know who Jerome's social worker was she had never contacted me and here she was gossiping to the School about my Child! Bastards always stick their noses into people's lives, meddling where their shit opinions aren't wanted.

I'll be honest with you I suddenly wanted to cry. I was pretty embarrassed that while trying to get Amelia and me out of this fucked up life on the block, Jerome was pushing us further back into it. Leonie and my Mother's words echoed around my brain "Once you have Social Services in your life, you never get rid of them" I felt like a deer caught in headlights. Was I going to go under the car or run into the forest? I didn't know what way to turn, and I knew one wrong move now, and our lives would never be the same.

Did I want to have child protection plans and more meetings with women who didn't have a clue about our lives? Mrs. Douglas, with her Welsh accent, sounded firm, and her face was squished up. She wasn't a beautiful lady; coupled with her harsh Welsh tones, she was formidable. She looked like one of those foetal alcohol babies whose mothers drank during pregnancy, and she had the most magnified glasses on her face that didn't help make her a beauty queen either.

Despite that, she warmed towards me a little "Don't worry, lassie, I'm pretty certain some input from Families First or even some parenting programs like Triple P would help you no end, courses that help with strategies for dealing with teens, getting them to co-operate and back into the school system, I know it's not easy the teenage years are the hardest of them all." I looked confused at all of them. "Triple P? What? I can't do any courses, I work long hours, and If I don't work, I won't get paid. And we need the money right now".

Everything felt like a trap. Should I even have admitted that I take extra overtime to ensure we can eat and heat so I'm hardly home? Zero points to me. Mrs Oxford felt she could put her two penny worth in looking me up and down. Because of course, she knew what it was like living on a council estate as a single mother. Her voice when she spoke was soft and patronising. "You may need to re-evaluate your lifestyle to ensure Amelia has proper support at home. Can you drop your hours to ensure you are home to support your daughter more? Amelia is a clever girl; it would be a shame to see her chuck her life away. We can refer you to the Citizen advice drop-in sessions to help you budget better. Would that help you? Perhaps the local food bank can also assist?".

I suddenly felt angry did they not realise that I didn't have money to budget with? We were purely surviving as it was! My salary went on bills, my credit card was for emergencies, and my overtime was for the little extras such as nice food, and when

I say nice food, I mean buying a branded item rather than the supermarket savers bottom of the barrel shit. Try budgeting with that! And as for the foodbanks, when was I going to crawl to them?

I was fucking working long hours until my back broke Saturdays was for washing clothes bending over my bath where I washed them by hand then hanging the washing over my balcony; I could never rest. I couldn't take a pay cut to stay at home. If anything, I would have worked more hours than was legal to put more money on our table.

Maybe I should have become a brass because I was getting fucked over no matter how I turned. At least I would make more money if I laid on my back. No, Louisa, I told myself not to go down that route because that was a step too far.

Did they think they knew even a second of my life? This was the most enormous pat-yourself-on-the-back bullshit I had seen in a while. I had to lie, think on my feet, and say my Mum helped me out, and I had many friends who supported me. Me and Amelia were going to be ok one way or the other. I had to make sure of it.

I knew how to play the game and what to say to these women so they could congratulate themselves on helping people less fortunate than them. They could go home to their semi-detached houses, drink their red wine, and feel good about themselves for working in the inner city helping these so-called lower-class women. Our lives must have made such a great topic of conversation for their dinner parties, discussing the East End women over their hors d oeuvres.

It was the typical white Savior's behaviour to feed their middle-class egos where they could be smug that they didn't have a life like mine. But I wasn't in the mood. I smiled and then, like an actress, agreed to all the self-help parenting bullshit they wanted to hear.

Boxes ticked, they could fuck off home to their perfect lives and Farrow and Ball painted walls, kitchen islands with bowls of pasta and prawns, leaving my Kid and me to eat our basic range meals from the microwave. And they didn't want the hassle of filling out a new social services referral on a Friday at 4.30 pm it's a pain in the backside when you have dinner plans that evening in a fancy French restaurant. And I knew that because I had heard them discussing it as they led me into the room, So I swerved that for now, promising that Amelia would be in School every day. I would attend the local community parenting classes at the local community centre. It was so much easier for them to hand me the leaflets job done.

So while I was mopping vomit-stained floors in the hospital and being spat at by crazy patients, Jerome was getting Amelia out of School and helping her run a trap house. Now I was oblivious to all this until much later on. I had no clue what the word cuckooing meant. I never believed for one second that my Child would be involved in taking advantage of Peter, our neighbour that lived above us, who I always told her to treat with kindness.

I never wanted to believe my daughter would get involved in something like that; it's not something I understood. After that meeting, I sat at home and cried tears that fell because I felt so alone and wished I had somebody to share this anxiety with. A partner or family member to offload, how shitty it was to have a child misbehaving and how money was so tight you weren't sure if this was propelling your child to make money in a very bad way. I knew I had Glenda, but I feared she would get fed up with me and walk away one day. If my blood had done it, then anyone could, I didn't want to burden her with my problems.

I was miserable! In a desperate situation, and I just wanted obliteration, for the first time in my life, I could understand why my Mum liked to escape with a bottle or whatever drug of choice she had to hand. Instead, I returned to work to finish my shift as I was scheduled to work until 8, and it was only 4 pm.

I briefly chatted with Amelia, and she made me a promise that she was now going to behave. She seemed excited and happy about something, not sullen and remorseful like usual. She told me she was going to a friend's house to celebrate Eid with them and would be back after sundown at 9 pm at the latest. I didn't disagree. I wanted this happy aura of hers to continue rather than me push her away again by laying down the law. "promise me 9 pm right? We need to chat, Amelia, I'm not going to nag you, but we can't have the school breathing down our necks like this, your dad was wrong to have taken you out of school" "Ok..Mum, I promise 9pm I will be back, let me just go and eat with a friend first, and then I'll come home, I promise you, no more messing about, hand on my heart". She kissed me goodbye leaving the residue of sticky pink lip-gloss on my cheek and she was gone.

It was 4pm now and I knew I should really go and finish my shift as I was due to finish at 8 pm. I rushed back to the hospital, feeling dizzy, and realised I had nothing to eat. I had to again steal some biscuits from the patient's trolley, hide in the toilet and eat them quickly, hoping the sugar would get me through my shift.

As I got home after my shift I went under the shower for a good 20mins as if I could wash away the stress of the day. I sat outside and was surprised to see Fatima sitting outside, too; Fatima came and sat next to me to enjoy the cool night air. She was escaping the excited shrills coming from her flat; she had been frying samosas and now needed to cool herself down. The smell of frying on her clothes made my belly rumble. I sat on the broken white plastic chair outside my door, looking as cracked as the chair I was balancing on.

The funny thing was, without me even having to say anything, Fatima knew that something was up, and it was undoubtedly to do with Amelia. "It's not easy raising Children here" She felt my pain as if it was her own, her hands squeezed mine tight they were covered in orange Henna. I knew that actually she was in the same situation as me a little lost.

Except Fatima was a religious woman who instilled those same morals and ideals into her Children, but with each generation in the UK, she could see the more Westernised they were becoming. Fatima's youngest boys were getting into more trouble at school. Fatima, not knowing good English, didn't understand the letters coming to her home. She struggled to understand the concept of Britain's schooling system, and she was still very much the outsider in this land that she thought would give her Children all the opportunities she never had. Fatima's sons seemed to now speak an entirely different language to her. They saw a quick way to make money and rebelled against their Mother's Strict Islamic practices. Fatima had no clue how her Sons made their money, but the rent was paid, and she had money for food. She needed to understand the landscape of urban living and Gangs. She was an older Somali lady whose life revolved around her family and Grandchildren. They were her Everything. Eid was a celebration for the family, and the boys gifted their Mother over £1000 in cash.

They told Fatima they had been helping in an uncle's shop. That's how they got the money.Fatima's boys were way over their heads. At least she had the excuse of English not being her first language and being in a land so different to what she had been raised.

I didn't have that excuse; London was running through my veins. I sat and wondered how many other Families on the estate accepted money from their Children to pay rent or feed hungry tummies. These Children were changing overnight, they were bigger, harder and entering a new world that was already becoming unknown to us.

Different slang words, Apps, Snapchat WhatsApp so much stuff online that us as parents had no clue about. Deep down, I knew cash in shoe boxes, and Chicken Boxes were not legit, but now with School and god knows who else watching our every move it was time to take a step back and not accept the money.

8

Louisa- Sanitary Pads, Microgynon And Hoods Riches

When a child does not return home there are so many conflicting emotions that run through your mind, fear, anger and then despair. I was terrified something may have happened to Amelia but also angry that if she was rebelling and staying out to cause me stress and wind me up then I would seriously consider taking all her phones and chucking them over the balcony.

It was now 10.30 pm she should have been back at 9 pm and she is not picking up her mobile even though I am continuously calling her over and over, she must have at least 35 missed calls by now. You would have thought that alone would have irritated her enough to just pick up and tell me she is running late.

The later it's getting the more anxious I'm becoming I am biting a 5mg Valium in half to take the edge off the unease that is cursing through my body making me feel sick. Every mother on that estate had their emergency medicines, Valium and Vodka, for when something awful had happened, it was the council estate equivalent of a first aid kit. Oblivion on an estate comes in many forms, but for me, I never really wanted to become like my

Mum so I was always cautious of getting too zoned out always ready and on the alert.

That's what happens when you live a life of trauma and heightened anxiety, You always needed to be on your guard and don't ever fucking let that guard down because that's when the bastards attack. It's now 11 pm and that's the latest she has ever been out and not to make contact, something is not right and a million different scenarios are playing through my mind.

A sick feeling of dread in my belly something is not right, call it a mother's instinct but something is off. Her second-hand school uniform is discarded on her bedroom floor. Amelia's mobile phone that I brought her still charging by the bed, but the SIM that I use to call her is not in that particular phone so I know she can see all my missed calls.I swipe under the bed and pull out her Nike Air Max box which she thinks I don't know is there and see the three mobile phones have gone. There is some cash in there and also some tablets but I will discuss those with her later, I just want her home.

Now the problem with being a single parent is that you have no other person to help in times like this. One parent could wait indoors while the other roams the street, it's safety in numbers when there are two of you.

If I have to call Jerome it will be the last resort because I never know what version of Jerome will turn up, either crazy Jerome or Normal Jerome, depending on if he has had his medications this week. Sometimes he would just cause so much more drama it would not be worth the risk. All of a sudden I'm panicking looking over the edge of my balcony, I can hear and see youths below playing basketball swearing and shouting, but none of them is Amelia. There is a bunch of girls huddled on the swings but I know, none of them are Amelia. I know the sound of my child and I know the silhouette of my child, and I always rely on my instinct and my instinct is now alerting me something is off.

The noise of the city, trains, buses, sirens it's never silent and I'm closing my eyes, can I hear Amelia in this noisy city that never sleeps? It's like I'm trying to home in on where she might be in this concrete jungle. A million thoughts scramble into my mind. Has she been hurt? Is she in danger? Every siren, shout or sound I link to her, the sounds all become so jumbled when you're trying to hear just one tiny voice.

Every scenario is running through my mind it seems that Stratford can be similar to Beirut some nights. And the money I had happily received in the chicken and chips boxes, I mean what kind of Mother was I? If anything has happened to her I was to blame, I felt sick, Amelia where are you? And all the new trainers and phones she has she says her Dad gets her as he always upgrades them. I suddenly feel old and off-balanced, I'm no longer streetwise I've just been going to work scraping by and coming home again oblivious to the outside world.

Suddenly I could see things clearly say if Amelia had got those new items another way? But No I couldn't allow my brain to go down that track, besides I would know wouldn't I? I couldn't think about it. Maybe I should have asked for help today, maybe I should have broken down to these teachers and support workers and say actually I'm not coping. Would a parenting course really teach me how to be a better Mum? To deal with the stressful situation that is now prevailing in me. Would the techniques they taught really make Amelia start to toe the line and be a model child? But No, I didn't need any more authority involvement, sticky beak women with their Cath Kitson rucksacks and bottles of Pellegrino water telling me how to raise my child.

I suddenly replayed the conversation about budgeting my meagre wages from that stupid teacher. Like that fat cunt could understand that I had days living off stolen white bread from the hospital kitchen to stop my belly rumbling, that's great for filling your belly without substantial food. Love the compliments from people on how I remained with a nice figure after having a child, yeah simple- I didn't eat!

This is what burying your head in the sand does, looking the other way and not confronting what's right there in front of you. It was my way of protecting my brain from cracking up, and now look where it had got me, well and truly in the shit.

A Daughter that was spiraling out of control and I wasn't sure how to put the brakes on. I pick up the photo of Amelia that I had made into a canvas a few months back she has long curly black hair beautiful caramel skin and almond eyes a mixture of mine and Jerome's genes – his purely Jamaican and mine Pakistani and English. She looks exotic and beautiful; I know all parents think their offspring are beautiful but I know that Amelia truly is.

This little girl whom I promised so much to has grown away from me and it's all happened in the blink of an eye. Treasure your babies when they are young and you can take them to the parks and the children's parties where you stand around drinking tepid tea with the other Mums. Enjoy those boring kid's parties with the jugs of juice and nuggets and pizza because when they get their independence and go out on their own and you don't know where they are it's terrifying and a whole new world. You will never be standing in the School Playground again watching them play, it all just changes so fast. So what do you do when your fifteen-year-old daughter doesn't arrive home on time? Call the police who will not really help, another ghetto child is a missing person it's only the white semi-detached housed children we look for. No I wasn't going to call the old bill that would be the absolute last resort.

And as ever in my time of need I ran to the woman who lived one floor below me, Glenda, my rock Glenda's was the door that would be opened any time day or night with no judgment, even if it was just to tell me I was being stupid and Amelia was just being a teenager. I needed reassurance from another adult that my child was ok and I was overreacting. A problem shared is a problem halved right?.

I ran down to her floor below in my sliders, I could smell the aroma of food cooking, fish frying, smells that told me Glenda was in her Kitchen cooking no matter the time, if one of her Children was hungry they would be fed.

I looked through Glenda's kitchen window to see her chatting and laughing with Julius and Adeola who towered over her, while one fried the fish the other chopped a tomato. The sight made me catch my breath because they all looked so happy.

Strong family bonds, shared times that were precious, they had it all without even knowing they had it. You know when something you want is within touching distance but you're still a million miles away from it. This was like window shopping for a family and I wanted to join this one. They may have been eating cheap cuts of meat and Glenda may have been on her feet dusting the NHS wards since 7am but the love in that small kitchen was incredible. You could have all the money in the world but that love is priceless it's not something that money can buy. If you offered me a million pounds or to have that love and belonging, I'd take the love. You probably think I'm bullshitting but I'm speaking the truth, what I was witnessing in that kitchen was something that we all truly needed at the end of the day a connection, security, stability and knowing these people had your back.

Even though it had gone 11.pm I was welcomed, Glenda's oldest boy Julius opened the door, the great protector of his domain. When he saw it was me, I was instantly welcomed, I was ushered into the tiny kitchen and made to feel as if I was entitled to be there. Nobody would knock on these doors after 11pm unless they were in desperate need it was tower block code. Glenda's oldest Children were always so polite, they always called me Aunty, and they knew respect I wished I could instil the same into my child, but Amelia was used to City life; these kids were shipped back to Lagos if they ever misbehaved so knew to respect their elders.

Glenda knew immediately something was wrong, "Glenda help me please, it's Amelia she hasn't come home, and she is not picking up her phone. I'm so worried this isn't like her" Glenda sat me down with a gentle hand, "When did you last hear from her?" It all came out then, the school meeting and how she had been skipping school, and she had promised me hand on heart she would be home. "Is Leon here? He might know where she went?. She said she was going to an Eid party but she didn't say whose?" I asked hopefully. Julius pushed a plate of food in front of me "I heard music coming from your flat around 4.30ish, it was the same time Leon left; he came home, showered and then he went out. They could be together. Let me try and call him" Julius went to get his phone while Glenda encouraged me to eat, I hoped Amelia was with Leon.

Glenda placed a bowl of food in front of me and encouraged me to eat, "Now sit and eat. You look like you're about to collapse. Julius will find her; she is probably just with a friend. You know how these kids can be; Leon is also not home yet" I tentatively

106

swallowed the food as my belly was rumbling now, reminding me I had not eaten anything much that day, and the Valium was making me feel a little calmer. Or it could be because I was with another adult. I felt safe in her presence like another adult might have the answer to what I should do. "Thanks, Glenda, honestly, I don't know what I would do without you. I just feel like everything is going wrong" The tears that I was holding back fell. I had been holding it all in so much I had given myself chest pains.

When the tears fell it was almost like a relief. Glenda pushed more food from the pot onto my plate, encouraging me to eat. "Shh... just eat the food because an empty bag cannot stand upright, you need to eat, or you're going to collapse and then be of no use to anyone" I hope that Leon and Amelia were together because the thought of her being out this late with god knows who and doing god knows what! Maybe she had taken something, maybe she was drunk, so many scary things I was conjuring up. It had only been 15mins, but time stretches on forever when a child is missing.

Without realising it, I had eaten the bowl of food, and then Julius was there sitting and putting his trainers on. "She's on her way back, I made a few calls, and she is just coming into the block, although I have to warn you it sounds like she may have had a drink".

The relief that washed over me was instant, she was safe, she was alive and if she had a little drink then that could easily be forgiven. I just wanted to touch her, smell her and know she was safe. I felt almost lightheaded as I got up to return home where I would wait for Julius to bring my baby home to me.

Glenda walked me to her door. "Louisa, no arguments tonight; deal with her in the morning, you're exhausted; when she is home, go to bed" I just wanted to lay my head down and sleep, the Valium was making me feel spaced out, and I hated it, I would never take this shit again I hated feeling out of control.

I was sitting in my plastic chair outside my flat, the night air was now making me cold and I was shaking, it might have even been the come down from the adrenaline of the evening. I heard the lift clunk its way up the block and when it opened on our level I was so happy my baby was home.

Julius was right she looked like she had been drinking, her clothes and hair looked completely dishevelled and she was holding her hands across her face as if she was trying to hide her face from me. It was dark on the landing as the outside lights were not working again, and our flat was in darkness except for a small table lamp in the lounge. "Amelia I have been so worried, where have you been?" "I'm Sorry Mum" just three words and then she ran to her room slamming the door shut.

The Vodka, Valium and the meal Glenda had given me all made me feel sleepy. Glenda was right I didn't want an argument tonight so I just collapsed onto the sofa covering myself with a blanket.

Tonight I could breathe Amelia was home; she was safe from harm. I had to be up at 6 am for work it was time to try and sleep. This was Motherhood, something I always dreamed of, a little person to call mine, someone to always rely on me, our little family. God, how did I ever think this would be easy?

I Sometimes had these moments when I would be working and I would forget my responsibilities and it was nice, I'd just be a woman cleaning and listening to the conversations of others, remember as a cleaner you are unseen; you don't count. I sweep, I empty their bins and they talk as if I'm not there because to them I don't exist and that's nice that escapism the world outside is left behind and I'm in my work mode.

Some people go on holiday to escape but, I go to work. One thing that I thought of before I closed my eyes, was no more envelopes of cash, I couldn't accept them from Amelia this was definitely the last time and I know I had said that before but it had to end.

9

Amelia- Red Wine, Lip gloss And A Burner Phone

I dry retched into the waste bin in my room. No more vomit left to come out; my stomach turned inside out, just like my life. Julius's face when he saw me rushing towards him said it all. I looked like a disgrace; I felt like a mess. I was 15 years old, yet I felt older. I had aged so fast in the past two years. What a lot of shit I had gotten into, and I was in too deep before I could say this was not for me.

Let me start at the beginning of how I ended up fucking up so badly and on a one-way path of destruction. I stayed hidden off the radar until I turned 12; Secondary School was a turning point. I blossomed quite literally and therefore was on the radar of boys. Estate boys would equal trouble as who you caught the eye of was linked to postcodes and gangs and all the crazy stuff that living on a council estate brings.

If some of these boys took an interest in you and you rebuked them, that could mean that level of disrespect would result in retaliation. Everyone liked to keep fac; even some girls bossed around like men. If you caught the eye of some of the top boys, then it was a safe bet, you had protection, and you were alright.

I was always part of the E15 crew and Leon's circle. Leon Mensah was my Mum's best friend's son, and the Mensah's were like the closest thing to a family we ever had. So it made sense that I would run with him and his crew. We were like blocks vs blocks and estate vs estates. My postcode and location dictated who I ran with. Your association was like your passport and you would not go into enemy territory without backup.

Leon and I had always been close. I loved him because me and him were on the same level. He was Mr Tough on the street, but behind closed doors, I knew the real Leon. He was a year older than me and always had girls hanging around him, but he and I were tight; we shared a lot, which was deep.

Both our Mums worked as cleaners for low wages, and he understood how complicated life was for me with a mad Dad. He never patronised me or held it against me that my Dad had mental health issues. To some on the block, it was a joke and something to be ridiculed. You know when you have something in your life that other people can mock you with. Many a time, I heard people chatting shit about it behind my back. It made me angry, but I ignored it as much as possible.

Growing up in this block meant you had to look the part. I like nice things, and cheap clothes and trainers were a no-go. I wanted to be unique; to be someone, you had to take that stance or be the odd one out. The feeling you have when you part of that crew is powerful- this was like the family I never had. A problem shared was a problem solved. Suddenly I was part of a network that had my back and cared for me. If I needed money, it was there. I was living the life. With Mum working long hours, these people were my family. Soon I had food, new clothes and a little bit of weed and alcohol, and that was better than being alone.

My Dad Jerome had always instilled in me that the Police were evil. I had seen them Taser and beat him when he was in one of his mental health crises, so I knew from Dad that protection would never be from this route. Many of the local boys would talk of the unfair stop-and-search policies and the beatings they would get. Mum also instilled in me to never trust anyone in authority. It could be dangerous. The people in authority never understood us or our lives. They caused trouble and removed children from their homes. The truth was if you were black, broke and had mental health issues, you were already at an incredibly poor disadvantage.

I had my Dad's relatives that would step in and out of my life like my aunty Leonie, but she was one fierce bitch, and as for Mum's family, forget that I never even knew them. I only knew that racism was rife in that family, and I was not wanted there, nor was my Mum, so a fuck up of a biological family all around. My Mum was a good woman, but she worked long hours and had nothing to show for it. She would bleat about how she wanted a different life for me, but I didn't know how she could realistically change anything. We had no money for the basics, so how could I compete with others? I'd always be the one wearing the cheap hand-me-downs, but I wanted more.

I started seeing young boys and girls on the estate making ready cash just by moving drug packages around. Some were going as far as Cambridge for the day or Brighton. It was easy in your school Uniform nobody batted an eyelid, and if you were a young girl on your own, then you were ripe to make ready money. When elders ask you to do things, saying no is sometimes hard. When you see the money, you get that nod of respect because you're trusted enough to carry it. It makes you feel good. I had nice things and good food like Nandos and McDonald's, and I suddenly felt connected to people and wanted and needed. That's how it starts. It's easy money; no one will say no to that.

When one of the elders took over Peter's flat just above our flat, I was angry until I went there and saw how happy he was with his Beano magazine and the fish and chips he got daily. He liked having people in and out; they all treated him kindly. That was important to me. I had to ensure he was ok. And you know they looked after him incredibly well and treated him better than the Government paid carers who were ripping him off. So The people I rolled with became my family because I did have an ingrained fear. What would happen to me if my Mum ever got sick or I lost her? Who would I have? It made me feel so scared, so I was desperate to branch out and have the security of a second family.

I think Covid made that hit home for me, my Mum had to go to work, and when I saw the news and all those people dying and the whole world fell silent, it was scary. I didn't see my Mum much throughout that lockdown, she worked longer hours, and she didn't get any extra money for the shit and the stress it caused in-fact she would have been better off claiming benefits-yeah, work that out, Mr Prime Minister I remember when Mum came home, she was afraid to kiss me, rushing straight to the shower and putting her uniform in a hot bath to sterilise it.

I was home alone for most of that lockdown. To get fresh air, I would step out onto our balcony; for once, it was like a new city. It was as if the earth had been given five minutes to breathe. You could hear the sound of birds, but no planes or cars; we were scared to leave our front doors. Remember that the first lockdown was hard for those who didn't have lovely gardens because we were trapped in our castles in the sky.It was at this time that Leon and I started having sex. We were both worried about our mums working on the wards and found solace in each other. Remember when we all clapped on our doorsteps for the NHS? Well, the first Thursday we did that, the block went wild. Every flat had someone who worked in the NHS as a cleaner or a porter. Low-level, low-skilled, low-paid, yet many of the migrants that did these jobs were highly educated. They just had Countries that were not safe to stay in, so they left to come to the Green pastures of England, ready to work their ass off for shit Money to try and make something of their lives. My Mum walked through the door ten minutes after the clapping had finished with tears in her eyes. "Mum, did you hear it? Did you see the people all out on the balconies?" I rushed towards her, and she pushed me away. "Yes, that's why I'm crying. It got me all emotional; let me shower first, Amelia. I don't want to bring no germs home to you". Crazy times when suddenly the cleaners and NHS workers were the heroes. I remember Mum sneaking home some toilet rolls in her bag because people had gone crazy buying up loads of it in bulk, and she worried we would run out. I wished I had told her then I was proud of her, but I Was a teenager, and that would never happen.

Amazing how the NHS went from people clapping for the workers to those same workers striking the following year over their pay. They were risking their lives, and all the Government could give them was a clap. A clap didn't feed us or pay the bills. After the lockdown, we got a hint about a new potential lead for a trap house over in Plaistow. It was an opportunity to get a salary without having to plug drugs. Now this place belonged to an old guy, an alcoholic called Paul.

He was originally from Liverpool and spent his whole life in the care system. He ended up in the Isle of Wight prison and we still don't know what for. He loved alcohol and young girls and the younger the better, now his little bedsit was surprisingly in a quiet little close in Plaistow, so slap bang in the middle of Newham but you could be forgiven for thinking it was somewhere rural. It was a prime location for us because the people that lived in these blocks were in their 60s; they were elderly. It was sheltered housing, meaning many carers would be in and out of the blocks to wipe the shit off the asses of the elderly for minimum pay. Ironically, it was a stone's throw from Plaistow Police Station and a tranquil cul de sac. So we first met Paul in Forest Gate, an alcoholic with a tale to tell. Junior, one of our youngers, robbed him of his Beats headphones and followed him to the Wetherspoon pub. Now Paul had victim written through him like a candy rock with the name running down its centre. An alcoholic with a lot of money around him; not sure how, but turns out he got the highest level for disability allowance.

I never knew at the time that Junior's Mum who was a brass had him as her regular punter. Paul would get so smashed out of his head take the women home, easily pleased with a quick hand job and she would snatch his money she never had sex with the geezer even once. So Junior had collected his Mother from this place many times, and he see first-hand the potential to use this base to peddle our shit low-key. Knowing this prick liked a young girl I was dispatched to lure the cunt in. Junior had done his work inside the pub, chatting about the young girl he could get for a reasonable price. I was brought into the pub, and when he saw me, he was drooling like a cat on catnip. I wore my school uniform and ensured my skirt was high and white socks and patent sandals the look of a virgin schoolgirl. He nearly blew a casket when he saw me. The trap was working well. He wanted me to come home with him, and he said he would pay me £70 for sex, so I smiled and said yes. One thing that worried him was that I was in my School uniform. It would draw attention, so luckily, a paedo called Mike stepped in with a plastic bag with a Niqab. Now a niqab is an item of clothing that covers your body, so only your eyes are on show which is why Mike loved them, he could move girls all around the place without arising suspicion. "Change into that, and nobody will know who you are."

There was a McDonald's on the corner next to the pub, so I went in and changed into my disguise, then I jumped on the 325 bus with him telling me his life story. I had a bottle of Vodka that Junior gave me and kept insisting Paul drinks it. Now we make our way to his little bedsit, and I'm pretty surprised that such a quiet place exists in Plaistow. Remember, I'm in the Niqab, the caring carer taking the poor man home. We get inside his place, and it's quiet, clean, and perfect for a trap house: no cameras and elderly residents.

As soon as we entered his bedsit, it was claustrophobic; there was a bed on one side, a desk with a computer, and a dirty-looking brown chair. The walls were green, and I remember thinking, why the fuck has he chosen this colour? It's like Kermit the frog has vomited everywhere I take off my Niqab, and he groans excitedly. I'm a virgin, I tell him, so let me have a little drink to loosen me up and calm the nerves.

He serves me the Vodka in a sports direct mug, one of the enormous cups and adds a splash of orange juice. As he goes to the bathroom, I crush a Valium into his cup and then top it up with Vodka, and when he returns, he also seems nervous too, so I hold the cup of juice out to him, and he drinks it, grimacing at the tablet dust but still pissed enough to swallow it. We chat about life, and before long, his eyes roll back, and he lays on

116

his stinking single bed comatose. I have my phone ready, so I Undress him and take a picture beside him. This is my collateral damage, and then I go through the silly cunts wallet, which contains his passwords to his bank cards. The job was done! I have the photographs of me in my school uniform with him, and I also have the bank cards and the passwords. We have this wanker stitched up good and proper.

When I know he is deep in sleep, I drop call Junior who pulls up in the car park in his car, smiling at the old lady whom he helps into the block. After all, he is a male carer here to do his evening shift. I open the door, and we take more photos of Paul naked with me and Junior next to him. We leave a lovely note saying we will be using this place as a base; if he so much as even breathes a word of this to anyone, those photos of us next to his flaccid cock will go viral and with a past like his, he will be back in prison before you can even say repent. He was well and truly fucked, I took that card to the ATM in Beckton, and I took out £250, which was my salary for the night, and I knew Mum was behind on her catalogue orders, so I was going to give it to her.

Me and Junior got chicken and chips on the way home, and I asked for an extra box and put the money in it, writing on a piece of paper that it was from Dad to Mum, my upkeep. She would never know it from a paedos pocket. He deserved it, evil cunt. I didn't feel bad; you play with fire, you get burned, and men like that deserved everything that would come to them.

After School, I often went to my friend's house; her Mum never worked but seemed much better off than my Mum. In fact, the whole thing with Mum as a cleaner was an embarrassment by that time. The only good thing was her hours meant I could do what I wanted, and as long as the evidence was removed, it was all good. So Tanisha, who I had known since forever, was like

117

the sister I never had, and DP (That's Tanisha's Mumma) was the most laid-back Mother you could ever have. She was a tall black Jamaican woman with the biggest bust you had ever seen, which is why they called her the black Dolly Parton, shortened to DP because her long blonde wig went all the way down past her bum. DP was curvaceous; all the men on the estate loved her with her false eyelashes, makeup and fierce stance. She stood out; you couldn't help but look at her. DP never nagged us; she treated us to wine and sometimes prosecco. I was in awe of her. She had her shit together, no man ever messed with her, and she kept her and Tanisha's flat spotless.

After School, there was always a feast in the flat with KFC, McDonald's and cheap wine from Iceland, which we could drink as if we were adults. I used to stay there until 7.45pm when I knew Mum would be on her way home. It was my safe haven where I learned about boys, make up and getting on in life. There was always a heavy bass sound of music coming from her flat, doors open, and smells of nail varnish, perfume and weed. It was a heady combination. The fact that I only had Sex with Leon used to make them laugh. They thought I was still almost like a virgin if I had only ever just had one guy. Having sex with multiple guys to them was seen as normal, they even spoke about having to have sex with the older guys to keep them happy and onside as if that was just nothing just something that had to be done.

Luckily, I wasn't tasked with plugging anything, which meant hiding drugs inside your ass or vagina. I'd still visit the Shine clinic; what a joke calling it that because we all liked to give shiners, right? Slang for oral sex. It was a sexual health clinic where young people could drop in for contraceptive advice and pick up free condoms. Now they must have thought we had incredibly high libidos because we would go along and literally get boxes and boxes of condoms and lube, but it was all for transporting drugs.

I will never forget being in the flat when my mate, having run out of lube, decided to use baby oil biggest mistake ever, the thing split, and then we were tasked with trying to get all the drugs out of her backside. That was a day I'll never forget, so remember that the cheaper way of doing things doesn't always work.

Leon and Glenda were the closest thing to a real family that my Mum and I ever had, so if I could cement it by being with Leon, I would. I mean, me and Leon knew each other inside and out. When we were alone, there were never any pretences. It was just us, and it was beautiful. I can't say that it was sex with him. It was love, we would lay together for ages, and he would kiss me and tell me how much I meant to him. I was confused the day he brought me a green packet of Microgynon; he wanted me to take the pill so I would not get pregnant. I was pretty upset if I'm honest. I felt that he maybe didn't love me enough. Would it be so bad if me and him had a baby together? I chucked the packet into the big metal bin outside. If he wanted to fuck with me, then he should be prepared for the consequences.

DP seemed to manage the little hood rats on that estate. Her stepson Malachi was one of the top boys. His Dad, Nico, was serving time but still maintaining his elder and well-connected role on the estate. Nico was doing ten years for a shooting, but DP was his right-hand woman. She visited him every weekend in Pentoville and kept her eye on Malachi for him. DP certainly kept all the little soldiers under manners; nobody messed with her, and the song Jolene by Dolly Parton- please don't take my man, was written about her.

DP was like a warrior; she let me and Tanisha do our thing

as long as we kept the top boys in the loop, but Tanisha was far more popular than me. She attended a Pupil referral school which meant she only went to School 3 days a week and had a support team around her because, my Tanisha could fight; the things I have seen her fake nails do, I don't even want to repeat. Mother and daughter had every designer bag from Louis Vuitton to Chanel; they may have been fakes from China, but they were good fakes. These women looked the part and acted the part. DP explained that as a young woman, I had to be wise. She said I looked attractive and sweet, so my County lines work was good for me. But she warned me that good looks fade and that my expiry date was already ticking.

Trapping powerful men was an excellent way to secure my membership in the Big Girls Club. It meant we would always be looked after. Working like my Mum for pennies while breaking my back was laughable. Mouth shut, legs open for the right ones was DP's advice. Tanisha was involved with Malachi, who ran our estate, even though he weirdly was her stepbrother. Malachi was 6ft1, looked like he spent his whole day in the gym and was always immaculately dressed. He drove a white Mercedes and lived in a flat over Canary Wharf, the really lovely apartments with the gyms and saunas underneath, and for Tanisha, he was the meal ticket she was looking for. Ironically around this time, Malachi planned to move Tanisha to another house in Bournemouth. She had recently turned 16, so she was ready to go, and both DP and Tanisha were over the moon about this.

This was graduating the hood way, a step up, more money and a nice area, what we would have achieved if we had gone to Uni. We had a flat and money but no debt. We graduated from the School of Life, which meant fast cars, fake designer goods and getting little roadmen to take the rap.

Some of the little youngers had already taken over an estate area in the borough of Dorset. They were rough boys from Stratford, so the little white boys acting as the big men in those areas never stood a chance. Even the elders in that area, the older white gangsters, couldn't compete with the heavy dudes that imported the shit in, they were the more senior East End white mob, so it was better to just let them take over rather than start a fight they would never win. You had gangsters, people hungry to make money with nothing to lose, and people raised in environments where crime was the only way. Trust me, the actual top tier of the drug-importing world was the white East End gangsters. They lived in their mansions in Hertfordshire while we peddled their shit and had black kids stabbing each other, all making money in their name. They would sit back in their huge houses, looking on, never getting their hands dirty, while sipping whiskey in the Ivy, having lunch chatting about the good old days when the East End was white, and people could leave their doors open. Really? Leave their doors wide open. I thought the East End was always a bit rough around the edges.

Tanisha had never seen the seaside apart from Southend on some council estate six weeks' summer holiday youth thing, so to her, this was like a lottery win. She couldn't wait to brag about the posh area she would be placed in and how they ate fish and chips like proper fish, not even battered, without coating on it by the sea. Tanisha told me she had calamari and had tried Swordfish. The girl was living her best life. A life that she felt she was entitled to, a life that her Mother had ingrained into her, was hers for the taking. She came in like the Lion but went out like a lamb; as the old saying went, she had even dropped her East End accent. Tanisha was out! Another area had changed her, and she didn't want back.

This was an opportunity for me, and she had to teach me how to survive quickly. Remember the golden rules in Estate Life? There will always be some girls younger, prettier and more willing than me. You had to make hay while the sun shone. Because for girls like us from the block, our lights would dim quicker than ordinary girls with everyday lives because of all the shit we were exposed to. Our beauty and good figures were all on borrowed time. A pregnancy or a fight and we were finished, or just years of hard living meant our shine dulled faster than the rest.

I had been getting more involved in helping Leon run the flat that Malachi had taken over in Peter's flat, which meant I could move about and ensure it was kept down on the low. I had been doing this since I was 14, but it was evident that with Tanisha out of the way, Malachi wanted me to step up and do more.

The Paedo flat in Plaistow was being managed by a new girl called Trish a runaway from a care home, she needed a place to stay and I was pissed off at first she would be taking my salary but that's the way it goes. They always took over flats of people that had learning disabilities or were junkies, easy to control, all paid up for by the council with minimal interest because these people were too scared to complain. The flat I was now responsible for belonged to Peter, and I was glad I had been assigned this one because I genuinely felt sorry for him. He had a carer, Joyce, who was partial to turning a blind eye for the handsome sum of £40 a week and his Valium, sleeping tablets, sidafil and Promethazine. Spastic Peter, as he was known, knew me well as my Mum had often helped him with shopping and seen him in the hospital wards when she was cleaning. My Mum was one of the first people that met him when he moved into the block, and he had never forgotten her kindness to him as most people treated him like shit. So he knew me, and he trusted me. He was easily pleased a Beano magazine and a Kebab takeaway would keep him entertained for hours. Give him that, send him to his room, and the rest was history. We had an empty flat, electricity, warmth and the space to cut up coke and cannabis. Whatever we had to package and send out, it was almost perfect. Malachi liked to keep a minimum of people in this flat, Leon and I mainly oversaw the youngers there, and we kept our business quiet, just as Malachi liked it. We heard stories of all-night parties in the neighbouring blocks which, of course, aroused suspicion, especially when it was the house of a vulnerable person. You might as well stick a light outside saying. Yes, we are here! We are fucking over this vulnerable person; you had to be sensible and move with minimal noise.

I had moved from nobody to somebody in the space of a few weeks, Tanisha took me to Westfield just before she left for Bournemouth again, and for the first time in my life, I had £250 to spend on clothes, a little thank you from Malachi for running the flat. He had gifted me a pair of trainers previously and a mobile phone so I was grateful it wasn't like I was not earning a salary from this job. I'd go to School most of the time unless some big shipment had come in, then I'd get Dad to call or even go into School to get me out of it, and then Dad would get a bit of smoke for doing it. Leon and I worked well as a team. We got some little hood rats from the estate to run about while we concentrated on packaging, cutting of drugs and bagging up weapons. It could all drop down onto the balcony below or sometimes pass across from the flat to the other balconies within touching distance. Most residents had younger ones in this block who were involved. Mothers would pass a package to receive a little cannabis or coke to get them through their dismal

123

lives. We were all in this together. There was no such thing as grassing. We were all one.

For the first time in my life, I felt powerful. My Dad was in awe of me; he would visit me and sit chatting shit while he smoked weed, telling me how proud he was of me in this big man's game. This was the first time my Dad said he was proud of me. To say Dad was unpredictable was an understatement, and he could sometimes be embarrassing. You always knew when he hadn't been taking his medication because he would look for arguments and start becoming paranoid, so if I could give him weed to mellow him out, it was all good. And I tried so hard I put Dad's tablets in Plastic boxes like you see old people have with the days of the week on it MONDAY TUESDAY, but I still think he skipped them, mainly because he didn't know what day of the week it actually was.

Tanisha had to school me quickly as her permanent move to Bournemouth had come entirely unexpected as a huge shipment had come across on a boat, and she needed to oversee the new flat in the seaside town. This oversized shipment required only a few of us to be in the know. We had lunch in Nandos, eating spicy chicken wings with hot sauce while she spat out the bones, telling me how my new life would play out. There were a few things I always had to do- Ensure I always carried a morning-after pill, Levonelle brought with a fake credit card. Use condoms with the low-level guys because the younger ones would have diseases the way they messed around the estate, and the last thing you wanted was Chlamydia or something worse that would put you out of action for a while. Always ensure I had Norethisone a period delay tablet just in case Malachi planned ahead and invited me to a party or a date. I would be expected to attend and perform, and a period was just a no-go whenever he asked me anywhere. I was confused at how she talked about sex as if it was just something you had to do it was part and parcel of life, nothing to be ashamed about, not something between two people but something that was expected of me, no time for niceties this was my weapon, my bargaining chip, suddenly I felt a little sick. She also handed me a small box of Doxycycline. She told me this was an Antibiotic to treat Sexually transmitted Infections, so if any of the boys from the other ends raped me, I was to take this the following day and continue taking it even if it made me vomit. I looked at her, aghast! Rape! She looked at me like I was stupid. This is pretty much part of the course. These rude little boys think they are men and take the piss at times. It's best to protect ourselves as much as we can, she told me. Besides, you can never tell when some rude little boy from some other ends wants to fuck you just to make a point; it's best to be prepared.

All this was said to me as if it was perfectly normal. How could I have been so blind to see what some of these girls had to do and how they lived? I must have seemed like such a sheltered baby; being Leon's girl protected me in some ways. I slurped down my giant Cola too quickly, feeling the pop of the bubbles on my tongue; what the hell was I involved in? burping up gas as quietly as I could as I waited for her to laugh and say she was joking, but she never did.

Decisions, decisions I could be like my mum sweeping floors and mopping shit for a pittance, never becoming anything or this. I didn't want to return all these clothes; I brought on the £250 shopping spree with Tanisha and have no money or nice hair. I needed to be someone and this was the only way! I finished my Chicken wings and chips, the first full belly in months, looked down at my bags of clothes, and knew which route I had chosen. I took the bag of medicines, morning-after pills, and period-delay tablets and knew this was my chance. I couldn't act like a pussy now and back out. What would I do, run home to Mummy and apply to be a cleaner? No way! The more I looked towards the shops with all the clothes and perfumes I couldn't afford, the more I wanted them. The more I saw that the expected route in life to work, for low pay, would not readily get me things. This honest way of living made us dishonest, and could you blame us?

So with my new Clothes paid for, I had to work a bit harder. I soon became more involved in moving stuff through to Hertford and Essex. We had a system where we would use some stupid little white girls from out of the area to take the drugs back on the over ground lines. We always had our rough little Stratford lads on the trains if we were moving large quantities of drugs. The rationale was that way if the feds got on the train, the black boys would start a fight, and the white girls in their posh school uniforms would not even get a second glance; it was genius, and soon we were making quite serious money from the southern borders these posh white kids were in just as turmoil as us. I was pretty surprised as imagine having your own house, two parents with a nice car, a posh school, and an Ocado home food shop with prawns, avocado and Malbec, and you still felt life was just too tough.

It was laughable when they stepped foot onto our estate; it was almost like they had done it for their Instagram, snapping photos of themselves with black boys in the hood. Listening to Stormzy and Giggs and thinking they were rude girls, it was laughable. Mainstream grime had a lot to answer for. I was just too naive, as I wasn't aware of the sexual abuse that was happening with these girls. The older guys would lure them in on Snapchat, private message them, and pretend they were extraordinary beautiful. Black boy's hood rich such a catch! They were Girls from affluent families, and once a boy had lured her in and made her do a few sexual videos, the rest was history.

Before they could cry to Mummy and Daddy and hide behind their gated homes, it was too late; they were being threatened left, right and center, their homes were burgled, their life was turned upside down, and they were petrified them rude photos and videos would start circulating, they were blackmailed basically.

But before I realised this, all I felt was anger and jealousy towards them my whole entire flat was the size of one of their bedrooms. It was ok to taste the poverty and roughness for an hour, but then they could take their Valentino rucksacks and Kickers shoes and return to their suburban life. They pissed me off with their Instagram poses. There was one girl Katy with her Moncler jacket, straightened hair and a face made up of expensive makeup, you know, the radiance of money. I can see it; their perfume even made them smell richer. No smell of Damp lingering on this sket.

So this one particular girl Katy made a beeline for Leon; now he said his interest in her was purely financial as this one was loaded. Malachi had strictly instructed him to keep her on the side, find out her parent's passcode for the burglar alarm, and we would rip the place apart when they went on holiday, which the family frequently did. What a mistake that little white girl would pay for her bit of roughness. Look down her nose at me as a peasant but would be on her hands and knees for a black boy because it was so bad and daring to be in the hood with a gangster. I hated them fucking girls; they were vile. Never think money makes you a better person because it doesn't; it just means you were born lucky. I never forget being forced to be nice to her, and she was a cunt on the highest level. Leon, with his sweet nature, had played the part well. You had never met such a self-entitled bitch in your life.

Leon showed her around Peter's flat as if this was some poverty safari, I was seeing red by this point, but Malachi had made an appearance, so I knew I couldn't cause a fight because that would be pretty foolish. We all sat eating chicken and Chips, and this bitch tried to pretend she was one of us. Then her phone pinged, and she got her iPhone out of a Mulberry bag it was time to go home. Malachi offered to drive her home with Leon, and I came along, which pissed her off. I wanted to keep my eye on her as I didn't want her to think that her money meant she could overtake me in Leon's life or Malachi's. I was thinking, keep your enemies' close kind of thing. This cunt loved the sound of her voice; all the way home, she yapped on and on about how she could make the boys a lot of money because her School had kids ripe for the picking; they had lots of excess cash. I will never forget we dropped her off at a house just off some funny winding country lane called the Crooked Mile. This girl didn't have a home. She had a mansion, a stable and horses and there she was fucking about with us in the slums; it made no sense to me. Guess she was hungry for some black cock. We parked just outside her house, Leon kissing her bee-stung glossed lips outside her gated doors while I raged in the car. It was then I decided, you know what? If he is doing this shit, I will play the game as well, fuck him, fuck her! Malachi seemed to enjoy seeing me so vexed it was almost like he planned it "Looks like you need a real man" He smiled at me, and I don't think I ever really looked at him, not in this way because I always assumed he was out of my league. But he was showing an interest in me and

I suddenly felt special. Malachi was Jamaican but light-skinned, and his eyes were hazel. It was a striking combination. "Girl, like you should be treated properly, why don't you let me take you out sometime and show you how a real gentleman treats a lady? You don't need any hood rat like Leon. You think he cares about you?" Malachi kissed his teeth, shaking his head and laughing, "Just look at him.".

And it would appear Leon was really saying goodnight to this bitch as he had one hand on Katy's bum and seemed to be enjoying this all a bit too much. "He's been bare-backing that little white pussy for months. She thinks they are in love, and the fucker seems to think she wants to invite him in to meet the parents." I turned towards Malachi, shocked. "Your fucking kidding me, right? Leon? My Leon?" I thought of all the times he had disappeared to do extra work. Malachi laughed. "This bitch has parents that don't even fucking notice when the Dom Perion goes missing. They holiday like three times a year. Even that stupid designer dog is worth a few grand, we are going to rinse this bitch clean, and she won't dare fucking grass us up, or else her Mother will be having a facial of an acid kind, and her little brother might just disappear for a few days you get me." I nodded. I felt like an idiot; every day after school, Leon and I had sex and he told me, he loved me and that this girl was just a business transaction, a way to make money. But was that the truth? Because it didn't fucking look like It from where I was seated, was he just like all the rest, only interested in one thing? "You know what, Malachi, fuck him. He has bullshitted me enough lately. I have not got time for all this shit, your right; I need a real man, not a boy".

I was rattled but had to play the tough girl; even though some part of me wanted to cry, I felt hurt and stupid. Malachi smiled and rubbed his hand up and down my thigh. The feeling instantly made me feel something I never really felt before for him. Malachi was dangerous, and his hand was rubbing me and making me feel immediately turned on. The way he looked at me made me think that I could have quite easily fucked him there and then if he wanted me to.

And I'm not a sket, but he was on a whole other level with his Stone Island Jacket, nice watch and flash car; it was like a taste of the big time, and I was hungry for it. Power is an aphrodisiac, well it is for a girl like me, playing at being a big girl, but in reality, I'm not that tough. I was pretty taken aback at why he would be interested in me. I'm sure he just took me along for this drive to wind me up and make me see what Leon was doing. When Leon returned to the car, he smelt of her expensive perfume. I kissed my teeth, moving from the front seat to the back so he could ride up front with Malachi. He could tell I was pissed off. Well yeah, no shit, Sherlock; he turned to face me, and even in the darkness of night, her pink lip-gloss was still on his lips "You know that was just an act, right Amelia? I have to keep that bitch on my side. It wasn't what It seemed. This one is mega-loaded." I turned my head towards the car window while Malachi blasted the car with music screeching away from the luxurious front door. I didn't speak to Leon for the rest of that night. It looked like good play-acting from where I was sitting. It hurt me that the one person I thought I could trust and had my back just saw me as another girl to mess about.

Did he think I was just some stupid hood girl who would count her blessings that he even looked at me? Nah, fuck that. I was going to show him I was worth more. On the drive back to Stratford, I was silent.

I could smell Malachi's aftershave, making me want him more

and more. I noticed he kept looking back at me from the car's mirror, and I stayed silent, just contemplating what being with him could bring. I didn't feel like being that loyal now to Leon after that night. When Malachi started messaging me, I liked it. He started sending me messages telling me everything he wanted to do with me.

I was flattered. I felt like this was going to mean something so much more. I was rising; I would become someone in her own right. I would never have to rely on the protection of the underdogs because I would rise higher than them and get my beloved Mum and me out of this sinkhole estate, and I'd look at Leon and tell him to go back to his white whore and fucking stay there.

Did Katy really think someone like Leon would be welcomed into her family and that life? Where Glenda would be made to feel like the hired help. No way, not in a million years, she might have been some rich girl playing in the hood for a bit, but she had taken the one person that meant so much to me, my Leon.

I could never forgive him, and I figured two could play that game. I didn't realise just what a dangerous game I was playing.

10

Amelia-Polyester Knickers And Dining Room Etiquette

Tanisha was happy in her new set-up in Brighton. Stratford was forgotten; she was out of the hood and in suburbia. I called her, gave her the low down on Malachi, and told her that he had asked me out because the last thing I ever wanted to do was make an enemy out of her.

Tanisha told me it was calm; Tanisha was seeing this older man a white gangster and they were getting on just fine. She told me how she lived a comfortable life and only had to do him a few times a week. He was older he was easily pleased. She had outgrown us and moved up, and who could blame her? Not me, that's for sure.

Lots of girls were desperate to be on Malachi's radar, and I stupidly thought I must have been something special to be invited out by him. It was a slap in the face for Leon, a little sign to show him who was in control of me, and it wasn't him. Malachi and I had been messaging back and forth, and we had arranged to go out for something to eat. He would be going to Peter's flat about 6ish to speak to Leon; he wasn't happy with him, and I hoped it had something to do with that sket Katy.

I planned on avenging her for looking me up and down like shit. I planned to ensure that I was on the job when they looted the house when the family were on holiday. It serves her right to flash the goods. She was going to pay the price. No rich girl should come into our hood thinking they were better than us. I wanted to dash acid in her face. I already planned what I wanted to steal from her. All those bags and the jewellery would give me a nice amount of cash. And we looked the same size, so I wanted to take clothes from her wardrobe.

School was pretty shit that day because it had all come on top about Dad getting me out of school. Mum had been called in for a meeting. But nothing could spoil the excitement of my date that night with Malachi. I was walking on air and I knew I'd placate Mum and say I would be back home at about 9pm as I was thinking Malachi would just be taking me to McDonald's or something where we would eat in the car and then drive around to the back of Tesco's and I'd let him fuck me. So I wondered what to wear. I wanted to look classy and wear something that would give him easy access. What do you wear on a date night with one of the Top boys on the estate? I wanted to get it right. In the end I decided on a tight black dress that showed off all my curves. My breasts were spilling over the top, and my bum looked good. I had a nice blazer jacket from Zara that Tanisha had given me, and I looked seductive but glamorous. I washed my hair and straightened it so I lost my curls, and my hair was long; I wore high heels, and when I looked at myself in the full-length mirror in our flat, I looked good. I looked like I belonged in different surroundings, well this was me, no little boys and their silly games. Alisha, another friend from tower block 2, came over and gave me a line of coke for confidence, and she also gave me a shot of blue vodka. It was my chance to shine! I'd never taken Cocaine before, but she expertly chopped the white powder on my makeup mirror with her library card, then got a small plastic straw cut small and told me to snort it. I felt good, as I could taste the powder dripping down the back of my throat, and my nose went numb even though I had been around drugs before, this was the first time I'd ever touched the hard stuff.

Alisha had already briefed me on what was to be expected. Men like Malachi wanted to bear back (Not wearing a condom). She checked that I had my morning-after pill in my bag and told me we would get an STI test online later, but enjoy your night and do everything he says. It was my chance to be a top girl, and I had to take it! And trust me; she knew because she had been involved in some top boys and had come out of it good, with new trainers, handbags, and most importantly, respect.

She had a baby now, so she was out of the game and keeping things low, but it didn't mean she wouldn't help me. Her baby's daddy was doing ten years for attempted murder, but she wore that badge proud; she was another girl you didn't fuck with. I see her boil sugar in a pan and then dash it in some girl's face who was knocking on her door, chatting shit about how her man had been screwing her. She was crazy, but it was never for tea when she boiled the kettle. It was usually for somebody's face. She was my new Tanisha, my new go-to, the one who, like DP, the Mother of the Block, was a solid woman that handled their shit with ease.

As I made my way up to Peter's flat, I could hear raised voices from inside. I stood and listened before I pushed the door open I could hear Malachi screaming at Leon, his voice threatening and angry. "I'm telling you, boy, nobody fucks with me and takes the piss; it was short by a ton at least...you think I won't notice that shit? It's happening too often". Leon's voice sounded strained, "It can't be right! I'm telling you, she wouldn't do that. And I wouldn't do that... I'm not stupid". The shouting continued, "She isn't from these ends, Leon. She probably thought she could take the piss or someone scammed her. Either way, this is your fucking debt and mess to sort out". Leon was scared. I could hear the change in his voice "Serious, Mal, you know me. I've known you for years. Please believe me, that money going missing had fuck all to do with me. I promise, I swear on my Mother's life,". Malachi kissed his teeth; he was getting bored. "You run this place right, so the debt occurred on your patch and your run and your manor, so you have to fucking sort it, do as I say over in E16, and then it's all paid up... let's see if you're a real man or just the pussy that I think you're looking like to me right now".

With that, Malachi swung open the door, smiling to find me outside, pretending I had just arrived and hadn't been eavesdropping. He looked sexy in navy blue Chinos and a Ralph Lauren knitted T-shirt. He didn't ever wear tracksuit bottoms; he always looked stylish. He smiled as he looked me up and down suggestively, whistling and turning me around as if he was inspecting the goods. I felt like a bag of meat going to the highest bidder at auction.

I struggled to follow Malachi down the stairs in my heels. He hated the lifts here and couldn't stomach the smell of them. So money had been skimmed off of the stuff being sold, only a couple of hundred here and there, but it was disrespectful and something you didn't do. I believed it was that bitch Katy as it was on her run that the money was skimmed, and I wondered why a posh little cunt like that would be so stupid.

I know Leon is meticulous about this stuff, so for him to be short-changed was pretty rare. And Leon was never a thief to his own; with my hand on my heart, I could say that. He was just not that kind of person. It turns out the money was correct, and Malachi was bullshitting Leon so he could be further in debt and couldn't say No to a little gang reprisal thing he had planned for later that night. If there was ever an evil bastard, it was Malachi, but I was blinded by the big lights for that night. Leon felt he had something to prove, his elder sister and brother were both going to Uni, and he needed to follow a different path than his siblings. Glenda spoiled him rotten, but she didn't understand him. It's like his childhood was so different from that of his siblings. Even though he had the golden ticket, the UK passport, and the UK teaching, he needed help to go down the right path. His siblings would go to Church with Glenda but not Leon, he was caught between his Nigerian family values and British values—a bit of a cross-cultural jumble of life.

Malachi's car was a white BMW, a different car that looked pristine, smelt like coconut wax and was freshly cleaned. It must have been a hired car. It was safe to leave on the estate. Everybody knew who was driving it, and nobody dared breathe near that car. I hoped everyone saw me walk towards the car and get Inside. I hoped being seen with him would give me more kudos.

Malachi smiled and opened the door like a gentleman, and I slipped into the front seat. My legs felt nice and warm against the leather seat, hot from the sun. As Leon got into the driving seat, he leaned across me, and I could smell a mixture of Weed and a strong aftershave; Tom Ford Black Orchid, he whispered into my ear, sending a cold shiver down my spine. "How about we go get some food over by the river? We'll go to a little place over Canary Wharf, just you and me" As he finished whispering into my ear, he bit my earlobe; it was the sexiest thing I had ever experienced.

I had never been out with a man like this in my life. I was used to cheap takeaway meals in a polystyrene box where you ate with your hands; I'd never gone on a date with three sets of knives and forks on the table, and dining etiquette was lost on me. The big girl was going to the table. This was just what I needed a night of fun. Besides, tonight I was going to tell Mum I was done with School I planned to leave early.

I figured I could earn more money by stepping up and taking more responsibility with the trap houses and moving drugs, and tonight I planned to test the water by mentioning it to Malachi. The Cocaine was making me talk more than I usually would, and my hands were twisting my hair around my fingers because I could remember reading in a magazine that it was supposed to look seductive. I was talking so much shit, and I felt euphoric as we drove towards the bright lights of the financial district of the East End.

We parked in an underground car park full of expensive cars; then he led me up the concrete stairs- riverside where several restaurants and Hotels overlooked the River Thames. This was fifteen minutes' drive from Stratford and the blocks, but a world away from my estate, there was money here, and it smelt and looked so inviting.

I would have been happier having a Big Mac Meal, but I suppose that this would be the way things would start to go for me. Eating in proper restaurants the more important I became. Hopefully, I had eradicated the smell of dampness which always clung to my clothes with some stolen Tester Victoria's Secret body spray, ironically called Pure Seduction, that I had doused myself in.

I had on Knickers that were cheap polyester from Primark and a bra from Asda that pushed my breasts together and made them look two sizes bigger. Girls from the hood always looked and smelled like what we were underneath the lights; you could tell it was all just a veneer, the bags were fake, the eyelashes were fake, and the jewellery was fake. Our accents and etiquette skills would identify us, trip us up, and our schooling would expose us.

It was pretty exhausting trying to be something you were not in a posh restaurant like this. It Would be nice just to sit back and say you know what, we have fucking tough lives, and we got here through sheer hard work and toil, just a different route from yours. It does not mean I am less of a human being because I didn't have the same opportunities as you or had parents that were loaded.

So here I was, walking into Gaucho, some fancy Steak restaurant on Malachi's arm, grateful that he asked for a table outside. I was sweating, and the night was humid and being outdoors, I felt more free and less in a goldfish bowl with the other diners looking at me. And you know those cheap polyester knickers? They could make you sweat.

The evening breeze was cool on my skin which was welcomed as I could feel my underarms sweating, with anxiety and probably from the Cocaine as my heart was beating so fast. My mouth was becoming dry and I was desperate for something to chew. I pulled my black dress lower as I suddenly felt cheap and exposed in my cheap dress with my fake Louis Vuitton bag.

I expected the waiters to say I could not enter and there was some secret dress code policy that Indicated I was from the tower blocks, too poor to sit on these seats. I was a fraud playing a part in a life that wasn't mine, but for one night, I was here, let me just have it. The waiter spoke to Malachi, not me, asking what drinks he would like to order. I had never had wine before apart from Lambrini cheap shit from supermarkets, so the waiter was correct Sir could order! Because I wouldn't have a clue, the table made me feel a bit anxious with glasses, knives, and forks all placed as if they were pawns on a chess board, and I wasn't sure what one to touch or where I should put them.

Malachi ordered the Argentine Red Bonarda at £45 for a 750ml bottle; I almost choked when I read the price. Malachi must have sensed my anxiety as I looked at the menu, I did not have a clue the difference between a Sirloin or a Ribeye steak so he ordered food for us both, and when the waiter asked me how I would like my steak, and I replied cooked, I could tell by Malachi's smirk I had fucked up a bit. Medium rare was the correct reply, and some lovely hand-cooked chips.

When the waiter poured the wine, he only filled the glass up a tiny amount. As soon as he moved, I swallowed the whole glass back, it burned the back of my throat, and the alcohol burnt down to my belly. It didn't taste that great, and I winced at the taste. It tasted like vinegar; how the fuck could people pay so much for something that tasted this bad. Malachi laughed, and the way he sipped at his wine, tasting it and then putting his glass down delicately, I knew I should not have swallowed the whole glass as if it was going out of fashion. He poured me another "Someone likes this wine" I didn't want to correct him and say it was disgusting because, at the price he was paying for it, that would appear rude and only highlighted that I was a hood girl who was not used to proper drinks.

My palate was primarily the bland type used to sugary alcohol-type drinks, cheap and potent to get you drunk with a minimum spend. Malachi was the perfect gentleman and sang my praises all night. As we ate, he chatted, "You Clean skins, right?" Gangs liked clean girls meant they attracted less trouble. These girls were not on the social services radar or known to the police. They crept, were discreet, and wouldn't bring drama to the door. I nodded as I delicately cut my steak, I had never seen proper steak knives before and they looked like blades the youngers on the streets would carry. "Yeah, I am. I've never been in any trouble or had any police or Social services involvement ever, and although I did get in a little bit of shit today with the School, I want out. I will tell my Mum I'm leaving School. I don't want college or a shitty low-paid job".

Malachi poured more wine. "And what will you do?" I looked at him, and suddenly the question felt loaded, and I wasn't sure what was the correct reply "I guess I want to get more involved in running stuff and helping out that way". Malachi smirked I wasn't sure if he was laughing at me or smiling at my reply. "Interesting…. you know where a lot of money is being made right now, and that's Girls". I continued eating, wondering what he meant. "Girls? What do you mean?" all the time hoping, I was holding my knife and fork correctly. He took his time to reply, sipping the wine that made his lips turn red. "Ok, as well as the dealing, I also supply girls to people for money. It's quite a profitable business". I looked confused. This was news to me. "And you think I can help you how?" He smiled and I felt safe when he looked into my eyes. "Girls like Katy, that out of borough sket, they think they are some tough little cookies. Maybe you and I can work together to supply them to some of these guys. I mean, you're so clever, Amelia, you have so much going for you, and I can see you going places".

I suddenly felt hot, made excuses, and rushed to the bathroom. I peed and then opened my purse, shutting the toilet seat down and snorting another line of coke. I was going places. I would show them all who I was and what I had become. I suddenly felt like I was in some crazy dream, Dinner in a posh restaurant with Malachi. It was better than a cheap chicken and chip box meal and a quick fuck with Leon. He always used to eat first and then want sex and it pissed me off because he always had chicken in his teeth.

At that moment, I felt invincible. I could make money to give to my Mum, and we could have a life that didn't revolve around budgeting for things and going without. I was looking towards the big time, and it looked good. Canary Wharf, the new financial hub of the city, the restaurants, the bars, the shops all dripping with new money and promise, and there we lived in its shadows, looking up at it all with our caps in our hands. But tonight, I was Cinderella, and I was having a ball.

The women here who I looked at as they strolled past with their heads held high, returning from the Gym in the Four Seasons Hotel that overlooked the dirty river dropping their glass water bottles into designer bags, then taking their Audi TT to flats overlooking the Thames. These women were in the same part of East London as me, yet they walked taller; They had confidence; they looked like it was their God-given right to life. That is what happens when you have a secure upbringing and are nurtured correctly. If they bled, they would still bleed the same blood as me. They probably still had the same hang-ups as me. They were still girls living in the East End getting by, and we were all different but just the same really, vagina, Tits, ass, man trouble. They had backup of a different kind and money and opportunities.

But here I was, and I thought I was special as if I had something about me that made me a bit better than other girls. It was a nice

141

feeling to be wanted for a bit. Little did I know what that night would bring, or I would have run away so fast you wouldn't have seen me for dust.

As the waiter placed the dessert menu on the table, Malachi dismissed him. "My Desert is waiting for me back home. Can I get the bill, please?" he smiled towards me, and I smiled back, the last drops of the expensive wine he poured into my glass. I was pissed and high, I tried to smile seductively, but it was all blurry around the edges.

The drive to his flat was not long at all; he lived in a gated block with the smell of chlorine coming from the vast air con units. He had his own pool and Gym in this complex. No wonder he hated lifts smelling of urine. I was still busy chatting on and on about how I could handle Katy and girls from out of the borough. Looking back, I was talking so much shit. I didn't stop acting the hard girl, hoping it would impress him and secure me a well-paid job to get some money behind me. Malachi parked the car and walked ahead, no longer listening to me. I remember looking back at the gates as we left the car, seeing them close behind us and wondering how I would get out If I needed to. The gates banged shut, suddenly making me feel trapped; this was a gated community. Malachi's whole mood changed; the sweet-talking stopped, and he just opened the door to his flat, expecting me to follow him inside, all niceties finished.

I realized another man was in the apartment, and that's when I suddenly felt unsafe. I can't explain it. Call it an instinct. But suddenly, the situation had changed; the vibe felt different. Deano was an older man, maybe late 40s, and he was sitting there rolling a joint on the coffee table, watching some American sitcom. He nodded in my direction and then took a long drag on his joint. There was something about this man that spelt trouble.

He was mixed race with gold teeth at the front and tattoos all over his arms, he smelt slightly of sweat, I had an instinct that this man would cause me harm.

Deano and Malachi started talking about some mad thing going down that night, and I was so drunk that I couldn't decipher the conversation. Malachi looked towards me and then shrugged his shoulders. "What you waiting for? Undress". He clicked his fingers at me, indicating for me to remove my clothes. I was momentarily stunned and laughed out loud. If there ever were a few words to render me suddenly sober, this was it. "Eh? What do you mean? I'm not taking my clothes off here" Was this some joke? Was he being serious? I had been expecting maybe to have sex with Malachi, but then who was this guy? Why would I be getting undressed in front of him? I wanted to have sex in the bedroom with the lights out. I wasn't brave enough to take my clothes off in front of them both, that was just weird.

Deano looked me up and down. "This one isn't bad, Mal; where did you find her? Off Block One? She looks clean and alright, unlike some of the other ones you've brought my way," he laughed suddenly, making him look sinister. Malachi walked towards me, shouting in my face, which made me jump back; holding my arms around my body, I was suddenly afraid of him.

I couldn't believe the change. "You heard me right, get your clothes off and stop fucking around, I am not in the mood for no games now" His eyes were suddenly cold, and he looked fierce. It was like the man with whom I had just shared a meal laughing and joking, was somebody else entirely. I had only seen a change in personality like this with my Dad in a mental health crisis. It was not a joke, and there was no punchline; he barked at me again, "Get out of your fucking clothes!" I felt so self-conscious as I stripped down to my underwear that didn't match and covered my hands across my chest. I felt exposed and swallowed back the tears. I wasn't such a big girl now, naked with two men leering at me. The words I spoke were so quiet that I wasn't even sure I had said them. "I've changed my mind. I want to go home" I swallowed, but suddenly my throat was dry, my saliva had dried in my mouth, and I was desperate for water.

The delicious meal that had made me feel full suddenly made me nauseous, and the wine made my mouth dry. The cocaine high that had me feel powerful had faded. The sweat was now cooling on my skin, and goose bumps prickled at my skin. I wished I could have run. I would have jumped out of the window rather than do what they made me do.

Malachi smiled and walked towards me. "What's your fucking problem, don't tell me you are going all frigid on me now. Where's the big girl, all mouth and action?" He grabbed me by my hair, pushing me down onto my knees. He dropped his jeans and started touching himself while moving my hands away so he could see my naked body. He thrust into my mouth when he was hard, making me gag.

I tried hard to hold back the tears, but they fell from my eyes. He roughly grabbed my hair and forced himself into my mouth. He did not care that he was hurting me and making me gag and cry. The other guy didn't even look our way. He just carried on reading something engrossing on his phone. It was as if this was nothing unusual; this was a common thing. Malachi kissed his teeth at me as I was not the compliant type of girl he was used to; looking at my tear-stained face must have spoken to some part of his subconscious brain he didn't like. For all their rough talk and bravado about Bitches and Skets, they must have some conscious, for they all must have Mothers, Sisters and females in their lives they respected. And getting a blowjob off a crying female wasn't sitting right with him.

He pushed me towards the kitchen island, slamming me against the little breakfast table. My stomach hit the surface so hard that I felt momentarily winded. He grabbed my hair again, so I leaned back while he pulled at my cheap knickers, splitting them as he pushed himself into me with no protection. Doing me from behind so he didn't have to see my face. The pain seared through me, I wasn't ready for him, and all the niceties of the evening were gone. He thrust so hard that I could hear him calling me every obscenity for a woman.

I was like a piece of meat; it wasn't even me. I closed my eyes and tried hard not to cry out from the pain. He finished quickly, pulling out of me, throwing me aside, and then breathlessly got himself a glass of water from the tap as if this was something he done all the time.

I crouched up from the floor, still exposed and naked with tears falling down my face I covered myself as much as I could with my hands to hide myself. There was a knock at the door, I wondered if this was an opportunity to get my clothes and run. Another guy entered he was a big man who I knew as Nutty Nsanda, a big Rasta man with a temper who everyone was scared of. He looked me up and down, smiling. "Sorry to break up the party, I need a word, Mal" Deano jumped up. "I'll finish this off in the bathroom; you know I like my privacy for the stuff I like, and I want to try this one out; she looks good." Malachai and Nsanda laughed at this. "The man is perverted; you go and have fun but don't mess up my bathroom, bruv, like last time you hear me, Deano?".

Deano dragged me into the bathroom and raped me, only stopping when Malachi banged on the door. "You are lucky shit has gone down tonight, or else we would keep you here all night" I gagged as the smell of them overpowered me and then I felt the vomit rise. I rushed to the toilet, vomiting up steak and red wine into the toilet bowl. I was empty inside and out.

As I was vomiting, Nsanda opened the door, laughing. I was going to have a go myself but fuck that Fucking hell, Deano; what is wrong with you? You do some perverted shit, bruv" he laughed and showed Nsanda the recordings. He pushed the phone in my face. "You say fuck all to anyone about what happened tonight; this video will go viral. I'll make sure your School, your family, and everyone in this area know what a dirty little sket you are and that you take it up the ass and when I call you, make sure you come running because Girls like you can make me a lot of cash you get me? I call and you are to pick up that fucking phone or else", he spat at me and made a slicing motion across his neck. He also took photos of me naked, sitting huddled on the floor, and then walked out of the room laughing.

My dress was in the other room, but I was scared to move. I felt numb and shocked at what had just happened. Was this what this life was? Is this what the top boys do? Is this what we aspired to become? Girls that have to endure being raped by men that wine and dine us. Malachi was pacing up and down, and I could hear raised voices. He kicked open the bathroom door, making me jump. "Come and get your clothes; we are leaving". The mood had changed. Both of them looked serious. I scrambled into my dress, unsure where my bra and handbag were. My knickers were still ripped and on the floor, and I scooped up my phone next to them.

I accidentally left my bag in a rush to get out of there. I just grabbed my clothes, wanting to be free. I didn't know how my feet were carrying me as I was starting to shake all over, and my trembling legs were finding it hard to walk, but I knew I had to get out of there quickly.

Fear can give you such an adrenaline rush, and I was focused on getting out of there alive. Keep walking, and do as they say, I could feel blood and god knows what else dripping down my legs, but I kept my eyes looking forward, following them in a trance. I looked around to see if I could run, but where would I have run? This area was gated, and besides, Malachi would have caught me. I could not have run when my legs were shaking so badly.

On that journey back to Stratford, I sat in the back of the car while Deano drove. He looked older somehow now we were in the harsh street lights, with Malachi in the front passenger seat cursing at the messages coming through on his phone. I sat dumbfounded, tears in my eyes, blinking slowly as if I was in a dream and would wake up any moment. Those bright Canary Wharf lights shining down on me no longer seemed so promising. They were tainted; I wasn't such a tough girl. Every time I would look at that building, I would think of this night.

The night when I once thought I was more important than I was. Malachi's phone kept ringing as we drove, with both of them screaming at whoever was on the other line. I was stinging so badly now and trying to swallow back vomit. The last thing I wanted to do was vomit in this car because I didn't know the consequences. And I knew it would piss them off no end.

Here I was, returning to the block a much different girl to the one that left, I was blooded and broken, and I knew I wasn't cut out for this life, but it was too late. There was no going back for me. I held my phone in my hands, trembling, I could see that my Mum had been calling me nonstop, but my phone had been silent. I couldn't walk away. I was indebted, invested, had clothes, money, phones and new trainers, and knew a lot. What would happen to my Mum and Dad if I went against them? It didn't bear thinking about. I hoped this older guy Deano never called and requested me to have sex with him or his friends. He was horrible, an absolute pervert. And that recording they had of me! I'd rather die than let anybody see that. Imagine the whole School or the people on the estate, everyone seeing me naked.

But I knew I was trapped that video would hurt me more than the physical thing they did to me; I was ashamed. The bottom line was that there was no escape for a girl like me. I'm not sure if this was a pity fuck or if I was supposed to feel elevated to a higher level for being with the top boys. I was confused, was this respect because I was chosen as being clean and not a sket, or was I just another girl that had been abused? This was the collateral damage, just like what I did to that paedo in Plaistow; video evidence and blackmail turned back on me because now these cunts had me indebted.

The erratic driving was making me seriously want to puke. I pressed the control for the window and wound it down enough for me to inhale the smells of the city. Inner city life had a smell; it was petrol fumes, Chicken Shops frying meals, Weed and pollution. Too many people in enclosed spaces, shops with their fronts on the pavement selling fruit and veg in bowls with the sounds of buses, sirens and voices of all different languages being spoken, it was a melting pot of all walks of life.

I heard the name Leon being spoken and I immediately got goosebumps. Something was wrong, if I had been in a better head space, I would have worked out what it was, but my thoughts were all over the place. I felt disorientated, no longer drunk or high but at the beginning of a bad hangover. As we pulled up outside the block, I saw someone waiting in the shadows, and I was afraid it might have been another man waiting for me. Until I saw it was Leon running down towards the car, looking both ways as if hiding from someone. My initial reaction was he was coming to rescue me, but I was shoved out of the vehicle by Malachi, and as Leon approached the car, his face fell when he saw the mess I was in. The way he looked at me, I will never forget. He was scared and running from something, but he knew something was wrong when he saw me scramble out of the car. "What the fuck have you done to her?" his voice was hoarse with anger. He turned towards Malachi and Deano, looking as if he could punch them both. I couldn't let him start a fight with them this was my battle not his "Leon. Please. it's ok…I'm alright" I was trying hard not to cry "But what the fuck Amelia… your bleeding" he looked towards my legs. I hadn't noticed that I also had a cut lip, as I licked the blood with my tongue; the taste of it made me gag again; it stung and tasted of metal, blood, semen and puke. Malachi shoved Leon inside the car. "I think you've caused enough drama for one night. Get in the car, big man".

Leon complied, shaking his head as he looked at me silently, mouthing, "What the fuck!" Malachi slammed the car door while Leon looked at me out of the window, confused. I will never forget the hurt in his eyes. Before they drove off, Malachi spoke, "Laters, Amelia, oh and remember." He sliced one finger across his neck, indicating a cutting motion. "And say Hi to your Mum for me… I know what bus she gets to and from work it would be a shame if anything happened to her; she's all you've got, right? I mean, your Dads a crazy cunt. Don't grass, Amelia. You know what happens to girls like you that do".Deano laughed as he spoke to Leon "I've got a funny video to show you later,

149

ain't I Amelia?".

I wanted to scream at him, not to show him. I wanted to say I would do anything but don't let Leon see that recording, because that was not who I was. I knew the message was clear. He would hurt me and hurt my Mum if I ever spoke about what had happened that night. My lips would be sealed. I just prayed to god I didn't have to go through that again. I'd move drugs, and I'd package gear, but sexual stuff wasn't my bag. I couldn't do that again. Now how the fuck did I get out of this shit ? I had talked the talk but it was pretty clear I couldn't walk the walk.

I knew girls like Tanisha could have handled tonight; she would have had sex happily with them and then boasted about it afterwards. But I was truly out of my depth and moving in circles that I couldn't handle but was so deep now that I couldn't see a way out. I heard Leon's Brother Julius call me from the door to the block. I ran towards my safety, but as the night air hit my lungs, my legs weakened, and I vomited outside on the concrete pavement. The car screeched away, and suddenly felt scared for Leon. He shouldn't have gone with them.

I thought at first that Julius was looking for Leon, so I motioned with my hand. Leon was there I wanted Leon to be as far away from them evil bastards as he could be. "He's gone, Julius, he's in that car". "I'm not looking for Leon. If he wants to act the big man, then let him. I'm out here coming to get you. Where have you been? Your Mum has been worried sick! And look at the state of you. You stink! Have you been drinking?" I just followed him into the sanctuary of my block, glad the lifts were working for once because I didn't think my legs would have carried me up the stairs.

Julius just looked at me like I was a drunken tramp; he shook his head as we entered the lift. "Your Mum has been worried about you, Amelia; it's unfair that you do this to her. She is a good woman, always trying her best, and you stay out late and get drunk. It would be best if you didn't do that. I'm surprised at you" I tried to speak, but no words came out. He continued talking, looking at me with such disgust "You shouldn't drink and run with those big boys. I thought you were different. I know this is not you. You were always such a sweet girl, Amelia, don't allow this block and this environment to taint you".

As the lift glided up to the seventeenth floor, I looked at my reflection in the glass mirror of the lift I wanted to cry and scream, tell him I'd been attacked I had been hurt. Every part of me, physically and emotionally, tonight had been damaged.

The girl looking back at me in that mirror was not the same one gliding down those stairs earlier, feeling like she was a big gangster's moll rude and not to be messed with. I was a scared child, and I'd been hurt big time. I wanted to break down and tell him, but for my Mother's safety, I had to keep my mouth shut.

I loved my Mum too much to put her in danger. The only words I mumbled were so quiet. It was as if I hadn't spoken to them at all. Julius kept saying repeatedly, "I thought you were different". "I am different", but he didn't hear me.

I was just another hood girl- invisible, silent, tormented and alone, returning home with a hangover and blood and semen running down my legs.

11

Amelia-Murders, Malbec and Mayhem

Between the smell of vomit from me and the smell of piss in that lift, it was like a metal box of hell taking me back up to my castle in the sky. As soon as I got onto my block floor, Julius pulled down my skirt, as if to make me look more presentable. It was done with such tenderness, so different from the animals I had just been with.

My Mum was already waiting by the door and looked relieved to see me. Part of me wanted to run into her arms, cry, and tell her what had just happened to me, but I was too afraid.

As soon as I stepped over the cheap, worn Welcome mat, Julius did all the talking, and I smiled and hid my pain as I ran to my room. My Mum liked Julius; he studied and went to church. He was Glenda's golden boy, and he had delivered me back home to her.

I clocked the discarded bottle of Vodka on the kitchen table and the small strip of Valium next to it. Mum was already in her warn cocoon of obliteration. There would be no lectures tonight. She was tired from work and already pissed. I couldn't have trusted myself not to have broken down if she had tried to question me or demanded to know where I had been.

Luckily, Mum fell comatose onto the sofa, where she slept with no questioning at the state of me. She would see the cut lip and bruises if she looked hard enough, but Mum or Julius hadn't seen my face in the light. Thank god for Council cutbacks that meant the lighting on the block wasn't working. The Microwave door left open was like a candlelight illuminating the kitchen where I got a glass of water. The shadows hid the majority of the carnage of the night.

I lay on my bed crying; I stung where they were so rough with me, and my body was already starting to bruise. I could still taste vomit in my mouth, blood and semen. I put music on as I dry retched into my waste paper bi, and I suddenly didn't want to get under the covers and have the smell of those men imprinted on it.

I knew I had to wash them out of my hair. I rushed to the shower and began to scrub at my body as if I could wash away all that had happened. My legs had track lines of blood and bodily fluids, and I burned my skin with how hot I put that shower on as I tried to wash the night off me. I felt sick that any part of those men could still be inside me. The smell of sex still hung on my clothes. It made me want to vomit, and again I retched, bringing up only yellow bile collapsing against the shower floor, suddenly feeling so tired.

I then chucked my dress out of the window. I didn't want my Mum to see or smell what had happened, and I never wanted to look at that dress ever again. I climbed back into my bed, put the covers over my head, and wished to be a child again when my only stress was who didn't invite me to their party.

I didn't want to be grown up. I didn't enjoy this life. I was still a child in the eyes of the law, but I honestly felt I was tainted

153

and impure. I scratched my fingernails against my arms, hating myself scratching over and over, stupid girl. What on earth had I done? The phone illuminated my room; it was on silent, but the light made me jump up in my bed, pulling the phone towards me and opening up the message in case the assholes had put the Video out. The message was cryptic, but I got the gist of it; there had been a fuck up of the highest proportion; no wonder Leon was being bundled into the car and taken away. If I felt that my world was falling apart, this was the icing on the cake, and the words I read made me cry even more.

Leon had accidentally stabbed the wrong boy in a retaliation thing which he was being forced to do to pay off his debt. A debt that he never really truly incurred, but Postcodes wars were all about face. It was a tragic case of mistaken identity; the boy had the same shoulder-length dreads and was in the same vicinity as the intended victim.

The blade had hit an artery, and within 15 minutes, the victim had bled out and was dead. Little did we know at the time that the dead boy was called Adimchi (Chi) for short, a churchgoing boy who had graduated the previous month, his Mum and Dad proud Nigerians. He's Dad was a Pastor at the local church that gave out food to the homeless and helped us all, and his Mum was a nurse at the local hospital.

This boy wasn't even from the E16 postcode, his only crime was to stop off and top up his Mums electric key before he collected her from her shift at Newham Hospital where she was working. Being the good son, he didn't want her getting the bus when it was dark. That one decision to stop to collect his Mum cost him his life.

The boy who was meant to be stabbed was a loudmouth, robbing drug dealing rude boy who was now smoking a spliff o his own tower block in Custom House. He was laughing at the massacre that was meant for him. The bastards had tried and failed to stab him. He took out his phone, ready to send his retaliation video to his enemies.The silly idiots had killed one of their own, fucking amateurs.

I never knew where Malachi had taken Leon, and I knew that from Julius's calm demeanour, he had no clue that his brother was in such deep shit. Julius and Leon were clashing all the time lately about Leon staying out late and needing a direction in life. So it was common for Leon to disappear some nights and come home in the early hours. I knew this worried Glenda but she had tried so hard to make him behave and she hated to see the conflict between her boys, Julius was starting to give up on him.

As I lay in bed that night with so much going over and over in my mind, I feared that Leon was not safe. I cried that night until my tears ran dry. One-night and absolute carnage had smashed into our lives, and many lives were turned upside down; amazing how things change so quickly in the hood. It really was like snakes and ladders. One day you could be at the top, but one wrong turn and you were falling down right to the bottom with the snakes.

My cheap fake Louis Vuitton handbag with my Morning After Pill was still at Malachi's flat; there was no way I could go and get it now. Luckily, my phone was with me, and I could see all the messages about Leon fucking up; it was entirely coded, but I knew the code words and looked at the clock; it was 5am.It was a school day tomorrow, and I knew I had to go because we didn't need any hassle from the School Teachers or Social Services. I looked around in my drawer next to my bed and swallowed half a blue tablet of Promethazine. I had stolen a strip of tablets from

155

Peter for emergencies and bit into it. I knew this would hopefully send me into some sleep. However, I had been twisting around in the bed. All my sheets were tangled as if I was trapped in a nightmare. I would have given anything to have been in a bad dream and wake not to feel sore in between my legs that were stinging so badly and my backside was painful.

But the real pain was inside my chest it was heavy, my life was never going to be the same again ever! The following day, I had such a hangover my head was literally banging. I stung when I went to pass urine, but I figured I had to carry on as usual.

Leon's situation and the killing drama would eclipse my own rape and take the heat off me for the moment girls like us ended up in problems with boys and men like this. The girls had explained this; hence the First Aid kit of Morning After Pill and drugs for STIs.

I should just put on my knickers and smile as if everything was ok. I had no right to complain. You roll with the big boys; this is what happened. Why couldn't I believe the bravado I repeatedly told myself, trying to convince myself not to break because I wasn't sure I would have the strength to put myself back together.

I swallowed paracetamol, red bull, and some Pro Plus tablets, put on my school uniform, and went to school. My mum had already left for work and left a note to say she was trying to get out earlier tonight so she could cook and we could chat. I felt alarmed at this. Did she sense something was up with me? Because to eat at a table with my Mum must mean something was up. We had not eaten at a table together in years, maybe a birthday or something but we tended to eat at different times.

That Morning the estate seemed quieter than usual. That's when you know something big had gone down, no little hood rats out and about; even though it was early, the block seemed to mirror how I felt dark, desolate and withdrawing. I looked at the vomit outside the lift, and there were still tire marks from the car where Malachi had driven away so fast. I cringed, replaying the night's event. It was like this was bringing me back to reality. The vomit on the floor the reminder it was real this was not a dream.

I walked to school in so much pain; every step hurt me. I was so bruised, and even though I had showered myself in the hottest setting again this morning, I still felt dirty. I didn't think I would ever feel clean again. My body had been violated in every way possible, and I could never make that right again. I was spoiled goods like rotten fruit, waiting to be discarded; nobody wanted the apple with the bruise.

My School day passed quietly, and thank fuck I spent lunchtime in the room where the safeguarding officer sits, a space to be nurtured and take time out. That alcohol rub they use to clean the whiteboard in school well; the smell instantly made me think of the red wine. I had to run from the classroom to puke in the toilet. I think the teachers could sense something was wrong with me. I looked pale, the dark circles under my eyes were terrible, and I still felt like I could smell the men on me.

Being asked by that one Teacher if I was ok nearly made me break down, but instead, I just smiled, saying I was ok. I think she could see the bite marks on my neck. If only she could have seen the rest of me, it hurt to sit down.

Tears stung my eyes, and I was so ready to tell all, to open up and tell an adult that I had done something so stupid and become involved in some crazy shit. I had been a bad person and now I was truly paying the price for that. And I truly did not know of a way out.

My Mums words echoed in my head, and Deanos's threat of violence and Mum's words of getting outsiders involved in our lives would cause untold problems. If I told the teacher, I had been raped. The teacher would alert the police and social services, and then what would happen- Malachi would harm my Mum, and that Video would go viral. I didn't want to be known as a snitch, fuck that. I bit back my tears. I'm not saying anything. Shut up and put up was the rule of the estate.

I was home early that night and lay in the lukewarm bath, trying to ease the aching. Junior was looking after Peters flat tonight so I could rest, I told them I was so hungover I needed a night off. They all thought it was because of Leon and I was laying low in case the feds started sniffing around so I let people think what they wanted. I had two polo neck jumpers, one black and one brown, so thankfully could rotate them to hide the marks on my neck.

Mum was home early. She had a takeaway bag that smelled like fish and Chips. But it was just chips, I sat and devoured them. This was a treat; we couldn't afford the fish if only she knew what I had been eating the night before, the best-cut steak and expensive wine, but I paid the price dearly for that meal. I would never eat steak again and when I think of it, seeing the blood on the meat would forever make me remember my own blood that was spilt that night.Mum couldn't stop talking about the stabbing from the night before. I wish we didn't have to discuss it because I was scared something I would say would trip me up. I knew how much Mum loved Leon. It would break her heart. Yet still, she was going on about it. "Did you hear about it? Everyone at work is in shock. He graduated last month from Cambridge. I know his Mother, Taiwo, really well, and His Dad is the Pastor of

Glenda's Church; they are such a nice family, it's scary out there now." Mum was pushing more chips onto my plate, and she had even stolen the little sachets of Tomato Ketchup and Vinegar from work, the TV was on in the background some nondescript TV program, I think it might have been The One show that intro always pissed me off with its upbeat song.

I shoved the chips into my mouth so I didn't have to talk, realizing how hungry I was. Mum gave me the majority of the chips, and I could see how what had happened had shaken her up. "Taiwo and Pastor Tim worked hard all their lives to put this boy through Uni, and then it is snatched away in a few seconds in the street. Such a waste of a life, and for what? seriously Amelia, I wish we could leave this place. It was never like this when I was growing up around here. I'm told this boy wasn't involved in Gangs, Amelia; you have to promise me that you are not getting involved in anything you are not meant to. It's Just the money and the new stuff you have and the help with the rent. Was it really from Dad? Or something else." I rolled my eyes, ready to shut off or storm out. "Mum, please just leave it, ok I'm not stupid. Dad gets me those things… please don't start. Can't we have one night together without you going off at me. I'm not involved in any gangs I promise you ok?" I could understand how Mum must feel the loss of a child in a tragic way made every Mother thankful it was not them that time. And I was happy to pretend I was a Child still laying on the sofa without a care in the world, except I wasn't a child without a care was I really?.

Taiwo had come to the UK with nothing and worked day and night to get the best for her child. Taiwo got her nursing degree and put her only son through Uni by working every hour god sent, only to have his life snuffed out on an East London street- He would have been safer in Nigeria, and that's painful for her

159

after all; she sacrificed to be here. The poor Boys Dad was a pious man who preached forgiveness and salvation. That must be hard now to believe in a God who would do this to this Man's son, his prodigy, his life, his reason for living it was tragic. The sad thing was Chi had been on his phone to Taiwo, who was at work then, to ask how much he should put on the electricity when the attack occurred. She heard every word and scream of her son's last moments while she helped save the lives of others less than a mile from where she was working, nursing in an East London Hospital.

Lady Luck is a bitch. She wasn't rolling that night for any of us from E15. That night was terrible, and many of us would pay the price. Life would never be the same again. I almost confided in Mum what had happened to me, but every time I tried, I couldn't speak the words, so instead, I let her cuddle me and held back the tears, so glad for the first time in months that I had my Mum here on our sofa, and we were safe. We watched some crappy American sitcom, and I tried to forget my life.

It had been years since I had sat like this with her, peaceful and content, what everyday teenage life should be; it was rare to get this time with her. She was always either working, washing up or doing something; this was calm. I do not think we had ever sat together like this in years.

Tonight I felt safe; I thought I could close my eyes and blot out everything that had gone on. The smell and touch of my Mum were comforting, like a warm blanket on a cold night, a hot water bottle and hot chocolate when your chilled, and just for that moment and that time, you're safe, protected and loved. Then my phone notifications started going crazy, I should have put my phone on silent, but I knew I couldn't. I had Junior and Jason, a little younger, running Peter's flat tonight. And I trusted him; he was an intelligent kid, but I knew I had to keep my phone on.

Then I opened the phone, and my WhatsApp notification made my stomach go over; it was from Deano; the words and then the Video made me sit up so fast my Mum jumped. As I opened the message, I could see from the image that it was me on my hands and knees with Malachi's Penis in my mouth; that was just the beginning. I knew it was 24 seconds long. I couldn't bear to relive that night again. I ran to the toilet and vomited up all the chips I had just eaten; my Mum was rubbing my back like she had done when I was a smaller kid and sick. "Oh my goodness, are you ok?" she held my hair back from my face as I vomited into the toilet bowl, struggling to speak. "Yeah.it must have been the chips" tears streaming down my face, my pain so evident if my Mum would have looked closer, if she would have just questioned and probed me a little more Still, Mum thought it was just because I had been sick I was in such a mess.

You know when things are going well, and then your instinct kicks in to say hang on a minute, girls, like you don't deserve happiness. Something terrible is going to happen. Amelia, you should never let your guard down; relax while you can, but then something really shit is going to happen to disturb your peace.

Being exposed like that on a recording, it's just embarrassing. Having the world see your naked body as a teenage girl that's horrendous. I would have rather been stabbed and lived with a physical scar than have the whole neighbourhood see me naked, exposed, doing things I didn't want to do, videos of me gagging, being raped.

At the same time, they laughed and watched me cry, except there was no sound on those videos, so what was happening was not apparent for all intents and purposes. It looked like I was

161

enjoying myself when it couldn't have been further from the truth. Deano told me he had sent the Video to someone close to me but had yet to identify who and that if I didn't meet him on Friday night, he would send the Video to everyone on that estate and my school.

I did something so stupid I still do not know why. I took the sim out of the phone. I chucked it over the balcony of my tower block so I didn't have to see messages anymore or see the replies or live with the threats. I had my old phone with just my Mum and Dad's number in it and placed that in my hand as if somehow removing that sim with my link to that world somehow eradicated it was me. It was a stupid move becoming uncontactable, but I knew it was something I had to do.I was scared, and If I didn't see what they shared, it couldn't hurt me, right? Indeed, it would all die down, as the wrong killing was the talk of the day.

I was going to tell people I'd lost my phone and get that message sent to Malachi; besides, he must have bigger problems than me now.But I was wrong; after school, Deano was waiting for me parked up close to the school gates I tried to ignore him, but as I walked along, his car pulled up slowly beside me, Aliyah, my friend who was with me, was dismissed. She ran knowing that older men like Deano spelt trouble. "Get in the car!", Just four words spoken with such anger and menace in them. I couldn't run.I could barely breathe his dark eyes looked more menacing in the daylight, and his face looked much older, He had fine lines around his eyes; he looked older to be about 50. I knew I was going to have to do whatever he said. With my heart pounding against my chest, I got in the car's passenger seat. He smiled leeringly. "Your Phones off, Amelia, I've been trying to contact you… that's very naughty of you. I thought you were warned about what would happen if you did not adhere to the rules." My mouth was suddenly so dry I could barely speak "I Broke my phone by mistake" I was scrunching a bit of tissue in my hand, feeling sweat pooling on my head and neck. I was so scared. "Well, that's very fucking unfortunate you broke your phone; you wouldn't be trying to avoid me now, would you?" I bit my lip. I could feel myself trembling and I willed my body to showing him just how nervous I actually was. "No, I promise. you know how wasted I was... I damaged the phone, and it won't work, I promise I wasn't hiding from you, I'm not stupid"

His smile unnerved me, I couldn't read by his expression if he was buying what I said or the complete opposite. "That's funny because when I sent that Video on WhatsApp, two blue ticks came up to show it was delivered and read...you wouldn't be lying to me now, Amelia, would you?" I felt my cheeks burn red with shame and fear could he tell I was lying? I knew he could make this so much worse for me and had the power to turn my world upside down with one click on that phone.

Deano drove towards the desolate arches of the over ground railway tracks that run down the town centre, overlooked by our looming Tower block; he undid his trousers, grabbed me by my hair, and forced himself into my mouth. I gagged but continued obeying him and blanked out what was happening. I was nearly sick as he finished all over my coat and uniform. Laughing, he opened the car door ready for me to leave. "This weekend, I need you, I've got some older dealers coming down from Kent, and they like young girls. I'll send a new phone to you, and I want you to wear school uniform, like... get some white knee-high socks and look really slutty... remember you owe a massive debt now Amelia we are meeting at the Holiday Inn Stratford, wear a long coat to hide the school uniform alright I don't want no

163

cameras picking up no jail bait pussy, or get the Niqab on its time for you to make a start paying back your debt "I was confused momentarily confused. "What debt do I owe? I have no debt." His smile was sickening and the smell of him on me made me again want to puke. "Oh, but you do, little Amelia…. Your Boy Leon fucked up big time, and he ain't around to pay the price, so it looks like you will be paying it for him." "What! Your joking, what happened had nothing to do with me. I didn't even know what really went down that night. You know that I was with Malachi and you. I wasn't even there when he killed Chi" .

Deano laughed, shaking his head "You both left that trap house wide open to the rude little boys who, in turn, thought they could take the piss; Money has been invested in this place, and you two abandoned it, now due to all this shit and it is a right headache I tell you, you will have to work for me for a bit to clear the money we lost over these two days it's only fair.".

Tears stung my eyes, this was all just getting so much worse day by day "How much?" Deano was suddenly serious, I could tell he was enjoying my discomfort "At the moment £4000" My mouth gaped open with shock. " What the actual fuck! I can't afford that that money, Deano, I can't do nothing this weekend. My Mum and the school are on my case and If I fuck up once more…" I stopped talking and let the tears flow, and I didn't know what to do. I felt wretched; my protector, my lifeline Leon was gone, and I was stuck between a rock and a hard place.

I had to protect my Mum and Dad; these men would be like lions on them, and the Video they had of me. I did not want that to go anywhere; how could I ever show my face again? It would be disastrous. And now I would have to carry the debt that wasn't ever really ours in the first place and get deeper and deeper into shit that I couldn't handle.I felt like an animal in a trap.

I was caged while my masters poked and prodded me, like one of those giant bears chained to the owner and forced to dance. Deano ignored my tears "You will pay me and Malachi back, you're a nice girl...look at you so pretty, I have big plans for you, Starting Saturday night, you ain't going to be on the rag are you?" I didn't know what to say so I said Yes in the hope it would deter them "Yeah... my period is due any day now" Deano shuffled around in the glove compartment of the car chucking a box at me it was Norethisone a drug to be taken to prevent periods "Take this to make sure your clean for the weekend and maybe think about getting on the Pill that way you'll be safer, all right sweetheart, oh another thing make sure you shave all over we want you to look as young as can be" Then his mobile phone rang; he shut the door and was off, and I was left standing with a box of tablets, semen all over my jacket as well as my School Uniform and a debt of £4000 for not overseeing the trap house and being raped the night before. Meanwhile my Boyfriend had killed a man he wasn't meant to. And it wasn't like I left the place unattended, but I couldn't trust Junior. He had tried to jump into Leon's shoes too quickly and had fucked up, and I should never have fucking trusted him I rushed home put my uniform and jacket in the bath and washed them with washing powder getting rid of any trace of that evil man. I hung them out on our balcony praying that would be dry for school the next day.

Some girls may enjoy the notoriety of being the top selection but not me I was done, I would have given anything to go back to being invisible and not caught up in any of this shit and sit in my supermarket trainers and Primark clothing with my vagina intact and my body clean.

But tonight I was sitting in my hood-rich jacket, Nike Air Max trainers and so sore I could barely sit down still two days later, It was not a good place to be, I longed for my childhood, I was so broken I couldn't even cry anymore.

I wished I could have just shut the door and never had to venture out again but I had to ensure the trap house was ok, or else I'd be incurring more debts I still had to make sure stuff was being moved correctly I had to show my face and make sure all the little rude boys knew they were being watched.

I suddenly had a thought about contacting Katy and seeing if I could perhaps rob her for one of her designer handbags or sunglasses to try and get the money back that way. But I had stupidly got rid of that SIM and besides I had the feeling she wouldn't be so brave as to venture to these ends without Leon calling her in. I couldn't disappear or else there would be trouble, ramifications like a job with a contract I couldn't not show up or they would be consequences and not just for me.

My mind and body felt like a washing machine turning over and over, what the fuck was I going to do? This was the time I started cutting myself with my razor so that the physical pain would take over the emotional pain I was feeling. I had seen someone doing this on Tik Tok, so when I started, it became addictive.

The first time I did it, I was alone in the bathroom, took the blade, sliced just a tiny part of my arm and watched as the blood trickled down my arm. It was like a release. I was in control of this; I was cutting myself; this was me; I was bleeding. I had the power over my body and nobody else.

Night times were always the most challenging time; it would take me a very long time to be able to drift off to sleep. I was tempted to smoke some weed but figured Mum would smell it, so

I took some of Peter's Sleeping tablets and drank cheap alcohol, but it made me sad at times; it didn't help clear my mind. It would just be more convoluted.

Every night my mind would just replay what happened over and over, the flashbacks of the rape were intense, and when they happened, only the cutting of my arms would stop me from remembering. The physical pain shook me out of that mental torture. My arms were becoming a mess, just like my life. I dreaded what was to come. My body would have to be used to repay the debt, and I wished I could die.

For the first time, I felt suicidal, Would I just become numb to having sex with men I didn't like?. Would I ever escape this horrible nightmare I was in? That same night a burner phone dropped through the letter box.

When I opened it up, Deanos message was already showing, "Hello Amelia, your Debt is now at £4500.". Turns out you going off the radar wasn't such a good move, was it?"

I knew then I was well and truly fucked. I had no way out.

12

Louisa- A Village To Raise A Child & a Hood To Mourn Them

They say it takes a village to raise a child and a community to mourn one. A photo of Adimchi (Chi) was pinned to the Domestic Offices door at work in the hospital, and a collection was going around for the family, and we all gave as much as we could, as much as our salaries would allow.

Glenda was close to Taiwo because of their church links, she cooked food for the family as soon as she got home from work, and I helped her carry the pots to the house the family lived in. The house was one of the few at the start of the entrance to our estate, the lucky ones who had homes on the ground, a small front garden and our tower block looming over them.

Jerome also had a home here he lived just a few doors along from Taiwo. I remembered being so impressed by Jerome's home when I was younger. I was the foolish teenage girl in her School Uniform, dreaming of having a garden and hanging out my washing on the line one day. That dream with him never materialised.

It was a solemn pilgrimage to the home. I helped Glenda carry pots loaded with rice and meat wrapped in tea towels to keep them warm, a small show of generosity in one family's time of need. We feed those who are mourning. It's what we do, we feel useless, but we feed because everybody has to eat right? I don't know how Taiwo got the money, but the funeral was booked, and I helped with the paperwork.

Adimchi was to be buried in the East London Cemetery, a large affair with no expense spared. I went with Taiwo to the cemetery to look at burial plots, don't ask me how, as it was pretty surreal. I was scared to think if anything happened to Amelia and me, we would end up in the Pauper's grave.

I couldn't afford my child in life and certainly not in death. Taiwo's pain was visceral, the noise of a woman crying for her dead child; it stays with you forever, a howl of pain from the depths of their souls, for it can never heal. It's a hurt that can never be erased. It is a pain we hear, and we thank god for our Children who are still alive and breathing next to us.

The funeral was to be a lavish event, and I was glad that, for once, I was helpful. I helped Glenda go to the local florist, where we arranged flowers and helped with the order of service. I had never been involved in anything to do with death and funerals, so it was quite an eye-opener. I had only seen those trolleys at work come and collect the bodies. I had never been to a funeral before in my life.

The mood shifts when something tragic happens on an estate; it's almost like a small pocket of calm, a tiny moment of reflection. Teenagers suddenly behave, Police do routine patrols, and people know shit has hit the fan.

My Daughter has been a different child. Amelia has been more withdrawn than usual, but I've just put it down to the mood on the estate and that Leon had been staying at an Uncles in

Kent. But now, I am grateful that she is under my roof and I can breathe. It's not my child in the morgue. We live to fight another day.

Amelia readily ensured her uniform was ready for school; something had shifted, yet ironically, this was when Jerome began to spiral out of control. I knew Jerome was ill by the phone calls that had been made to me and the comments on the street. This was typical of my life; Jerome was a loose cannon when Amelia behaved.

I could never get a true sense of peace; one was always out of balance and off-kilter. I knew to put our cheap white ikea dining room chair under the door latch to keep him out; he was unstable, signaling danger. I wouldn't be able to sleep unless I knew me and Amelia were able to shut out the outside world.

It made me think about my childhood and that feeling of not being safe until something physical was between me and the door. I could be sleeping but waiting for that noise at the door that would signal danger and disruption; funny how it had followed me into Adulthood.

I gave Leonie the heads up, but she was busy over Croydon Way and didn't want to make the journey to sort her brother out. She had a new man, and he was busy taking up her time, so to get the train over to East London to ensure her brother swallowed some pills was something she didn't want to do.

As I was on annual leave using up some well needed down time, I decided I'd cook Amelia and me a meal, it was only a Ready Meal Lasagna from Iceland with some Garlic bread, but I thought it would be nice to eat together at the table again. I couldn't believe it when I heard Jerome's voice with Amelia as they let themselves into the flat, both laughing. Jerome had that look about him that meant he was in one of his manic episodes.

I had to hope for the best.

I wondered why Amelia thought it was OK to turn up with her Dad in tow because he and I didn't talk much. But she might have found comfort in having us both together, so I complied. I wouldn't cause a fuss as that would be like lighting up a firework, he would explode and I'd be the one left burnt and picking up the pieces. Worst-case scenario, I would crumble a Valium into his beer, and hopefully, he would mellow. I was wrong.

He was on edge, shaking his leg, grimacing his face. I knew the signs he hadn't taken his medication for a while; thanks, Leonie! I hope this new bloke was worth it. Jerome was looking around the room, convinced we had cameras. Oh shit, the paranoid Jerome was in the building, and I knew this would not end well.

Amelia must have sensed this, too, as she began to try to appease him; it worked for a bit before he started to bring up Leon. "Where is he, Amelia? Do you know? Because some stupid little rude boys are causing havoc in Peter's flat, I need to sort it out for Malachi because who knows what's happening. And Deano, he is so angry. They won't just give me my smoke, and I need that it's like my medicine"" Amelia was suddenly alert. "How do you know Deano?" Jerome gracefully took the beer that I gave him with the crushed Valium in it. I was pissed off, to be honest with you, to be wasting one of my beers and emergency Valium on him. "I've known Deano for years; he recently got out of prison, Me and him are good mates. We go back years; he knew you when you were a baby. Is he a spy? I'm going to have to keep him under close watch.".

Amelia slammed her fork onto the plate, causing it to crack right down the middle, which shocked me as my child was not prone to emotional outbursts. Something was wrong. "Don't mention Malachi or Deano in this flat, Dad! Ever!!!" Amelia

171

jumped up from the table, breathing heavily. "Deano is not your friend, Dad; he never was. He is evil" Amelia placed her hands on the table, breathing heavily as if she was having a panic attack. I had never seen Amelia raise her voice to her Dad, she was scared, and I could sense something was off here. Who was Malachi and Deano? Why had their names created such a reaction in my child? Call it a Mothers instinct, but I knew the shit would hit the fan.

The noise of Jerome's phone receiving message after message started pinging through. Jerome's phone had automatically connected to our Wi-Fi. Our one indulgence, a cheap Internet connection enabled Jerome to download all the messages on WhatsApp he was being sent and had missed; due to having no data, this signed his death warrant. Amelia tried to get the phone from Jerome's hand, but it was too late; he snatched it away from Amelia's grasp and started downloading the video and messages on his phone. All I could hear was the voice of a male saying, "Yeah, you like that, don't you, you dirty bitch on your hands and knees begging us for it".

I started to scoop the Lasagna out of the black plastic tub it had been cooking in, gently putting it onto plates as if this was some homemade dish rather than a cheap supermarket one, Family value. Keep calm and pretend it's all fine, the mantra of my life. Look, the food is here; let's pretend everything is normal.

Jerome watched, entranced with the image on the screen, repeatedly shaking his head and saying No over and over to himself. His words, even though they were spoken quietly, were loaded. Amelia looked from her Dad to me, tears welling in her eyes, then threw her plate of Lasagna towards the wall to get Jerome's attention away from the phone he was engrossed in. The Lasagna hit the cheap magnolia walls, the whole lot sliding down, looking like a bizarre art piece. "Please, Dad, stop it! Please. Enough, just put the phone down." Jerome then pushed the phone into my face, and I could hear a girl crying and moaning; my blood ran cold because I knew it was Amelia before I even had to look at that phone.

I didn't want to focus on the image before me because I knew my child's cry of pain anywhere. Every Mother has that instinct, you just know your child's sound, it's something that is programmed in you. It wasn't pleasure; I was hearing; it was torture. I refused to look at what happened on that phone because I knew it was my Amelia. I couldn't face it.

I almost smashed the phone out of Jerome's hand to stop the image from being real and being seen. "Get that phone away from me. I don't want to see it." I pushed Jerome with all my strength as if moving him away could make the video disappear, and then we could all pretend this hadn't happened, paper over the cracks, which was the story of my life. Scrape the Lasagna off the wall and pretend that everything is OK. This was not happening.

Jerome shoved me back, and I fell into the living room, falling backwards and hitting the coffee table as he kicked me in the stomach. "It's all your fucking fault, you fucking bitch. You always were a slag, and then because of you our girl becomes one." I was winded. I curled into a ball, knowing that when he was in a psychotic episode, there was no calming him down. His strength became almost superhuman. I had seen three or four Police officers try to restrain him in the past, so little old me had no chance. I just curled into a ball and hoped he would stop without doing me too much damage that I needed a hospital because that would have been bad. You couldn't just turn up to A&E after being assaulted now, they asked too many questions.

It was Amelia's screaming that eventually made him stop kicking me. Our child's scream was so loud and guttural that I'm surprised the whole block did not come running.

Amelia was clawing at his back with her nails, and when he turned around, I was scared he would hit her. Seeing her face full of tears and so much pain, he stopped. He was breathing heavily, exerted from kicking me. "Why Amelia? look at me! He is an old man why?!" he grabbed her face, squeezing his hands around her jaw. He was hurting her, and I knew I had to get him off her. Her voice was muffled. "I had no choice". Jerome's eyes were now wild; he was manic. I tried to stand, the pain in my ribs made me cry out, but I knew I had to get up and get him away from Amelia.

I reached towards the only thing I could see, a glass that had luckily not broken, when I fell onto the coffee table. I grabbed the glass and smashed the top end against the wall to break it. It cracked at the top, and a large shard fell to the ground, so all that was left in my hand was a sharp weapon. I struck him from behind and dug the glass into his back. He reared up in pain and released his grip from Amelia. I threw the glass away from him, terrified he could use it against us. He was momentarily stunned, "I'm going to kill them all. Amelia, I will stab the lot of them. Give me that glass", But it was too late. I couldn't pick it back up because my hands trembled too much. When I screamed out, my voice didn't sound like me, it was as if it was someone else entirely. "Get out of this flat and get away from my Daughter!" Jerome raced out of the flat, tearing off his T-Shirt, revealing a cut that was bleeding from where I had glassed him. "Where are they? I'm going to kill them all" he ran out of the flat.

As he ran towards the door, Amelia started following "Dad, No! Don't go up there!" he ran out the door with Amelia on

174

his heels. I had no clue where they were running to, but I was barefoot and following. I needed to get my baby back inside the flat, "Amelia leave him. Let him go, for fucks sake, come back."I ran after them treading on stairwells that contained god knows what, but I knew I had to get Amelia away from him as quickly as possible; he was dangerous.

Jerome knowing exactly where Amelia had been hanging out, ran up to Peter's flat and banged on the door. Junior, who was keeping watch, almost shit himself, thinking it was the Police. When he saw it was just Jerome, he breathed a sigh of relief and opened the door, and even if he hadn't opened the door, Jerome would have kicked the flimsy wooden door off the hinges.

How that boy had wished he would have kept that door shut, Jerome was wild, incensed, talking to himself now and banging his hands against his head to stop the voices, a sure sign we were beyond talking him down when he was at this head hitting stage we were really in the shit.

Amelia was crying and screaming, her words not making sense. I must have cut my face when he was kicking me, as my tears were now mingling with blood as I tried to pull Amelia back out of the flat back to ours so I could shut the door and put a chair on the handle of our door and call the Police, they could do their usual routine take him to hospital and get him sectioned. My priority was to get Amelia to safety.

Peter's flat was full of drugs and a few teeange boys, the whole place stunk of weed, and a string pulled the packages down onto the other balcony. I was momentarily stunned that this was happening above me and never even knew. Peter was sitting in the corner with giant Beats headphones on and reading a Beano magazine. He smiled and waved to me, oblivious to the carnage that had just crashed through his door. Even my blood-soaked top, crying child and psychotic ex-partner didn't stir him. He saw me and knew I was a safe person to be trusted, one of the good ones. With me in his flat, he knew it meant safety, one of the very few in his life.

Jerome smashed the coffee table into the air, drug paraphernalia smashed to the ground, weighing scales, plastic bags, lumps of weed, white powder and Peter's medication all over the dirty floor. Jerome's sweat beads glistened on his skin. "Where is he? I'm going to kill him," he yelled in the faces of the young boys, and they were all jumping back, laughing and getting their phones out, recording the circus. Then they ran when they saw the mighty strength that people in mental health crises could obtain. Jerome was like a lion, teeth bared, poised to attack. There was no stopping him now. He was beyond the point of control, I would have called the Police, but I had run out with no phone. I was just there in my bare feet, trying to get Amelia to me so we could run and get away from him. But I knew Amelia was not going to leave him alone.

The teenagers had escaped outside and no doubt called in the elders. It was a show, alright Jerome was riled up on lack of medication, mental health and rage at seeing his Daughter having sex on his phone. Then, realizing something was amiss, Peter started to get scared and started crying and rocking back and forth on the sofa, emitting a low-level moan a vulnerable man with learning difficulties, caught up in some crazy shit just because the council deemed him safe to be cared for in the community.

With the teenagers outside the flat, Jerome ran out towards the stairwell. I was shouting at Peter "It's OK" and to lock the door. I saw Amelia going up the stairs, so I followed. Jerome was approaching the top of the block. My stomach went over; I knew this was not good. He went through the fire escape, which gave him access to the top of the tower block where the pirate radio station tannoys once were, now there was mobile phone masts everywhere.

I scrambled up the stairs, following my baby girl, who called for her daddy to stop and get back down. I had never felt fear like this in my life, and like a lioness protecting her cub, I just wanted to get her off the top of the block and back behind the door of our flat. Too many people pushed past me, phones in their hands, sensing a show, a drama. Good old Crazy Jerome, off his meds, was always a source of entertainment. Anything for a click would be all over Snapchat and socials very quickly.

As if his child being violated wasn't bad enough, here was the crazy Dad to top off the show, excellent viewing. Amelia's screams were becoming more hollow as she was losing her voice. Jerome was pacing up and down right near the edge of the tower block, talking to himself. Time seemed to go in slow motion, and everyone seemed to fall silent; there was a change in the atmosphere. It was no longer a joke. This was some serious shit. The laughter and the chatter behind us stopped. I could only hear the city's soundtrack, trains in the distance, and the gentle hum of traffic, but we all fell silent on top of that block. Amelia walked closer towards Jerome with her arms outstretched. "Dad, I need you to walk towards me, Dad, please! Look at me… get away from the edge". My heart was pounding so hard I could feel it beating against my chest as the realization hit me he could fall. He could make Amelia fall with him; my body went cold. I didn't know what to do, my instinct was to run towards Amelia, but I knew any sudden movement now could be disastrous.

Jerome was pacing up and down, muttering to himself and hitting his head with his hands; his tears mingled with snot as he broke down. I knew the voices in his head were terrible this time, so he was punching his head to make them stop. When he was at this stage, no matter what me and Amelia would do, we couldn't calm him. I watched him pace back and forth and then scream with such intensity we all drew back. It was as if he was going to charge towards Amelia. He beat his chest and roared so loud it reverberated around the top of the block, and then silence.

It happened so quickly that it was like a figment of my imagination. One moment he was there, and the next, he was gone, just a collective gasp from everyone on the top of the block. Rather than charge towards Amelia, he ran the other way. A bird with no wings, an angel or a devil falling towards their death from a cold tower block that should have been condemned years ago. He never stood a chance falling nineteen floors to cold, hard concrete. He had jumped over the side of the block. There was no way he would have survived falling from that height.

Amelia fell to her knees, the cries of my child made me run to her, scooping her into my arms and collapsing on top of her to ensure she didn't follow Jerome, like throwing a fire blanket over a raging fire, I needed her to be calm and be still and for me to cover her and protect her from what had just happened.

I can't remember much about what happened next except for the strong smell of aftershave and a large black boy scooping Amelia and me into his arms and shielding us. I did not have a clue who he was. Voices were shouting, so many people running around all over the place, then someone calling 999, someone walking me and Amelia back down the concrete stairs, me holding onto Amelia while she sobbed, and me just looking down at my bare feet and noticing how dirty they were. It's unbelievable how you remember things during traumatic incidents, and mine was, what will they think of me with dirty feet? Drama reverberated around us, hurried voices, people rushing to depart the news of what had happened, doors being opened, and people coming out the smells of their homes opening up into the night

I remember breathing in the scent of my Daughter's shampoo on her head as I held her to me while she screamed the smell of coconut oil and Victoria's Secret spray; even amid the carnage, the smell of my child was my comfort. She was in my arms; she was safe. I know I didn't want to let her go, but somehow I was being pushed and pulled and shouting so much noise and, eventually, blue lights and uniforms.

I ended up in Glenda's front room rather than our flat and felt dizzy and disorientated; then I fell to my knees, and the world went black. I was on her sofa with its plastic covers, and my body was sticking to it. I still had no clue why she covered that sofa in Plastic but it was just something she had always done.

Nineteen floors up and down onto the concrete. When Jerome hit the ground, it was not a pretty sight. He landed right outside the back of the block where luckily, nobody else was walking. His body was smashed into pieces; the impact was like an egg hitting the ground, you get the idea., blood, body parts; whoever ran down to take a picture for their social media was pretty shocked. It was disturbing; You see something like that, you can never un-see it again. It was horrendous, the stuff of nightmares.

The Police and the ambulance, even though there was no need for one, arrived pretty sharpish. And drama in the Hood gets around quickly. It is exciting when something dramatic happens, something different from the normality of everyday life. EastEnders was playing out right outside your door, which broke up your ordinary day. They could gasp and gossip. My

179

goodness, you think our life is terrible; look at them!

The news and the buzz of the shock of Jerome's Suicide provided the evening entertainment for the block and the opposite blocks. It was like Chinese whispers within an hour of the suicide everyone knew.The police and ambulances drew attention the blue lights made people go and have a look like moths to the flames.

I woke with Glenda sitting next to me in a plastic garden chair by my sofa while I pieced together what that night had brought for us all. I can't even remember how I got back to my flat, but it had been tidied up, the glass swept away, and the Lasagna placed in the bin.

I momentarily thought it might have all been an awful dream, then I felt my ribs ache and knew it was not a dream. This was reality. I sat up too quickly, my blood running cold; where was my Daughter? "Where is Amelia?" Glenda placed a reassuring hand on me, sitting me back down "It's OK. You're safe. Amelia is safe; she is sleeping." I breathed a sigh of relief and realized I must have been talking in my sleep; how could I have passed out or blacked out? For a few fleeting moments when everything is OK, then it hits. It wasn't a bad dream; this was real Jerome had jumped from the top of the tower block in a rage after seeing his only Daughter having sex with more than one guy, already mentally ill from not taking his medication; this had just exacerbated his psychosis. Amelia had been given a sedative as she was hysterical; that's all I knew. Glenda provided something to help her sleep, and she was curled up in bed. The Police had taken down many witness statements, and they all knew Jerome by name and weren't surprised it had come to this. Jerome was bound to either harm someone or himself sooner or later. Case closed. A crazy fucker who is a pain in the ass commits suicide.

I felt a mixture of emotions and anger that he would do this. I felt relief that I would never have to live in fear of a man and his moods, always waiting for the next argument or fight that would make things go out of control. And sadness, he was still the Dad of my only child, and her pain was mine too.

No matter how I dressed this shit up, this would be a mind fuck of the highest proportion for my baby, forget me. It was Amelia that I was hurting for. I fell out of love with Jerome many years ago, and I knew we had built our life together on rocky foundations. I was just a child escaping a complicated and broken childhood. He was the older mental health patient enjoying the pleasure of a young girl, no wonder it all went to shit.

When a man keeps you in fear of him because of his moods, your forever premeditating about what's going to happen next; it's hard. There had been so many fights and trouble over the years. He always had that link to me through Amelia, and I hate to admit it, but I was petrified of him.

Now having that link to him broken through death made me feel like I could breathe. Always waiting for his abuse, always knowing you had to keep away from him when he was in one of his bad moods.

Living off your wits wasn't easy, and now that spell had been broken, I was free. I no longer had to fear another person. He was gone, so as much as I cried tears of sadness, they were also tears of relief. I had my life back.

There would be no more violence, no more fear; it was just us against the world. I didn't think our life would turn on its axis again, but I should have really known.

I wasn't allowed peace in my life. Something always shit was going to happen

13

Louisa- Only In Death Do You Finally Become Someone

When someone dies, they quickly become heroes; no matter what they have done before, it's forgotten so fast, and they are immortalised as gods. People complaining about Jerome were suddenly his best friends; he was their closest brother. I was given time off work- Bereavement leave, and people rallied around Amelia and me. In Death- Jerome was great, a good man, a legend. Everyone suddenly was his best friend; saying the NHS had failed him, he soon became the new poster boy for the black men on the block. Leonie was well on this latest bandwagon; the system had failed him because he was black, constantly being criminalised, and always denied services he was entitled to.

Leonie suddenly had all the documents and letters from when he was arrested and subsequently sectioned and how many times they used brute force. She had spent relentless nights typing up every interaction with the NHS, police, GP or mental health services her brother had ever had.

But this had nothing to do with any of their services at all. Leonie had taken her eye off the ball and left him to his own devices; the unthinkable had happened. He was a loose cannon, out of control, like a ticking time bomb waiting to explode. It's just a shame that Amelia was involved in taking the pin out of the hand grenade, as this would be something she would be living with for a very long time. Nobody said that Jerome could be a pain, that they would cross the road when he didn't take his medication and when they saw him coming. Nobody knew that a life living on the edge was finally over for me. If you have ever lived with someone with mental illness, you know the score; medication not taken means arguments started and fights they create over things that are so silly that they blame you.

I had lived so much of my life in fear because of him that only now I could finally be free now that he was dead. Even though we were not together, he did have a hold over my life. Imagine if I had dared to get a new boyfriend, the drama that would have caused it would have been not even worth it. Nobody on the estate would rile up Jerome, so I was invisible, un-dateable; no man wanted to take on a woman with any links to him.

Jerome was now just a dead black man forever to be immortalised in the folk tale of the estate, the crazy black man that jumped off a tower block. Let down by Community services and the Government.

Only me and Amelia knew what had happened before Jerome jumped and it was something that I would never share with another human being. To everyone else, a man in a mental health crisis had flipped. No one knew he had seen that footage of Amelia, and nobody knew how I had to smash a glass into his back to get him away from her. Nobody knew the guilt that my Daughter would carry for the rest of her life because for her Dad, his last moments on earth were at rage at what she had done. I tried to broach the subject of that awful footage and the fact she said she was forced, but she shut me down, pushed me away, and I didn't want to break her any further. She was already like a porcelain doll, and I was terrified she would crack.

People left flowers, bottles of rum and lit candles at the back of the block where he died. It was quite a large and impressive display. It was ironic that it was all given in Death because if Jerome had asked the same people for £1 to get a drink in life, they would have told him to fuck off. Yet, they had come with their flowers, rum and candles and all snapped themselves on social media next to the Suicide scene, no expense spared in Death but fuck all in life.

I purposely didn't get involved in any of the funeral arrangements or any of the night-time vigils outside the block. I pretended Amelia and I were too grief-stricken, but we enjoyed the downtime. People left us food and drink, and we huddled together in our tiny flat, and she barely left her room, but I figured the Death of Dad and the guilt she was feeling would take time for her to come to terms with. I let Leonie update me by Text of the arrangements and just sat back and let the circus play out, thank fuck I was no longer the ringmaster.

The day we cremated Jerome was one of the most surreal days of my life. Amelia and I left the block together and took a small bus ride to Jerome's Mother's house, 15 mins away. I had never been there before. I was surprised she lived that close. Amelia had only met her Nan a handful of times, and this woman never went to Jerome's flat to see her son.

We knew where the house was by the sheer number of people dressed in black standing outside. We couldn't have timed our arrival better as when we arrived, the funeral cars were pulling in, and Leonie ushered Amelia and me into a vehicle with three other people I didn't know. Thank fuck for that because I wasn't in the mood for small talk.

The small church area was packed. All of a sudden, he had a family and he had so many friends. He had a mother wailing for her lost son even though he had been lost to her for years. It was all a massive show of black clothes, lots of flowers and a service where the priest spoke as if Jerome had been a born-again Christian.

Was this the same Jerome we knew? Because I was a little confused. Only me and Amelia knew the truth; despite all of this bullshit, he was still her Dad. I would have felt the same, it was still a loss for her and a major one in the most traumatic way.

It made me wonder who my Dad was. I asked so much about what type of person he was. I never knew anything, no full name, nothing. He was from Pakistan, that was all. Last time I checked, there were 223.77 million people in Pakistan so I had no chance of finding my Dad. But it's times like this that make you wonder about your biological makeup.

Family members were kissing and hugging us, so many people we had never met. Amelia's siblings were all older and looked bored to be there. They were glued to their phones with no interest in their half-siblings. We didn't return to the local community centre for the food and drink as Amelia was too overwhelmed, so we just trundled off back home, where Glenda was waiting with a big pot of stew.

I remember being so grateful that she had thought of feeding us as my mind was elsewhere and just concerned with getting us through the day in question.Glenda had always come to the rescue, she had cleared up my flat of glass and blood and Lasagna the night Jerome had gone crazy. And now she provided Amelia and me with a hot meal and comfort and to know we needed space and time alone. Amelia and I sat at our little kitchen table

185

and silently ate the stew.

Our world was certainly freer with Jerome out of the picture, but equally for Amelia, it would never be the same. I grew up never having a Dad, so I couldn't relate to her pain and the hollowness that her only other living relative was gone. She now only really had me.

Amelia was off school for that week, and we sat indoors contemplating life, but I spent the time worrying if my job was secure.I called my supervisor every few days and convinced them I would be ok to go back to work the very next week. I couldn't lose more money; I needed to get back out there. And again, I had to escape the flat and get out of the block, just like Amelia had to. She was undoubtedly more subdued, but I let her go out; she needed it as much as me.

Your environment can become a prison, and you must escape after a while. The hardest thing for Amelia was, of course, she would have to walk past where her Dad had died. She would have to still live in the block where the worst thing that could happen to a child, the Death of a parent, happened. And, of course, she blamed herself because of that video on Jerome's phone.

If it wasn't for that, he might have eaten the food and fucked off home. I walked down to Glenda's flat. I wanted tea and the smell of home-cooked food to provide some comfort. I planned to return to work the next day, so I tried to catch up with her and let her know I'd be at the bus stop with her tomorrow.

But I found Glenda on edge packing clothes into some large floral suitcases encrusted with years of dirt; they looked like antiques. Something was up, and her usual relaxed demeanor had been replaced with panic and a sense of urgency.

The words Jerome had muttered came back to haunt me. Had Leon had something to do with Adamchis's Death? Glenda certainly could not afford a holiday, and I knew how much saving it took to take a return trip home. Something was seriously up, and it was some nasty shit. Glenda looked like she was set to collapse. "My Susu money is for this month like fate. It's my turn to get the money, and I'm using it to get Leon out of here" A susu is a form of savings between friends. People paid monthly, and then each month, the recipient would get cash; it was a popular form of saving in Africa. Glenda's face told me all I needed to know, this shit was serious, and she needed out. I nodded, "It's ok. I know why." I don't know if she comprehended my words. She was too busy rushing around packing up what little she had.

Glenda had risked everything to bring her family here, and now she had to return temporarily to her homeland to ensure that her baby had freedom, the home she had fled for a better life. Tears filled her eyes. "You are like a daughter to me, Louisa. What I tell you here must never leave these walls". I nodded towards her taking her hand in mine. I didn't even need to begin to voice how much she could trust me, Glenda knew I had her back, and I always would. "It's Leon". I nodded. "I know, Glenda, I know.... Before he jumped, Jerome told me." She sighed, and all of a sudden, her age showed, and her tiredness showed.

At that moment, a woman that had been trying so hard to keep it all together on her own slumped down onto a rickety chair holding her head in her hands and crying. She was spent, she was beaten she was mentally and physically drained, and the life she had carefully created was falling away like a landslide. For the church-going pious woman that she was, this was beyond comprehension. "Leon has got involved with things way beyond his means" Her tears fell, and she broke as the enormity of what

187

had happened hit her . "He killed Chi. He stabbed this poor young boy because he thought he owed money on some crazy debt he didn't even owe. These gangs are evil. They poisoned his mind with the devil. My boy ….my beautiful son." As Glenda broke, I held her tightly in my arms, just like she had done for me over the years I cried with her. This woman was my rock whenever I felt like I was going to crumble, this woman was there for me. She looked deep into my eyes. "He was forced, and he was scared, and he hurt the wrong boy. We have to get him as far away from here as possible. He is an innocent trapped in this cycle of stupid boys thinking they are something they are not. He is not a killer. He was forced to do this to save his brothers and me." I could feel the pain and the anguish, knowing she was right. I felt the same when I heard Amelia on the recording, knowing she was caught up in something beyond her control.

Leon was not a killer. Leon didn't have an evil bone in his body, he was caught up in a stupid cycle of Gangs that thrived on poverty, and no matter how hard we tried to shield our kids from this crazy shit, it was futile. It was like walking on ice when a fire was underneath; we were bound to crack and fall.

Leon had killed Adimchi. He had sliced an artery as the boy had gone to top up his mother's electricity. His only crime was having the same shoulder-length dreads as the other boy whose life was meant to end that night. The Lord works in mysterious ways. Poverty is a killer; we were all victims here, just trying to make our way and achieve better for our Children.

The streets were so different from when I was young. It was a whole new world. There were elders always on the lookout for fresh young clean skins, and there were social media that led us to believe everyone was living the perfect life. The truth was indeed madder than fiction; everyone had to look perfect and

188

have designer labels to make themselves feel worthy. Our photos were filtered to make us look different to what we actually were, pretty and perfect all imperfections could be erased. We were led to believe that to succeed in life, we needed money, designer clothes, and expensive bags.

Now for kids living on a sinkhole estate with no real chance of ever getting a mortgage or a job that could pay them a decent wage that could feed them and still have extra for a nice holiday. Is it really surprising that they get angry, they get restful, they want quick money and to look the part because we are all led to believe happiness is only attainable when we strive to be picture perfect with white teeth and a Hood Rich Tracksuit? It's a dog-eat-dog world out there, and we have spoon-fed all this commercialised bullshit from the moment we can walk and talk.

Our kids never stood a chance; on our salaries, we could never have given them everything they see online, the influencers on beaches in Dubai, the trainers, the cars. How is some little hood kid going to achieve all that? Trust me. It's not by going to school and getting a good job because things like that couldn't happen for people like us. The hood offered quick money, easy cash, status and belonging with people who felt as marginalised as you, as criminalised as you and as angry as you, a product of a postcode in which you were raised.

Glenda had tried so hard to give her children the best in life, and she worked hard; she went to Church, instilled in them right from wrong, and looked where it had gotten her. She was strong for all the years I had known Glenda, but tonight she looked defeated and worn out. Her eyes were red from tears, and her hands shook as she knew she was conspiring with the devil to protect her son, but she had to save him because the alternative was unthinkable. This made in England a child, her youngest boy Leon her baby, and now they had to run. Glenda's only Daughter Adeola had moved away by now, living in Norwich working and studying. And Julius would be doing the same soon and her other boy Nnamdi worked hard studying to be a mental health nurse. But her youngest was her undoing, and she knew she had to get him out of the UK, or else he would end up in jail and their family name tarnished forever.

Leon had free education, free school meals and look what the land of opportunity had given him. Glenda thought coming to England would herald a new beginning and give her children the freedom and life chances that she would have taken with both hands if she had had the chance. But instead, she was a mother who had saved every penny of her hard-earned cash and for what? What had she achieved, she had tried and failed for one of them. The tickets were booked. I didn't ask how long she would be away.

They were flying to Germany and then onto Lagos before returning to her mother's Village, which she had left many years ago. She was taking her boy to live with her sister and her elderly mother, he would experience village life, and she prayed for the day when it would all die down that he could return to them in the UK. She knew that going back here would teach him so much more than she ever could. He was to live amongst people that had nothing, and he would learn to appreciate life again. Life was a blessing, and he would have to learn to go back to basics, the upbringing that she herself had, one where you went to Church and you, respected your family, and you didn't step a foot out of line.

I held Glenda so tight I didn't want to let her go, she had been a mother figure, a voice in the dark, and I always felt safe and protected knowing she was just a floor below me. She was dependable, like a security blanket for me, and the thought of her not being there scared me more than when I lost touch with my mother.

Glenda's leaving would affect me more than losing Jerome because she had always been there for me, and it was like I was losing part of me. For a long time, Glenda had been the mother I had never really had, and even though she would return, it made me anxious, not knowing when.

Not having her near or knowing I could run to her for help scared me. It made me feel like a child again, vulnerable and unsure of where to turn in a crisis. I mean, I was a Mum now. I really should have got my shit together and known about life, and I had another person depending on me, my Daughter and I didn't want to let her down. I had to be strong.

So much of our block was changing; austerity measures meant more families moving in, pissed off and poor, and youth violence was making the headlines more and more. The local community centre had closed due to funding, and the children's playground was tatty and broken.

It was as if the Council had given up on us, and just like the block we were in, we were left to rot. Work was my salvation where I could put on my uniform, pick up the mop and become invisible; my only task was cleaning, so monotonous it was good for my mind that it was whirling in a thousand different directions. Work is a distraction, and it's an escape. It's a place where I am a worker, and I can relinquish responsibility to the school for those hours I am there. I am me, just a woman working to make some small change, Louisa Mary Doherty, NHS Cleaner and invisible.

Not a Mother responsible for another life -for 37.5 hours a

week, I can breathe. My only responsibility at these hours is ensuring I sign the sheets to say the toilet has been cleaned. And that's pretty shitty; that is my escape.

14

Amelia- Misoprostol, Bleed Outs & Self—Harm

People rallied around after my Dads death, our small kitchen was laden with food, my dad had never really been productive in my life apart from getting me out of school. I realized in death he was helping me out far more than he ever did when he was alive.

Dads mental health stigma had vanished; he was a black dad let down by the system.I had people I never knew come to my home and all of a sudden due to the utter tragedy of what had happened people respectfully didn't share my video anymore or comment it just went off grid out of respect.

Dad had taken the spotlight off my rape, it was the first time he had ever done anything productive for me, even if it meant he killed himself in the process. People respected that it was pretty fucked up to even share that video now with what had happened. And I wasn't contacted by Deano or Malachi I guess they realised I wasn't going to be any good to them sexually while mourning my dad.

So the death of my Dad passed such darkness over my life

that the incident with Malachi didn't haunt every single waking moment of my day like it used to. I had new guilt to carry, I felt responsible for killing my Dad, his suicide made me feel that it was his blood on my hands.

I was cutting my arms more at night time when things just got too bad. I would go to the bathroom and slice little cuts into my arm so that the physical pain would stop me thinking about all what had happened.

Dads funeral was a lavish affair where I met a lot of his family for the first time and many of my siblings, that was surreal I can tell you. Mum and me just sat in the pew with our eyes forward still feeling as if we were caught up in some nightmare at all that had happened, these people had never been in our lives before and there was no way we needed them now. Nobody had ever helped us, when mum had to choose between electric and food did they help us? No, so now we were suddenly all family. I don't think so; my mum had taught me several times that blood is not thicker than water. Glenda was much more to me than these blood family members and she had done so much more for me and mum.

One thing that had been playing on my mind my period was late and I had vomited a few times since dad's death. I put it all down to grief, but then a cold fear crept through my body, the bastards had had unprotected sex with me. I didn't want to bring my mind back to that night in question because it was just too painful to think about. Every time I thought back to what they did to me I just wanted to cry or cut myself. But the reality was I could be pregnant and I knew I needed to confide in someone and soon.

I called Tanisha in a mad panic, I was suddenly really scared. Tanisha sent Alisha to my aid, I was to meet her in Stratford and she would help me out. The pregnancy test was stolen from Wilkinson's in Stratford and I done the test in the toilets in the small market in the poorer part of Stratford called the mall. The toilets where they have florescent lights to stop the junkies shooting up in the cubicles. I didn't even have to wait three minutes, it was positive! a real strong double line. I opened the cubicle door to find Alisha filing her nails looking bored "Well, you preggers or not" My hands shook as I held the test towards Alisha who shook her head and kissed her teeth "You should have taken the morning after pill like you were told, this is some serious mad shit fam" I looked at my face in the mirror I had huge dark circles under my eyes and could hardly recognize who I had become "what am I going to do?".

Alisha told me she would help me sort things out, this kind of thing happens all the time a few tablets and life was back to normal. Alisha would get me some abortion pills on-line from her cousin who got good shit off the dark web. To her this was nothing just part of the course with this lifestyle, you get pregnant you get rid of it problem solved. My own mother had me at 16 and I know it was hard for her and there was no way I could have confided in her what had happened. Part of me wanted too, this was a child that could have belonged to any one of them monsters.

How could I bring another life into a life of pain, our lives were hard enough, imagine having a Dad that was a rapist. I didn't want to continue the cycle of a long line of women before me who had got pregnant young, ended up in the repeated nightmare of low incomes, poor housing, all believing that we would be the ones to break the mould and get our asses out of this trap. It was an incessant cycle like a hamster on a wheel going round and round and getting nowhere fast and I had once again hooked my chain to a life of poverty and no hope. I really had no choice but to swallow those abortion tablets and pray the link would be broken because I didn't want to make this mistake again.

I wanted the next time that I see those lines a positive pregnancy test, I have a warm home, a bathroom with plush towels, a man who has married me and a home with food in the fridge. Not this, in a piss smelling toilet not even fit for humans with me vomiting in a bowl full of shit and an overflowing sanitary bin with blue lights above us making me dizzy because the druggies wanted to shoot up in here. I had to get rid, there was no way I could contemplate bringing an anchor to the devils that had abused me into the world, because those men were evil, and I know it wasn't the babies fault. But I couldn't do it,I couldn't risk looking into the eyes of a monster it would terrify me.

Leon had txt me to let me know he wanted to see me and say goodbye before going to Lagos he had been laying low over in Kent with some distant cousin. Tonight he was coming back to collect a bag then he was off with Glenda first thing in the morning and I agreed to meet him. I wanted him to know that whatever had happened in that video it wasn't my fault, I needed to tell him I loved him with all my heart and I always would. He had no choice, if the truth got out who had killed that innocent boy then his life would really be over.

And for Glenda I know this must be one of the hardest choices that she had to make but she had to protect her boy. I couldn't believe I was losing him, he meant so much to me not just in a teenage crush way, but a deep way because he knew the real me and there was no reason to pretend or try to be something else because with him it was always me being me and that was calm. Even with my female friends I always felt that I still kept a part of myself back, smiling being harder than I usually was when deep inside I wasn't so tough. I can't say I had any normal male role models in my life apart from Glenda's boys. And to have Leon so far away left me vulnerable, it was another person who had my back gone from my life.

The night we met up it was still humid, the day's heat not abating with the sun setting, the smell of the communal bins was quite overpowering the heat had made all the rubbish smell worse than usual. It would appear my sense of smell had heightened since becoming pregnant and every smell was making me nauseous.

Leon stood next to the wall a dark shadow looming, he looked sinister but I knew it was him so I felt safe. He was dressed all in black with his hood up and I could only tell it was him because I knew his body shape and smell, his signature aftershave and it made my belly go over with either nerves or excitement.

I wanted to run and hold him but it was too late how could he ever trust me or forgive me now, I had to tread carefully I wanted to ensure our last words were good and kind and not bad as I didn't know when I would be seeing him again, little did I know back then this was the last time I would see this precious boy. He's voice came out sounding broken almost like a cry "I'm sorry about your dad, that's some fucked up shit....and I'm sorry I've not been around to look after you" I bit back my tears and tried my hardest not to cry "it's OK... I just want you to know they forced me Leon. All that shit with Malachi it wasn't what I wanted to do, I never wanted to do the things they made me do" I broke, the tears when they started poured from my face and I hated the fact that this ugly crying face would be one of the last memories of me he may have. I didn't know what else to say, I would have rather they cut off one of my fingers than for Leon to see that video but it was too late, the damage had been done.

The words when he spoke was said with so much pain behind them so softly spoken it was like he hadn't actually said them at all "I know. I see the state of you when you got out of that car. I know you Amelia and I know what they do to girls and I never wanted that for you. I just wish I could stay and make this all go away...but I have to go" I moved towards him and he cupped my face in his hand, he held his forehead against mine looking into my eyes "You have to be strong while I'm away Amelia, look after your Mum and My Mum when she returns...get out of this lifestyle if you can...You're a beautiful human being with so much to give and you and I know you can achieve whatever you put your mind too" I was broken and I was looking into the eyes of a man who was a condemned man if he stayed, I could see the pain in his face and knew by the way he swallowed he was trying not to cry. "I love you Leon. I always have and I always will" the words came out before I could stop them I needed him to know he was my everything and how I wished I had never ever thought I was some big girl messing about with the big boys. "None of this is anyone's fault Amelia, you think we both wanted this? me on the run you caught up in something so crazy" I was sobbing but I knew I had to tell him the truth "I only went out with him that night because of you and Katy, it fucking killed me to see you with her" He shook his head "You know why I was doing all that shit; you think that stupid little entitled bitches like that would ever mean a thing to me Amelia?" "It looked pretty genuine from what I see, Malachi told me you were sleeping with her" Leon shook his head kissing his teeth "Can't you see that's why he made you come along for a drive that night, to make things worse so that you would turn on me and be further indebted to him and all the shit they create, that's how they work Amelia, they lure you in with promises of being

198

the top person having this and that, but in reality they are only interested in themselves and what they can make and take, they aren't interested in the likes of me and you, we are just the foot soldiers the ones to take the shit and do their dirty work!".

I suddenly felt stupid, why did I ever think I was going to be something more than what I was. I had to tell him about the baby "I'm pregnant Leon and I'm so scared. They raped me and they didn't use protection" "What" he pushed me back but held me still at arms distance looking into my eyes, his anger evident but it was an anger that could go nowhere. "I don't know if it's yours or theirs" it killed me to say this but I had to tell the truth He fell back against the wall breathing out as if I'd punched him "Fucks sake..., Amelia you have to get rid of it, you can't keep this baby ...I'm not going to be around to protect you or take care of you. I don't know when I'm going to be back" he fell against the wall his words hitting me like a bullet shattering a glass I was broken into so many pieces that I could never be put back together again.

I wanted to run away with him, or hold him forever I inhaled the smell of him as if it was my favorite perfume knowing it would be a long time if ever I held him again. "I have to go, until this all dies down, but trust me Amelia get rid of that baby, you don't know what type of man Malachi is, they are bad people and if he knows your pregnant then I don't know what he could do, it's no point having any connection to them, listen just get rid of it and lay low for fucks sake get out of this lifestyle while you can while you're not so indebted and do Something with your life" My tears mingled with his as he kissed me "I love you Leon" He kissed me hard on the lips and with that he was gone. All that was left was the smell of him the taste of him still on my lips and the bleakness of the block. Before I could beg for help, demand to know when he might be back he was gone. Doing what I never would have ever believed he could ever do which was to walk away from me. I knew he had no choice, he had killed someone he had to run but part of me wished I could have gone with him.

The pain I felt from all this loss it was like a genuine pain in my chest, I just couldn't take anymore, my dad had gone, now Leon was going and now I had to end this baby's life. I had to try my hardest not to think of it as a baby, it was just cells it wasn't even formed properly yet was it?

A video of me being fucked by two guys had been seen by everyone how could I ever go back to normal life again I was damaged goods. I wanted to end my own life, I just couldn't see a way out of all the shit that was happening around me. I had £10 in cash on me and I brought a bottle of vodka from the corner shop they assumed it was for my Mum and they knew us so it was no big deal the bottle was handed over with a wink.

Then I made my way home with my heart so heavy. I could see flashes of lightning in the sky a storm was approaching and then I heard the boom of thunder, I counted between the lightning to seven so the storm was seven miles away. I looked up at the Tower Block my home and the home my Dad had jumped from the top of, my prison and my safe place all in one.

How could one place be my safe space and also the place that made me feel so much guilt. As I stood looking up into the night sky feeling the oppressive heat still rebounding off the city walls. I blew a kiss up to my Dad and prayed he would be looking over me to make everything alright.

Then the rain began to fall, big heavy drops that soon became a deluge. It had been a long time since I had stopped and looked up at my surroundings and breathed in the air. I liked the smell the rain brought to the city it almost cleaned its dirty streets, I inhaled the smell of the rain cleaning the hot dry pavements and lifted my head up letting the storm rain down on me as if I was being washed clean.

My girl Alisha was waiting for me for me by the door to the block she called me over, already pissed off she was getting wet, she handed me a brown paper bag that contained my abortion pills "Swallow this tablet tonight and then tomorrow when you wake up, insert the second one up your vagina" and with that she was gone, rushing off into the night pulling her hoodie over her head yelling as she ran towards her own block in the rain.

To me it was like a sign from above from my dad, to tell me what I don't know, I had a problem and here was the solution. I walked up to the seventeenth floor convinced these would be my last steps on this earth I was finished, I didn't have the heart or the strength to go on with this life. I was scared and I didn't know what to do, this was the first time in my life I really thought about killing myself.

I wasn't brave enough to jump from a tower block like my Dad, I wasn't brave enough to jump in front of a train, I just wanted to go to sleep and never have to wake up ever again. I'm not sure what I was really feeling I just felt scared, unsure what was going to happen to me or who I could trust.

I didn't take the lift I took the stairs and I stopped at every level that I knew floor Ten the block with the Somalian family who gave me food, floor eleven Mamma Victorine from Guyana who had always brought me Christmas presents and birthday presents and whom I helped carry her shopping up the stairs when the lifts were broke.

All these different floors contained neighbors who had enriched my life with the inhabitants reaching out to me helping me at some point in my life. And with every footstep part of me wished I could knock on one of these doors and just collapse and tell the truth let this heavy burden that I was carrying be offloaded because the burden of it all was becoming too much to bear.

It took every ounce of strength to act normal in front of my mum, I hid the bottle of vodka in my coat. Mum had treated us to a takeaway just a box of chicken and chips. This was to be my last meal consumed on earth, I swallowed down the first abortion pill with cheap supermarket own brand Lemonade and cuddled up to my mum I wanted her to sense something was wrong and ask. But she never did I could see that she was in her own turmoil, we were both in so much emotional distress we were living like actors playing pretend, not wanting to show the other the amount of pain we were actually in.

I was just so mixed up inside and the words were on the tip of my tongue so many times but I just couldn't speak them. I mouthed the words to myself in the bathroom mirror "Mum I'm pregnant, I've been raped" But I just couldn't say them out loud. I was going to break her heart, what would happen? I would destroy both our lives. She would hunt down the men that hurt me or tell the police and that would make everything ten times worse which in turn would hurt her and I couldn't let that happen.

I knew killing myself would break her too but I was a coward at least this way it might protect her. I knew how much my Mother had sacrificed for me, sleeping on a sofa every night, working long hours for shit pay just to put food on our table. Not once did I ever tell her how much I loved her or how grateful I was. I just see all the things she couldn't give me, I was selfish.

I realized now that Tanisha and DP may have all the material things that they want but it's all fake, down to their eyelashes, lips and nails. My Mum was a kind woman and hardworking and I just prayed that in some way whatever God was watching us be it Jesus or Allah they put things right for her one way or the other. She didn't deserve a crazy partner and she didn't deserve a fuck up like me. With Dad gone and hopefully me too I hoped she could start her life again. She was still young to perhaps marry have a nice new family in the suburbs and forget all about this life, she had chances and in a way I was almost holding her back.

I wanted to tell her to move away, live her life and be free from all this shit, I had anchored her here enough this way at least she would be free.I pretended I was going to school and even had my uniform on when things started to really fuck up. I had set my alarm for 6.30 and I listened as my mum got herself ready for work knowing as soon as she was out of the way I had to proceed with part two of the abortion.

I heard the door shut and Mum making her way to work and I went on-line to read the instructions I had been emailed. I inserted the pessary and then re-set my alarm for 8am enough time to nap before school. The alarm woke me at 8am and I found I had started to bleed and my belly was starting to cramp, at first it was just like a really bad period pain. By 8.30 when it was time I should have really been getting my ass out the door for school things started to get bad, the bleeding was getting heavier and I was seeping through the sanitary towels that were now piling up in my little bin.

The blood was red and there were clots coming out, almost like jelly. This was the worse pain I had experienced in my life. The clots were now dripping down my leg onto the bathmat coming thick and fast. My school skirt was now covered in blood.

I quickly run a bath and sat in it hoping the water would make the bleeding stop and help ease the pain that was contracting through my body. I lay in the bath for 5 mins but the pain was too much, I decided there and then to just swallow some painkillers as many tablets as I could find because I felt like I was already dying.

I stumbled to the medicine cabinet and swallowed down a pain killer called Naproxen that mum had been given for her back pain from sleeping on the sofa all these years. I then swallowed some Paracetamol as my stomach was contracting with pain and I was still bleeding quite heavy.

Sitting at the table I remembered the vodka and swallowed down some of the bottle, it made me gag and burned my throat. I was retching as the chalky tablets I was trying to swallow kept coming back up it felt like they were stuck in my throat that dry horrible white chalky taste, swallowing tablets was not pleasant. Then I started to feel really sick and woozy and for some unknown reason I called Alisha the girl who had got me the abortion pill, crying to her that the pain wasn't right and something had gone terribly wrong.

The pain was searing through my body the blood was still coming it wasn't easing up. I tried to scoop out the blood clots from the plug hole of the bath and as fast as I was scooping them out there was more. I was flushing away a life and I couldn't bear it, I can just remember thinking I didn't want my Mum to find me like this or for there to be any evidence of what had gone on. I knew I wanted to die but at the same time I wanted to live, my mind was all over the place. I guess this was my cry for help. Alisha's face when she opened the door and see me was one of horror, the blood was seeping down my legs and she could see all the packets of pain killer tablets surrounding me, her face was angry. "what the actual fuck have you done! Have you swallowed them pills" She looked at the bloodbath that was the bathroom then She pulled out her phone dialled for an ambulance. I was begging her not to "No Alisha don't... Please stop... I only took a few tablets it's not what it seems. It was the pain...it's just so bad" She kissed her teeth "No one is going to get nicked because of your fucking stupidity Amelia, now fucking make yourself puke before the feds start looking at where and from whom you got them abortion pills from" she shoved me onto the sofa got a bowl and told me to stick my fingers down my throat, but I couldn't, my hands were covered in my blood, I fell onto my hands and knees begging her and pleading her to leave "I'm not going to tell anyone just go, please leave me alone" "Damn fucking straight I'm going..., this place is a mess, you fucking say where you got the tablets from I'm going to fuck you up bad, and your mother, I'll burn you fuckers while you sleep, give me your phone I ain't having no evidence linking you to me" She spat at me left leaving the door on the latch so the London Ambulance Service could find me, she snatched my shitty little phone and left. She was not playing no part in this she was getting as far away as she possibly could and taking my link to her with her.

She disappeared in a cloud of perfume and a look of disdain, I mean what kind of hood girl doesn't know how to handle a DIY home abortion, I was a failure a real fucking top notch idiot. The room was spinning and I was finding it hard to focus then I felt as if I was drifting off into a dreamlike state.

Next thing I remember is feeling cold and a breeze like someone had left a door open too long and two ladies in a green uniform now whom I know were paramedics calling out "hello" before they entered the flat through the open door.

Then I swear I see my Dad standing there smiling at me and

beckoning me to follow him but I turned back and run from him, it was like I was hallucinating. I didn't want the darkness I wanted the light, and then everything went black.

I had reached rock bottom and it was dark, cold, desolate, it was full of blood and vomit and a feeling that I was swimming in a sea where the tide was just too big and powerful and I was drowning, I closed my eyes I didn't want to be saved.

15

Amelia- Resus, Regrets & Time For Reflection

I opened my eyes so confused; there were bright lights above me, almost blinding me like I had stepped out into sunshine from a dark room. It hurt my eyes, and I struggled to focus.

There were so many people rushing around and noises of machines beeping and alarming. It was confusing, like waking from a pleasant sleep so disorientated as to where you are. It was hard for me to take it all in. It felt like I was outside with so much noise and confusion, but I was lying in a strange bed, a hospital trolley. The sheets were caught in the side of the trolley, and I tried to pull it up, and that's when I looked at my hand and saw the drip being fed into it.

There was a strong smell of urine and vomit; where the fuck was I?. My head was pounding with each move I made. I felt like I was on a boat and was seasick. Every move was making me feel queasy, and my mouth felt dry. I was either in hell or hospital; it turns out it was the latter.

I was in resus a busy space for the sickest people. I had been rushed into the hospital, and then I suddenly remembered all that had happened the abortion pills, the pain, and me swallowing painkillers and vodka.

I looked down to see my arms on display. All the cuts I had done over the past weeks that I had tried to cover up were now exposed under the harsh bright lights of the hospital, making them look much worse. It almost illuminated them, making them stand out against my skin, revealed here for all to see.

Hospital gowns are not one of the most dignified items of clothing ever to have been made. There was no hiding in one of them, with the arms of the gown short and the back open for easy access. I tried covering my body with the white sheet but couldn't move my hands. I was attached to so many wires and machines.

As I moved my head, the whole room spun, and I felt vomit rise, and then my Mum was holding one of those grey round hospital vomit bowls as I vomited bile into the pot. My Mum took the bowl away when she was sure I had stopped retching and then wordlessly put her hand over mine. She looked broken; you could tell she had been crying; her eyes were puffy and red as if she had terrible hay fever; they were red and raw. Mum looked so pale, like a smaller version of herself. It was like she was a child. She looked young sitting there, and I felt like I was seeing her for the first time without her guard up, that shield she always put around herself, part of the Oh, I'm alright crew of Mums. They never moaned about themselves. They just dedicated their lives to their children without ever considering themselves.

I couldn't work out if I were dead or alive or stuck in some weird dream. My Clothes were in a yellow hazard bag, and despite the smells of the hospital all around me, the smell of vomit, blood and urine was so strong it made me want to be sick. Mum couldn't throw them away as it was my school Uniform and we could never afford a replacement.

I was told by a friendly English nurse called Rachel that I was being moved to a children's ward, a bed had become available, and I would finish my NAC Infusion in the Paediatric ward. I wanted to say my what? What's an infusion? Why am I being taken to a children's ward? I'm not a child, but I was in the eyes of the law. I didn't even have time to question anything. I was just being pushed on a trolley along a hospital corridor, looking up at the white stripped lights as they passed above me.

The porter wheeled me into a ward that was designed for younger children. There was a Winnie the Pooh and Mickey Mouse and lots of colorful pictures on the walls, all designed to be Child friendly and happy. I wasn't in the mood for cartoon characters and balloons. I was in the mood for darkness and solitude.

The air smelt of lunch but not a pleasant smell. It was a mix match of all kinds of foods, a mixture of curry and cabbage. There was all sorts of Children on that ward, some older bending over on crutches, babies in see-through plastic cots with tubes coming out of their noses and attached to oxygen.

Nurse Rachel dropped me off in a bed, handed me over to another nurse and then wished me luck and was on her way. I was left with my Mum sitting awkwardly on a plastic chair while we avoided the eyes of the other children and parents, who gawked at us. We were new people on the ward; curious looks glanced our way, a new patient to break up the day. So there I was, lying in a bed in a children's ward, yet I felt so far from being a child that I wanted to scream. I just wanted to get me out there, away from the crying babies, taunting me. Don't they realise I just killed my baby? I didn't deserve to be here.

I wanted out of this hospital gown, so I can plan my escape, give me my clothes, anything to cover these scars on my arms that I can see. My Mum kept looking at me, my arms on display with the cuts all over them, getting emotional and looking away.

My Mum looked drained, as if she didn't know how she was standing up. I pulled the crisp starched bed sheet up to my neck to hide myself and then closed my eyes. The nurse on the ward allocated to me was a young girl who introduced herself as Aisha; she looked as young as me and looked uncomfortable nursing someone probably bigger than her. When they signed up to be Children's nurses, they imagined cuddling sick babies back to health, not baby killing, suicidal teenagers like me.

Part of me felt like I was in hell with no way out. The other nurses walked past and glimpsed at me, fake smiles, constantly wary, wondering what I might do next. Then the crazy shit happened a lady in a lilac uniform, a healthcare assistant was instructed to watch me, as I was being put on something called a one-to-one. Nobody explained to me what that meant, maybe they told my Mum, but the lady just grabbed a chair and sat at the end of my bed yawning and reaching for her phone, an easy end to her shift. She was paid to keep me safe. I never knew until much later that I was deemed high risk. I had tried to kill myself. So to prevent anything from happening in the hospital, in case Winnie the Pooh or Mickey Mouse sent me even more over the edge. I was to be watched to ensure they didn't have a lawsuit on their hands. If I went to the bathroom, the door had to be unlocked.

A one-to-one meant someone had to watch me at all times, literally. On paper, I'm trouble; a 15-year-old overdosed, swallowed abortion pills, and bled out. I didn't even know at this point if I was still pregnant, and as for my Dad, did I see him at the front door? I hoped I wasn't having hallucinations like him. Oh my goodness, imagine if I became mentally unwell like my Dad. When that thought entered my head, I had to squash it right away, and I wished then that I would have the opportunity just to cut my arm a little to make the physical pain get rid of that thought, but with being under such scrutiny that was not going to happen.

I must have drifted off to sleep because the next thing I knew, I had a different nurse looking after me, another young girl. This one was called Aniqa; she was to be my named nurse, she explained, and she would be the one to be chasing up CAMHS and Social Care. I'd heard of CAMHS before. It stood for Children's and Adolescent mental health services, it had been offered to me after my Dad's suicide, but I had declined. I didn't need that shit in my life. Mum had taught me to be like her literally and deal with things without involving authority attention.

The next healthcare assistant to watch over me was a prominent African woman called Gladys, who introduced herself, grabbed herself a computer on wheels, and then logged onto Netflix. These people were being paid to watch my every fucking move. Do you know how fucked up that is from spending years alone when Mum worked to now having someone watching me keeping guard? I couldn't even take a shit without them checking that I was not strangling myself with the shower head.

So many hours I spent just looking up at the ceiling because I didn't even have a phone, which was quite a relief in some ways. Not having a connection to the outside world was freeing. I didn't know what drama was happening on the estate or what people were saying about me. I felt like I could breathe. My mind wouldn't let me start to think about the consequences that going off the grid could have for me.

The next day I had visits from the Child and adolescent mental health services; they were a team that would come into the hospital each day to assess me and my mood. I was under their team, and I was also under general Paediatrics for my overdose and Gynae for the abortion or baby I still didn't know. I had so many blood tests, and then a kind female doctor sat with me and explained that I would have a scan and more blood tests to ensure that my HCG levels (Pregnancy hormone) were depleting —the good news, or so they made it sound like, I was no longer pregnant. I know, idiots, I took the pill to get rid of the baby, and I just wanted out of the situation, but now I felt hollow and regretful at what I had done.

I was starting to feel like a murderer, and the fact I was now surrounded by crying children was like payback for what I had done. My Mum was like a cat on a hot tin roof; it was hard for her to sit still, she had colleagues that kept popping in to see us, as they were all cleaners, but she was embarrassed. How can you explain your Child tried to kill themselves? If it was something like appendicitis, it was OK; that's not something Mum would have to feel guilty about, but Mum felt like I had stabbed a dagger right through her heart. I could sense her embarrassment, not wanting to tell the truth; my Child had a DIY home abortion and then tried to kill herself, but we are great. Thanks for asking!

We never even had the chance to talk one on one because I always had to have someone with me, and there was never any privacy. I was unsure if it was a combination of staying strong for so long or Dad's Suicide, but now Mum was just a shadow of her former self as if she had finally been defeated.

In the hospital, they pull the curtains back every morning, so I keep my head under the covers as much as possible, as I do not wish to look across at the other patients or let them see me on display. Too much of me feels broken and exposed, and

212

what else is there to do when you are all trapped in a small ward but to look across at your neighbours. And when the Drs come in for ward round, they pull the curtains around for privacy, but we can still hear every spoken word. You know they aren't soundproofed curtains. I get curious glances from other parents and patients. I mean, what's so special about me? Why do I need to be constantly watched like I have a bodyguard? I wait for my Mum to arrive with more clean clothes, but she doesn't, and then I notice the note she left by my bed, and my stomach lurches like I'm on a roller-coaster.

My first thought was she had gone to kill herself like my Dad. I grabbed the note fast, which made the healthcare assistant that was supposed to be watching me jump as I guessed she thought I would use the blunt NHS catering knives to stab myself or her. Mum's handwriting was unmistakable; good handwriting was always something she was proud of. I breathed deeply and began to read, with my heart in my mouth hoping this wasn't a suicide note, please don't tell me Mum was also leaving me.

Dear Amelia, I'm writing this letter to you on a broken table that keeps moving around, but I can't speak while you're sleeping, so I have to put it down in words. The nurses must think I'm a pain requesting paper and a pen, which they had to go and pull out from the A&E reception desk printer, but I needed to explain how I felt. I'm wondering how I got this so wrong; I always believed I would be the type of mother that was laid back, that you, as my daughter, could tell me anything. I envisaged us having coffee and shopping trips together and laughing like best friends at some in-joke that nobody else would understand but us. Watching you sleep, I remember you as a tiny baby, the small hand that would reach for mine. Now in your hospital gown, you look older, vulnerable yet childlike without the makeup and hard stance that seems to be your permanent look

213

lately. I can see the cuts on your arms from months of self-harming, which I never knew about. You always wore long sleeve tops or jumpers, so It never even entered my head to check. They are striped like red zebra lines; some are white and faded, meaning this has been happening for some time.

The NAC infusion being dripped into your veins protects your liver from the overdose of paracetamol you have taken. My baby girl, how could you ever feel so much pain that you couldn't tell me? You mean so much to me, Amelia. I will always be by your side no matter what you do but never try to leave this world, my darling Girl; you are just too precious, and no matter how bad things can be, we can get through them. I'm sorry you never told me you were sexually active; I could have advised, I wouldn't have judged, I was young once, too, and you know I got pregnant at 15 with you. I wish to god I could swap places with you. I wished I hadn't been so blind to what was happening. You could have told me. You may think all I do is moan, but I love you and want to protect you. You always hated that I worked long hours for shit money, but my baby girl, you don't understand; I could never sit home in that flat receiving government handouts as that would feel like I had failed. If an immigrant to this country can come and sweep floors for a wage, then so can I. I always dreamed that somehow, some way, we would escape. Working was my way of keeping myself sane. I was working as a cleaner, but I was hoping it would lead to a Healthcare Assistant job, and then, from that training and perhaps Nursing, we would be set for life. In doing so, I failed you, and I am sorry. I should never have worked to 8 pm picking up other shifts to get the extra cash, but it was all done with love and hope. Never feel you are to blame for what happened to Daddy, he had his own demons but don't carry that guilt with you, its not yours to hold. Please always remember how wonderful you are. I never wished for you your life to be anything like mine.

And every decision I made for you was out of love and the hope for
something better than I had. Love Mum) xxxx

I read the note with tears streaming down my face and my hands
shaking because of that great fear of her leaving me like Dad. I
couldn't take the pain and almost felt like I would have a panic
attack. Deep in my heart, I knew she was a good woman; she
wasn't like DP cheating the government, drinking, and screwing
around with men. I knew all that, and I had caused her so much
pain.

I knew that in a world littered with no opportunities, she still
got up, showed up and gave a fuck. I wanted to scream at her
how now I see all she had done for me! I know how you tried to
raise me in your cheap second-hand clothes on an estate where
our address is notorious and even the delivery drivers don't go.

And I prayed it was not too late. I'd lost so much and couldn't
lose the only person I relied on; that made me go cold.I was ready
to speak and do anything to get me and mum away from that
life. She only had me; how the fuck could I think leaving this
world would benefit her? I had been selfish. I see that now, and
I was only concerned with myself, suicide was never the answer
it just shifted the pain onto the people that were left behind. I
knew that better than anybody due to my own Dad, except me
and Mum knew his Suicide was caught up with this own mental
traumas.

My first review with CAMHS was uneventful; although I felt
ready to speak, this worker still needed to get me. She was a
middle-aged white woman with short brown hair and a slow,
condescending voice. Her name was Ruth, and she had a script
she was reading from and clearly had a million other things to
do. I was just someone on the list, a tick-box exercise to say she

had been to the ward and reviewed me. She spoke to me as if I was stupid. I mean, I was damaged; I know that. Yes, I'd lost my Dad in a traumatic way, but she was not the one for me. Some people don't gel, and me and her would not work well together. Did they expect a stranger just to come in and expect me to open up suddenly? This was a middle-class housewife with kids that paid for their school meals. She ain't got shit all in common with me.

Ruth told me a colleague would review me again tomorrow, and I could see what she must be thinking; what an almighty fucking mess; they weren't even aware of the rape. There was no way I was planning to disclose that. I sensed that this CAMHS worker was overworked and busy; she even checked her watch while assessing me; it's OK, lady; write your notes and get out of here. You will never understand me, and I will never understand you. The fact that you have a Leather bag for your laptop and a Waitrose coffee cup speaks volumes to me; you've never had to live how we have lived for a day in your Cambridge-educated life. Fuck off because I will never open up to you. It will be like opening up an umbrella in a tornado pointless.

I was sitting in bed when a young woman arrived, and she looked different to the rest of the professionals that had peered at me from the end of the bed. She was dressed in leggings and a Nike Hoodie; she was mixed race like me, and her smile seemed to have that genuine warmth of someone who had been there.

This angel of the streets explained her name was Kendra, she was from an organisation called St Giles, and she told me she was not police or social services; she could chat with me and advocate for me if I felt I needed more support.

I looked towards the healthcare assistant watching over me, a big god-loving African woman who I heard describe me as

216

cuckoo to her colleagues.

I suddenly saw Kendra as someone who might be trustworthy, and she didn't look like she was leading me into a trap. She seemed down to earth from her nose stud and the tattoo of a rose climbing up her neck. I said yes, I'd like to chat; I immediately wanted to see what she was about. First, I explained that I wanted to know if my Mum was safe, that she had left a note by my bed, and it worried me where she was. Kendra took me to a small room on the ward for teenagers because she said she got better mobile reception there, and it also meant my one-to-one could go and have a Tea Break; yeah, it is hard sitting on your ass all day watching me, who didn't move.

It was also a good move by Kendra to enable us to speak away from the ward, where there were eyes and ears everywhere. I knew Mum's number by heart, and Kendra used her phone to call Mum for me. Mum had to visit the GP to get a certificate to be signed off sick from work, and she would see me later.

The relief of hearing that my Mum was OK, she was alive, and she was safe momentarily made me place my head In my hands, crying from relief. I had not let those tears fall since arriving in hospital. Everything was just bottled up inside me like a shaken fizzy drink, ready to explode. Kendra touched my back and told me to breathe; it was OK. I was in a safe space. I must have been hyperventilating.

Everything flashed through my mind, like when you are on a train, and another train goes by. You just see flashes of light, Deano and Malachi raping me, Dad jumping from that block, Leon disappearing from my life, the pregnancy, the abortion, everything just overwhelmed me. I was trying to breathe. Still, I felt so spaced out and out of control. I had opened the floodgates, my tears fell, and I needed a barrier to stop them. I managed to calm myself and count to ten as Kendra did; she placed her hand over mine and safely brought me back to the present with calming tones. "Your Safe. I'm here with you. It's OK; take deep breaths in and out".

Kendra asked if she could get me a drink, to which I readily agreed I wanted coffee, but the nurses were treating me like a child and refused to get me one. After all the crap I'd just done, all the drugs and the OD did they think a coffee would be so detrimental to my health. Luckily Kendra got me a coffee from the Hospital Costa, and I finally felt someone was seeing the real me.

We sat at a little table so we could place our coffees on it, and the moment I sat and my eyes fixated on the sexual infections poster that was displayed in the adolescent room, I broke again. Kendra clocked me, looking at the poster, and asked, "Did you need a test, Amelia? An STI check?" I nodded my head. I couldn't trust myself again to speak, but the silent tears that poured down my face were an indicator something painful had happened to me. And it all came out about the video, the way it had gone viral.

The only thing I kept back was that it was rape because I knew that would involve police and a trial, and I couldn't face that. Kendra continued in a slow, gentle voice, "Amelia did you consent to have sex with those boys?" I nodded, and when I spoke, my voice was quiet. "Yes, I did. Well, kind of. I knew I was going to have sex with him. It Just all got a little crazy" I knew I still had to tread carefully, I needed to be sure that I could trust Kendra, and as we were still in hospital, I had to be careful, one word spoken it could all unravel for me massively.

I had said the words out loud to another human being. I was almost relieved but then scared of what this would mean. I couldn't hide it any longer; I was in every pain I could feel physically, mentally and emotionally. I'd lost my Dad, my boyfriend, and now my child and almost killed my mother with the stress of it all. It all came out like verbal diarrhoea.I had kept everything in for so long that once I started, it felt cathartic; it all came out, the trouble with gangs, the trap house I'd run and finally, my Dad's suicide which was my fault, and aborting my baby.

Kendra sat and listened, her face showing understanding. "I've been there, Amelia and I know how hard this must have been for you, and I appreciate you confiding in me." I was immediately alerted she might betray my trust "You can't tell anyone they will harm my Mum or me, and besides, I don't want any trouble; my Mum still lives in the block of that trap house. My words will have consequences." Kendra nodded her head. "I understand the implications and why you are so afraid, I'm guessing you do not feel safe going back home?" "No, I don't want to go back there; I can't; it's too painful." By the time I had finished talking and crying, I just wanted my bed, I was emotionally drained.

A nurse was waiting for me with a small blue tablet of Promethazine. I was no stranger to that drug, and part of me wanted to ask for something stronger. I swallowed the tablet and fell on the crisp white sheets to sleep. The crazy thing was it may have been a hospital bed, but it was the most comfortable bed I had ever slept in. And despite the constant noise all around me, I did manage to get sleep. The following day I was discharged from the general paediatric team.

My toxicology blood had normalised with no liver damage. This meant that I wasn't being kept in the hospital for any medical reason. It was all purely for social reasons. I guess with the children's ward security of locked doors and someone sitting at the end of my bed to ensure I didn't harm myself I felt safe for once. Gynae had also discharged me, My HCG levels were back to normal there was no baby.

I knew that Kendra had to share any information that would put me in danger, and I had swabs done to test me for Sexually Transmitted Infections. We also discussed me naming the boys involved, and I strictly declined. If I named Malachi, he would kill me or harm my Mum; there was no way I was putting us through that. I voiced in every session with CAMHS that I would kill myself if I had to return home.

They tried to question me as to why I felt this way, and they probed if I was involved in gangs. I blamed my Dads suicide from the block we lived in as triggering me. It wasn't exactly a lie.The stupid CAMHS workers who changed each shift, I felt like I had to retell the whole story, although they knew the gist of it from my notes. I could not and would not go back to that flat. I was vulnerable, scared, and had reached rock bottom.

The social worker that was allocated to me, I hated on sight. She was a small fat white woman with hair coming out of a mole on her left cheek and short brown hair nicely dyed. She looked incredibly like Dawn French, that actress. She came from money she had an expensive looking leather bag and an air of entitlement.

This was not a woman that ever graced a council estate. She told me her name was Carol, and she smiled at me in such a fake way I could write the story already. She was Overworked and tired; here I was, another case for her already exceeded workload. Yeah, great, let's get this show on the road and get this shit done with. She spoke to me, but I didn't speak back to her, I couldn't relate to her, and I didn't want her stupid interference in my life. This was like Ruth from CAMHS; why the fuck didn't these people just go and work in a posh area with their own type of people and their middle-class problems. Like having a meltdown because your Dior bag was delayed at Customs or the air con in your house was broken, first world problems.

I pulled the bedsheets back over my face. I didn't want to talk to someone who would not get me or be able to help me. She just looked like the usual stuck-up white woman who would pretend she was interested in my life but then secretly write notes to say how fucked up my life was. There was no magic wand. I wish she would just fuck off back to her Council office and drink her herbal tea as far away from me as possible. Walk a day in my shoes, then be qualified to tell me how to live my life.

Relate to you? With your University degree paid for by Mummy and Daddy, yeah, lucky you to have had the 2.4 nuclear family. Well, I'm fucked if I'm allowing you into my life. Mum was right; don't trust outsiders; they will never understand or never know what our lives were like. It's OK to pass judgment and look at us derogatorily when you go home to your semi-detached house with your wine and AGA oven every night. Fuck you all, and don't come preaching to me about how much better than me you are. I'm stronger than all of you put together.

Not only had I been through the biggest mind fuck known to anyone watching my Dad commit suicide and me to blame. But I had been raped and abused by vile men that I thought were my ticket to a better life. And then, just to put the icing on the cake, they got me pregnant, and I had to kill that baby with those stupid abortion tablets, so yeah, I really was not in a reasonable frame of mind.

I was 15 going on 50 the way I felt. It was as if I had already lived a lifetime of pain in such a short time. Suddenly I was angry; I didn't want to talk to anybody. I hated the hospital food and the fact that nobody seemed to genuinely give a fuck. All the nurses were only bothered about doing their shifts and leaving. They introduced themselves first thing in the morning and then in the evening when they changed shifts and that was as much interaction as they gave me.

A healthcare Assistant was still allocated to me to sit at the end of my bed and keep an eye on me. They never really spoke to me, they moved the stupid tables that go over the bed for me to eat food, and that was just about all they done for me. They were happier sitting and watching their phones even though I know they weren't meant to do that, but they did.

I was surrounded by adults who should have been able to help me, they should have been my saviours, but I felt even more alienated. The hospital should have been the safe space, a time for me to confide and get the help I needed, so why wasn't I feeling it? That's why Kendra from St Giles saved my life because if it weren't for her, I would have just shut down and not engaged with anybody. Here was someone who I felt listened to me. She got where I was coming from. I didn't need to explain things because she knew street life. None of these others could get it because they hadn't lived it. It was like I was talking another language to them. They couldn't understand me, but Kendra and I were on the same page, and when you are stuck in a Hospital bed shit scared, to have someone like that walk in to help you is like when you are drowning. Someone throws you a float. Suddenly, I can breathe, and even though I was still far from the shore, I felt Kendra might help me get to land.

16

Louisa- Hospital Corridors & Tepid Coffee

Even though I work in a hospital, I become blinded to people's anguish when I'm working. I'm used to walking the corridors and seeing the signs someone is dying because families would gather en masse outside wards.

I walk past people whose lives may be changed forever, be that good, bad or utterly traumatic; because I'm working, I walk on continuing my day, numb to it all and unseeing. When you have your Uniform on, you are invisible, and when you are in your civvies your normal clothes, suddenly, you can't just walk into areas you previously passed unseen with your bucket and mop. The day that Amelia decided to end her life, I was supposed to be on a training course some statutory and mandatory shit. I had been sitting having a coffee in the staff room in my jeans and t-shirt, waiting for my other colleagues to arrive when my phone rang, and my life changed forever.

The person on the other end of the line was calling from the same building I was in right now to ask me to make my way to the Hospital as my child was in Casualty. I don't remember anything else except running as fast as I could to the A&E department and thinking thank fuck I had reception on my phone as it could be a little sketchy to get reception on the ward. And if it wasn't for me going on that training course my phone would have been in my locker.

I rushed to the front of the Reception of A&E, but people were queuing. If I had run to the glass window to beg at the reception, jumping the queue, there would have been world war 3. I luckily had my work pass around my neck. I swiped myself into the main section of A&E. There were so many cubicles all surrounding the large open plan office area for staff where Drs and nurses typed on computers, engrossed in what they were doing, either ordering blood or documenting notes, requesting beds.

Not one person met my eye as I rushed to the front of the desks. I then frantically started opening doors to rooms to find my Baby. Some doors I opened contained older people that looked up with hopeful eyes thinking I was a relative or someone finally arriving to see them. Other cubicles had drunk people swearing, covered in vomit, looking at me with hostile eyes, none of them my Baby. All staff were busy rushing around, clutching blood and urine samples, running paper back and forth, everyone with their mind on their task, afraid to catch my eye in case I asked for something more from them in their overworked chaotic shift. I rushed to a bedraggled-looking nurse at the desk. She was busy typing on the computer and ignored my gentle cough and stare to get her attention. "Excuse me, My Daughter is here, and I need to find her" She looked briefly away from the screen towards me, with no smile, no compassion. "Name and Date of Birth", I reeled off Amelia's name, half hoping she would say there had been a mix-up and no one with the name Amelia Doherty was here. It was all just some silly joke, some big misunderstanding.

She clicked on something then her face suddenly changed. "OK, I need you to follow me" For a woman that was obese, she could move, and she shot up from behind the desk. I followed behind her as we walked towards the large sliding glass panel with the words that made my stomach turn inside out -Resus.

We were heading to the unit that held potentially the sickest patients in that Hospital, I don't know how my shaking legs carried me on, but they did. I was told to sit in a tiny room while she went to get the nurse looking after Amelia. A large African lady with a huge smile and a reassuring air about her with a big yellow name badge, "Mercy", smiled and gently guided me towards Amelia. She was talking, but I couldn't retain what she was saying. I kept thinking that Mercy was smiling, and she wouldn't be smiling if my child was dead, would she? The words overdose was the only thing I could recall, and the words stable; she was vomiting but had been found just in time. Pinch me. I'm in a nightmare, and in a minute, I will wake up and thank fuck this is not real.

Amelia was hooked up to a heart monitoring machine, she had fluids running into her body through a drip in her arm, she was in a hospital gown with a Grey vomit bowl next to her, and she was retching into it. She looked drunk; her eyes were glazed, and she could not sit unaided. A kind healthcare assistant, a girl about her age, was holding her hair back while she retched, struggling to be upright and vomit. Her clothes were piled into a yellow bio-hazard bag covered in blood and vomit, at first, I thought she may have been stabbed because there was a lot of blood. Then Mercy pulled the curtains closed and held a sanitary towel that was a maternity one, and I couldn't comprehend what was happening. Why was she bleeding so badly?

225

Had she overdosed, or what has happened? Why were they using such a large pad for her, nothing was making sense? Yet it seemed so many people were talking at me simultaneously, and I couldn't understand what was happening. An overdose would not cause vaginal bleeding would it? I had been mopping those hospital floors for long enough now to know that was not the case. I'd seen adults that had overdosed with mental health nurses watching their every move but never had they been bleeding vaginally.

Mercy took away the tissues they must have put into her knickers while someone went to look for the maternity pad, and it was soaked. This was not just an overdose. My world had tipped on its axis; I remember falling into the plastic chair beside the bed with Mercy's big strong arms holding me there.

The realisation this was my child in this bed and my legs just gave way beneath me. A young English Dr who looked younger than me, a very polite speaking woman was called to update me on my Child. She led me to a tiny room to the side of Resus -the death room, the breaking bad news room, with glasses of water and tissues on the table. This Dr seemed busy and frustrated, she sat on the edge of the chair as if it was sinful for het to sit even for a second they were that busy. She cleared her throat and then began to impart the news. Let me give you the heads up if you ever visit a hospital and are led into a room with a small box of tissues awaiting you, it's not good news.

I had so many questions that I couldn't even begin to ask, my mind was jumbled, and my hands shook as I held a plastic cup of tea with too much sugar in it. I can't remember asking for the tea or being given it yet here it was in my hand with me shaking, I drank it to give myself something to do while the enormity of what was happening sitting in this stifling hot room with no windows and artificial light waiting for the bad news.

Amelia had overdosed, and the ambulance had brought all the packets they had found in the flat; they were presented in front of me in a clear see-through bags which looked like Sandwich bags. The display showed Naproxen, Paracetamol, one Promethazine and half a yellow tablet which I knew was my emergency Valium. The Dr explained they had started an Acetylcysteine infusion which was being given to reverse any liver damage to prevent serious hepatoxicity. Speak Fucking English. She then said something that made me drop my tea. I splashed it all over my jeans in shock; how could it be worse than this? Her accent was white middle-class mummy, and daddy were probably Drs, and she was slumming it in the East End.

She cleared her throat and spoke "It would appear that Amelia has also taken an abortion pill; we have found some tablets called mifepristone and misoprostol also on the floor. Your Daughter had the empty packets, and with the presentation of heavy bleeding, we can assume that she has likely taken these tablets to induce an abortion. We have sent bloods to the lab to measure her HCG, which should be back very soon" I looked at her dumbfounded. What? I didn't even know that she was sexually active. "HCG? I don't understand; you mean she was pregnant?" The Dr nodded, and the bleep she was carrying chirped to life, making her jump up; she had to go; there was

227

another emergency, a paediatric trauma call for another child, one who was genuinely sick, a child with a medical emergency that wasn't self-induced needed saving. "Sorry, I have to run. We will know more when these levels are back. In the event of a miscarriage, hCG levels typically decrease from previous measurements. For example, a baseline level of 120 mIU/mL dropped to 80 mIU/mL two days later can indicate the embryo is no longer developing, meaning that whatever tablets Amelia has taken has done the job" She smiled and then ran.

I was left staring at the tissues in front of me, feeling like I didn't know what to do. I wished Glenda was still around. I longed to call her and have her sweep in with sound advice and that motherly feel to her; instead, she was a thousand miles away, and I cried with the realization I was out of my depth, and I didn't know what to do or who I could now turn to. Honestly, these people needed to brush up on their customer service skills; You can't just impart news like that and run away. I was angry it seemed to me the higher you went up the NHS pay scales, the more of a cunt you could become.

Then I had to breathe this was not the Drs fault this was all my fault, I was just looking for someone to blame. I was the Mother and what had I done? I worked all the hour's god sent me, I left my child, my only child to suffer and enter into a life I was supposed to be protecting her from. I was a failure and a massive one at that, the realisation that Amelia could have died made me want to vomit. I stood up too quickly and ran outside that room through an opening where the ambulances rushed patients in and I collapsed against the wall crying.

I can't remember how I got back by Amelia's bed, I think the nurse come to find me and led me inside. I could tell people were staring at me and I wanted to scream at them to fuck

228

off this was not a show this was my life. A social services referral was made because a child overdosing in a flat and taking abortion pills warranted that and also they thought there was Gang involvement. That really threw me because my Daughter was not involved in Gangs and it made me angry that they had the nerve to say she was. Why could they not see my Baby for what she was? She was a victim, she was not some rude little gang member.

It suddenly occurred to me she had many labels being placed on her head- Gang involvement, teenage pregnancy, single parent household, council estate fuck up. I had lived with these labels and over my dead body would these cunts treat my girl bad she was a CHILD and a VICTIM. The Children's adolescent mental health services (CAMHS) were going to come and review Amelia when she was medically cleared, but at the moment, we had to get through the storm of the overdose and ensure that she would be alright.

Mercy the nurse explained that we had to get her medically stable, but she was doing OK when her blood levels were normalizing, she didn't need a blood transfusion, and her vitals were becoming stable. While Amelia slept, I decided to go and get some fresh air. I was feeling faint and needed to escape the noise and the smells of the Hospital.

Trauma and stress can make you do some crazy things; I sat outside A&E on a cold bench sitting next to drunks and mentally ill patients asking for cigarettes. All humanity was out there. I was useless to them all, I had no cigarettes or alcohol. I just looked like one of them, lost, looking like I had wet myself, but it was the tea all over my jeans.Once they knew I had nothing of value, I was left alone. I sat next to cans of cheap larger discarded in the gutter, bottles of cheap Vodka; it looked like someone had been having a party on these benches. There were cheap polystyrene containers that contained cheap chicken and chips discarded all over the pavement leading into the Hospital like the people had given up on life and didn't see the point of putting their rubbish in the bin squalor was part and parcel of their lives, much easier to chuck your rubbish on the floor if you looked like shit and felt like shit.

I can't remember when it became morning until I realized I was trembling with cold. I must have just sat in shock outside, trying to process all that had gone on. I went back into the A&E department and must have looked like shit because Mustapha, one of the cleaners I knew who worked in that department, got me a hot drink and put one of the blue blankets around my shoulders to stop me from shaking. Then I was told Amelia was being moved to the general paediatric ward. Amelia's infusion had finished. She had spoken to CAMHS, but I wasn't present at the time, so I had no clue about the extent of how she was feeling. She must have disclosed that she still felt suicidal because when we arrived at the ward, a healthcare assistant was to sit with us and watch Amelia as she was at high risk of further self-harm or absconding.

These were words that were alien to me. The situation was tough to comprehend in my shock and naivety. Nobody explained it to me, we were just taken to the children's ward, and a burly lady came and sat down on the plastic chair, saying she was our one-to-one. The only time I have heard of one to-one was the old phone company, certainly not in the NHS. No other children had anybody else by their beds, just us, so obviously, we were a source of intrigue for the other parents.

When we arrived the nurse asked us questions like GP address and are we known to Social Services. When I said No we was not known I'm sure I see her raise an eyebrow, next question please! We felt exposed, broken, and raw, and the curtains to the bed had to be kept open at all times unless for dignity reasons like changing clothes, so we also felt so like we were in a Zoo. We wasn't just being scrutinised by professionals but the other parents would all smile and look towards us and ask why we were in.

We were under several teams, Gynae for the abortion, paediatrics for the overdose, CAMHS for the mental health support and last but not least social services to come in and determine how I had fucked up as a mother. With so many different teams, it wasn't evident who was who; so many Drs; I was overwhelmed by different faces introducing themselves, nurses and CAMHS people. When I thought about my Baby's abortion, I had to rush off, vomit into the toilet, and splash cold water over my face to bring me back to the present. What animals had harmed my Baby?

Except I knew I wasn't stupid, I knew exactly what type of boys ran that estate. How could I have been so foolish. I would have given anything to have taken her pain. How could this have happened? Was I so blinded to it because I knew I couldn't change anything?

As a parent, you feel out of your depth so quickly. I mean all the different Apps on the phone, the different lingo they used, it was like the youngsters lived in a parallel universe at times, and it was so easy as a parent to be so out of your depth that you just ignored it and prayed it would never happen to you or your child.

That night I returned home at 11 pm. I felt safe to leave Amelia as she was fast asleep and had someone watching her. The nurses told me to go and try to rest; I would need my energy.

Usually, Glenda would be there with a plate of food and a cup of strong tea to hold my hand, dry my tears, and impart some wisdom. The Mother I never really had, a woman that stood firm for me and always had my back.

There was nobody to greet me but the darkness of the tower block, whose lights seemed duller than usual. The ironic thing was that song by Nik Kershaw was playing out of someone's speakers on the bus "Wouldn't it be good to be in your shoes, even if it was just for one day, wouldn't it be good if we could wish ourselves away" those words really resonated with me tonight.

With a heavy heart I exited the bus feeling that song was an omen, the words of that song playing just for me. I often looked in through other people's windows when I was younger on many nights wandering around town. Looking at families sitting together on sofas or at tables having food sitting together, enjoying life. I always wished I could knock on one of those doors and sit in the rooms and be part of something where I felt safe. That I had somewhere where I belonged with people who didn't have much, but at least they had each other—it had always been such a massive part of my life being the outsider looking in.

The flat with a lingering smell of dampness was now mixed with vomit and old blood. The bathroom looked like carnage. It smelled like copper coins, old blood had a distinct aroma, and it seemed to be all over the flat. Handprints on the wall and the bathroom looked like a murder had been committed. Blood was all over the floor, and the toilet bowl was a mixture of vomit and blood. It was hard to believe that so much had come out of a tiny body and she had survived.

So many bodily fluids were all over the floor like a jigsaw. I had to wipe away each piece, knowing what part of the picture it painted—chalky vomit overdose, blood, the abortion. In anger, I threw the Razor Blades out of the Bathroom window, knowing that rather than use them for shaving, Amelia had been cutting her tiny arms, letting them rain down on the estate let them feel our pain.

I took bleach and a mop and bucket and got to work scrubbing, picking out the clumps of blood clots from the plug hole; the good thing was working as a cleaner, I had plenty of experience of just shutting out the world and cleaning, and this was a time for that.

I wasn't cleaning up the remnants of my Daughter's abortion or the vomit from her overdose; I was elsewhere; I couldn't think about the task at hand. I just had to get through this and get out. Remove the evidence as if, in some way, by doing so, it had never really happened.

I was broken and lost, but suddenly it was like a spotlight shone on me, and I had to make the right choices or risk losing my child for good. I was having sleepless nights. I felt anxiety kicking in every time I remembered what had gone on.

Part of me felt that I didn't deserve Amelia; she would have been better off being taken away because what had I achieved for her. My Mother didn't set a great example, and I may never know how to be a Mother. Perhaps it was in our genes? Amelia had deserved so much more than I had given her, and it pained me now to know that all the time I thought I had my shit together, it was all just bullshit and based on lies. Because what the fuck had I done for her? She had grown up in the same cycle as me living in this shitty tower block and sleeping with something pressed against the door to keep danger that seemed to follow us like a moth to a flame out.

It was fucking incredible how could I not see it. I had lived it myself for years and swore I'd never repeat the same mistakes again, yet here I was, re-living it all. I had hardly any money left in my purse, and I wanted obliteration. I went to the local shop and brought the cheapest bottle of wine I could afford and a £1 beef curry that was probably made of horse meat but would sustain me for the moment. I sat on my sofa and guzzled the drink as quickly as possible. I microwaved the meal and ate it so quickly realising I had not eaten in a while. The wine burned my throat as I burped up the gas, it tasted disgusting, but I wanted to feel the alcohol burning through my system for tonight. I just wanted an escape from the life I was in.

I had to go to the GP to get signed off work to be at the Hospital with Amelia. I broke down on the phone with the receptionist when she started questioning why I needed an appointment because where could I fucking start. My child's overdose? My ex-partner's suicide? fuck knows. I want a medical certificate to ensure I can be by my Daughter's side. And believe me, I'm on a zero-hour contract, so I know I won't be eating correctly for the next few weeks because I won't be paid, so believe me, I'm not doing this lightly. I need a DR to say I can't work.

When the prim Marks and Spencer blouse sour-faced receptionist is telling me she has to screen my call as a gateway to the DR, I have to break down her barrier; she has heard it all before another scrounger needing a sick note, but that was not the case with me, yet she almost lumped me into the same category. Was my story so unbelievable? If it sounded wild and disillusioned, that could be because it was.

On the way back from the Drs, an older guy was hanging around the front of the block he asked me where Amelia was, he looked in his early 40s, and my suspicions made me stop still. "Who are you? And what do you want with my Daughter?" He laughed at me. "I don't want anything ...She is a friend of my Daughters, and I heard an ambulance come to take her away. I was checking she was alright; no need to get paranoid"

He smiled, showing gold teeth and the way he leered at me; call it a mother's instinct, but this man spelt trouble. I looked him up and down and walked away. There was something not right about him, and I suddenly felt scared.I shut my front door and again pulled a chair to keep the door handle firmly locked shut. I couldn't bring Amelia back here.

The next day I rushed back to the hospital; going there as a visitor and not a worker felt really strange. It was lunchtime when I got to the ward after dropping off my Sick Note and confiding in my supervisor what had happened.

Walking along that hospital corridor out of my Uniform, I was stopped by many other cleaners to ask how I was. How was my Daughter? Of course, I never told them the truth. I just said she was sick and getting better.

Amelia was not at her bed when I arrived, which made my belly go over with fear. The Nurse explained to me that she was in the adolescent room with a worker from the St Giles Team, a charity organisation that helped young people in crisis and advocated for them, turning a past into a future was their motto.

Kendra the specialist caseworker from St Giles and Amelia sat together in the adolescent room of the Children's ward, a small space for the older kids with bean bags to sit on, a TV, and a notice board full of advice for teenagers- Need Sexual health/ Drug Advice. It was all there. Amelia was sitting chatting with this girl, and she did look like a girl to me, except she had a St Giles lanyard around her neck.

She had brought Amelia chicken and Chips and her favorite bubble tea. This was the first time since she was admitted to the hospital that I saw my Daughter smile. Before I knocked on the door to alert them that I was there, I just watched to ensure I didn't break up the moment. It was so important to me that this girl, whoever she was, had broken down the barrier that was so clearly up with Amelia not wanting to engage with anybody. Amelia spotted me and motioned for me to come inside. Her face looked animated for the first time. "Mum, this is Kendra from St Giles" The girl shook my hand and offered me a chip. I could see that closer up; she was probably around my age. "Amelia has told me all about you", she smiled.

I shifted, uncomfortable in my seat. What had my Daughter told her? I crossed my arms across my chest, unsure of how I felt. "Well, nice to meet you, Kendra. How are you feeling today, Amelia? You are looking much brighter." Hopefully, Kendra will get the message. I didn't want her here if she was going to start being intrusive with me. Amelia started to prod her straw into her bubble tea. I could feel her bringing down the barriers again. "So, So.. It's boring in here. There is not much to do." I suddenly wanted to slap her. "It's a hospital, Amelia, that's why! It's not a playground." Amelia kissed her teeth. "I didn't say it was, don't start Mum." Before I could feel a fight brewing, I wanted to mention the man outside our block. "Last night, there was a man outside our block, an older man that said he knew you and was asking how you were. He said he was the Dad of one of your friends." Amelia's eyes widened, and she shook her head, looking between Kendra and me. "No! What did he say? Mum, what did you tell him? Does he know I'm in here?" Kendra sensed that Amelia was working herself into a panic attack and quickly calmed her. "It's OK, Amelia, your safe; nobody can reach you here, OK.... breathe." Then I knew what my gut instinct had told me. This was someone who was

236

dangerous and meant Amelia harm.

The last time I saw Amelia like this was when Jerome had that video on his phone. If I'd known, he was the cunt that had hurt her in any way. I would have killed him myself. I would have got a knife and stabbed him right through the heart for causing all this pain for my beautiful girl.

But now I had to reassure her because nobody would ever hurt my precious girl again, absolutely nobody! "It's OK, Amelia. I didn't talk to him...." I started to cry even though I was trying hard to keep my emotions in check and keep it all held back, but I couldn't because I needed to know. "Was he the one who got you pregnant? I mean, did he? Oh god, Amelia. I know you're scared, but was he the bastard that hurt you?" She shook her head. "No. Mum, please leave it. I won't say, I can't say, I want to forget it, and we get on with our lives." I was angry, I wanted to shake her and make her tell me the truth. "Amelia, if he had sex with you, then he has to face the consequences... they can't do this to young girls and think they can get away with it." Amelia's eyes when locked into mine. I could see the pain in them, the face that was so beautiful but now looking lost and sad. Her voice when she spoke was so quiet I had to strain to hear, "Mum, we would never be safe ever again...they know where we live, where I go to school, where you work. I just can't". I knew she was right. I wasn't stupid, and we were stuck. I had nowhere else to take her, no money, savings, or family. It was just us. What was I to do? There was no magic wand to make this right. Forget Police protection for something as low down on the radar as this. We weren't getting shit; it was as if nobody could help us now.

I wasn't stupid; I had been young once too, but we were nowhere as bad as today's kids. We drank, had a lot of sex and skipped school, but this was a whole other level shit. I was once the teenager sleeping with the older man- Jerome, Amelia's Dad. Had she forgotten that? I was once her, a vulnerable young girl who needed to improve her life, but opening up your legs was not the way. I wanted to scream at her that having sex and engaging in risky behavior trapped you further in what you were trying to escape.

Kendra and I walked Amelia back to her hospital bed. It was strange because all the other little patients seemed so much younger. Amelia was more like a young woman compared to them. Kendra and I were going to grab a coffee. I could have done with something stronger, but even that would have gone against me. My parenting skills were under the microscope, and getting pissed to blot out the pain wouldn't have looked good. The drink the other night just made me feel worse if I'm honest. Kendra and me walked outside with our take-away coffees, she explained the STI swabs, HIV and Hep C had come back clear, but we would repeat the HIV bloods in six months to be sure.

The Crux of the situation was Amelia did not feel safe to go home, and who could blame her? The complexities of the case were more than just a suicidal teenager. She was vulnerable and at risk. She had suffered such a traumatic event with her Dad's suicide, and now the sexual abusers were sniffing her out.

I received a call on my Mobile that a social worker had been allocated to us and was coming to meet us. Kendra could see by my face this was something that completely threw me. I felt scared, it's like when you are young and you are afraid of what's hidden under your bed, well this monster was coming out and I was going to have to face it.

I had always feared the big corporate parent swooping in and taking my child away. I had spent my whole life avoiding this, and yet here I was being led into another nondescript hospital room to meet this social worker. I asked if Kendra could remain with me as I wanted someone who I thought could be on my side. Nina the social worker was an Indian lady dressed like a hippie with a large flower in her short bobbed hair which was almost Grey she looked to be in her 60s, she seemed motherly and kind. She smiled and said she worked for Newham Social Services and had been allocated to us. It was like we was a football team and on loan for this month we have this player except in this case it was an interfering cunt that I would have to try to impress.

My back was up just because of who she was; she could have been the nicest person on the planet but I would have felt she was here to trick me in some way. With her slow speech, I felt Nina was treating me as if I was stupid. We chatted about a safety plan for Amelia. Did I have a support network that could step in? a relative to provide another place to live temporarily? No, I fucking didn't. I only had me, myself and I. I had no clue where my own Mum was, and there was no way she would step in now to be Grandmother of the year.

She had made no contact with me or Amelia over the years, so she would hardly have a conscience now and help me. My glorious Mum managed to avoid all this, but in the 80s, child protection issues were not so mainstream. Still, nowadays, schools have safeguarding leads, it's more noticeable when a child is being neglected, and the parent has no support network. Most of us when I was growing up must have gone to school smelling like ashtrays passive smoking was all the rage back then.

But now parenting was different and everything you done and every move you made was being watched by someone, ready to pounce and criticize you. The same raised eyebrows of disdain raised with my mantra- I could cope, I have before, and I will again.

Nina had a colorful notepad, that had a logo that said Good Vibes Only, and I could see her writing stuff down and pausing to sip her herbal-smelling tea "Have you thought about temporary Foster Care for Amelia?" she said tentatively because she knew the reaction it would provoke in me. "What! No...I want my Daughter with me...she needs me. I'm not putting her into foster care." Nina exhaled sensing the barrier I was now putting up. "I know and I also know that you want what is best for Amelia and to keep her safe and protected. She has been through so much, Louisa, its traumatic she needs time and space to heal from this." I swallowed down my emotions, this was not good. "I know, and I understand that, but I just...I can't. I feel like I'd be failing her, if I put her into Care". Kendra looked towards me, ever the voice of reason. "Lou, you aren't letting her down. You are protecting her. You're giving her the space to come to terms with everything. If you sign what they call a section 20, you still have parental responsibility for Amelia, you are still her Mum, but she will live somewhere else and begin the healing process. She can't do that in that block., if she goes back there I truly think we would be setting her up to fail". I nodded as the tears fell, I knew what she was saying was right, it just didn't sit right with me, but what choice did I have? "I love her so much...all my life has been about her, protecting her and wanting the best for her and look what I've done. I've fucked everything up for her" Nina took my hand in hers, which made me flinch I wasn't used to tactile behavior from outsiders. She had so many rings and bangles on that she jingled as she grasped my hand in hers. "Listen to me Louisa , you would be doing the best thing for her, it's been a truly horrendous time for you both, and I know this is probably going to be one of the hardest choices you will ever have to make, but please understand I am going to try and help you too. I will try and see if I can speak to a Housing Association I know and to see If they have any properties for you both." I looked up at Nina. "We have been in inadequate housing for years. There aren't any new homes for us. I've given up the fight to get moved." Nina tightened her grip on mine. "Let me try, OK? These are very different circumstances now that leave you both incredibly vulnerable...Louisa, you don't need to worry about asking for help. I'm on your side, and nobody is trying to take Amelia away from you. We are trying to keep you together and safe." The sad thing was I had been so ingrained in people not to be on my side that I found it hard to trust. I always felt I had to have my wits about me; it was just how I had lived. She couldn't just expect a few words and for me to roll over signing my daughter away into potentially a life in care that would kill me.

After the meeting, I went to the chemist to collect the prescription the Dr had prescribed me, which was Fluoxetine, otherwise known as Prozac. I deliberated about taking them and decided what harm they could do. I wasn't sure what way to turn, and even though this was a step I didn't really want to take, I knew I had to try them. In my mind, a temporary measure to help me deal with all that was going on in my life because did I feel anxious and fucked up? Yes!.I held the paper bag that contained the tablets as if contained a miraculous pill that, once swallowed, would suddenly make me happier, calmer and more in control of my life.

But there was no instant miraculous comfortable feeling, the Dr said it could take 4-6 weeks before it started to work, and I may have a few side effects, but it was a step in the right direction. I could see the GPs face looking at me, thinking, how could you have gone through all this crazy shit and still be standing?

I felt like saying don't have a fucking choice, do I? Was I becoming my Mother? Was this always the way it was going to be? Generation and generation of ruined lives, early pregnancies, shit housing, and poverty. I had to make the change. I had to ensure this ended right now with me and Amelia.

We were at the bottom, so the only way was up, right? I made that first tentative step for help, took the tablets, and signed the section 20 paperwork to put my only child into foster care. It was probably one of the bleakest days of my life.

17

Louisa- Section 20 & Corporate Parenting

There was to be a meeting in the hospital with all professionals to establish a plan for moving forward, now I had signed the paperwork a temporary foster home was being sought for Amelia. The Social Worker met with me at home she sat in our decrepit flat while she probed me with questions and our family history.

She gave me a document and read through it with me I couldn't even offer her a cup of tea; I had no milk, but Nina seemed to be the type of woman who didn't judge like others. I could tell she had sat with the broken before. So it was clear- a Section 20 was part of the Children Act 1989 and therefore it was temporary respite because I as the parent could not provide suitable accommodation or care.

Nina helped me write down a schedule of expectations and she was going to help me contact a Housing association that she knew who helped vulnerable women in situations like ours. I was feeling so overwhelmed, I was living on edge, every time I left my flat I was expecting to bump into that older guy. I felt the groups of Boys that hung around the estate looking at me and without Leon or Glenda around I felt exposed.

Fatima's son Mohammed had knocked a few times to give me some food which Fatima had cooked, I kept missing her because she was working the night shift to make extra cash. I could tell he knew what had gone on with Amelia his words when he asked how she was were probing and I didn't want to give anything away. I said she was going to stay with a family member for a while and left it at that. I didn't trust him as far as I could throw him, which wasn't very far.

Julius had also kept on the low; I wasn't even sure he was in the block. When I walked past Glenda's flat the place was in darkness and I knew it wasn't my place to knock and burden this family any longer they had bigger burdens of their own. Amelia had apparently confessed to another CAMHS worker that she had been involved with Gangs. Apparently this was a case worker who dealt with vulnerable girls caught up in this lifestyle.

It worried me that the professionals might label her and judge her, Amelia would be categorised as being 'One of them', I knew deep inside was not one of those rude girls that marched around the estate. She was Amelia, a sensitive soul with a big heart. Yet ultimately she had sent people younger than her out on trains to sell and distribute drugs; she was good but vulnerable and yet tainted by the gang association at the same time. It really was difficult because she fitted two profiles, one vulnerable and the other potentially dangerous. I had tried so hard to make them see her as the victim, but when she started saying about some of the things she had done I didn't want to believe it.

Kendra from St Giles had been such a massive support to us; she was the go-between professional. Amelia had asked Kendra to sit with in with us while we discussed what was going to happen. Amelia said she was happy to go into Foster Care but if she didn't like where she was we would have to try another way. I promised her even if I had to get us a hotel room each night, one of those cheap ones she would not have to face feeling like she had no safe home. I didn't know how I would afford it but I would.

Kendra told me the Social Worker we had was ok, one of the better ones, and she broke everything down for me without making me feel stupid. Amelia really liked Kendra and she was really starting to open up and make decisions about her future because Kendra made her see there was a way out, it might be hard for the moment but things would and could get better we just had to believe.

I Can't even put into words how grateful I was for the relationship that Kendra had built with Amelia. I was relieved that Amelia felt she could at last talk to somebody because, without Kendra, Amelia would have just shut down or, at worse, known the right things to say and then just walked out of that hospital and killed herself.

I contemplated so much, during those days sitting in a hospital ward sipping tepid coffee and smiling at the parents opposite. What if my Mum would have got help, would my life have been different? And thus better for my Daughter, I thought a lot about my Childhood while sitting there and it hurt me at the similarities. All the things I tried to prevent, but I had repeated. The discharge planning meeting for Amelia was to be held on a Thursday morning. I woke up feeling sick with nerves. The word 'meeting' evokes terrible feelings in me, professionals may have 'meetings' as part of their regular jobs, but for me, it conjured up bad times or trouble, being called into School, interviews or being told bad news, nothing good in my life had ever come from the word meeting.

The way the professionals positioned themselves didn't help matters either, they were all on one side of a large table with one chair opposite that was mine, to sit in like I was on Mastermind and the chosen subject was my child. It made me feel it was them Vs Me. I'm on the other side of the table, awaiting them to seal my fate.

I felt like I was back at School being led into a brightly lit room with cheap plastic office chairs with a cheap pale wooden table that had seen better days, standard MDF office furniture. The NHS was no different. There were four of them sitting to face me, the social worker, the CAMHS nurse, the ward nurse allocated to Amelia for that day and the School safeguarding lead. I wondered what was going to happen I had signed the paperwork in my flat and now it was all eyes on me.

Was I going to be punished for what had happened? I started to bite the inside of my lip feeling suddenly nervous and not sure what to say. There was one other chair on their side of the table that was vacant, but I knew my place was on this side of the table, the one closest to the door and away from them. This way it was professionals all facing me they didn't want to sit next to me, Poverty is contagious don't you know. This way, they faced me, ready to scrutinise my every move.

I felt hot, and sweat started to pool under my arms. I would have liked to have taken my jacket off, but now I was scared that the sweat stains would be showing, my cheap deodorant was failing me. The last thing I wanted to look like was flustered and smelling of sweat, but with their eyes on me, I could feel myself becoming that Child in School that always smelt and looked dirty because of the life they lived. I was in cheap black leggings, a striped t-shirt, and a cheap denim coat, a mixture of supermarket budget and hand-me-downs. I looked poor, and I felt inadequate. The others looked smart with their leather brogues. The power of dress can make you feel powerful.

Kendra rushed in late, apologising as she was with another client, but she immediately grabbed the chair from the other side of the table and placed it next to mine. It was like a game of Chess; the power imbalances tilted somewhat as I had someone sitting on my side. Nina, the social worker, made introductions, and then the discussion began. I nervously began to chew my chewing gum because I was so anxious. I could already taste blood from where I had been biting the inside of my lip, this was not a good look, but I needed to chew to stop my mouth from becoming dry. I couldn't reach for the water on the table because my hands were shaking. It was reiterated that home was not a safe place and left Amelia vulnerable. Nina was supporting us to move due to this vulnerability, we were going to be prioritised, but I wouldn't hold my breath on that part. The School was going to ensure that Amelia was supported to do her GCSEs even though she had not been engaging much at School and then, like a clap of thunder, the news, a foster placement had been found.

I felt the room suddenly become hot. This was actually happening; shit just got real. A foster placement out of borough, in Broxbourne, a country house with a lovely retired couple whose Children had flown the nest. They wanted to give something back which is why they had decided to Foster. Amelia would be their first Foster Child that they would be taking, and Nina droned on about it being the perfect fit; how lovely they were. I wanted to shout her down and yell. No, the perfect fit is with me. I'm lovely and HER MOTHER!! The CAMHS support would continue, and Amelia would be seen weekly by the team there. They all looked smug with the plan. The boxes were ticked, the perfect solution sourced, and oh, how lucky to find a placement so quick, and how great it would be so easy for me to visit her as it was just 40mins by train from Stratford.

But I wasn't feeling joyous, I was feeling numb, broken and angry. They may all be smiling at this fantastic bloody solution, but I wasn't, I was hollow, I felt like someone had ripped my insides out. I was losing my Child she was being taken to another home to keep her safe how the fuck did they expect me to feel? Joyous? I was hurting badly inside.

I looked towards Kendra, and she knew without me having to speak how hard this was. "This is just temporary, Lou, remember that" I wanted to laugh because how many times have I heard those words? Growing up in this shitty housing it's temporary; as an adult again bad housing its temporary, another cold, damp shit home its temporary. Poverty, don't worry It's temporary. That word didn't necessarily mean what it read in the Dictionary because many of my Temporary situations were permanent.

Amelia joined us at the end of the meeting; she was wrapped in an oversized hoodie she looked at all the faces around the table and raised her eyebrows. Her skin seemed paler, and there were dark circles under her eyes, as if the hospital was zapping the life from her. Her main worry was what would happen to me, and I explained I would be ok. Nina explained we were exploring some options with the local housing team as a matter of urgency to move us due to the situation. I knew Amelia took this with a pinch of salt as most of our life we were dangled the carrot of a new home, it never materialised.

I felt sick, I didn't know if it was the Fluoxetine tablets that I had started or just the situation, but I felt nauseous and had zero appetite. Amelia's voice seemed just as quiet as her demeanor; it was as if someone had turned down her brightness; she appeared almost guilty to look at me, which was the last thing I wanted. "Mum, I just need some time away; I don't feel I can come home just yet" She started to cry then, big angry sobs that racked her body Kendra immediately asked the others to leave the room so we could have time together in that tiny little space without the prying eyes of Nursing staff this was not a circus show this was our lives.

I held Amelia close, breathing in her scent; as a Mum, nothing is nicer than smelling your child. Even if it's not the pleasant baby smell, it was still like a calming balm to me. My hug will give her the strength to go forward. "I am so sorry, Amelia, I never wanted this for us…. I just wanted to give you everything and be a good Mum, but I now realise I fucked up, and I'm so sorry" I hated myself for breaking down in front of her, her pain was my pain, and I don't know how our lives could ever go back to normal again, and would we even want them too? I didn't want my burden to be her burden, I didn't want her worrying about me. "Mum…please, it's ok, just give me some time and space…I love you. I know you always tried so hard; I never told you how much I appreciated all you did for me. But I see, Mum, I truly, truly do."

I didn't know how I was going to cope without my baby. She was the reason I got up I the morning, she was the reason for me to smile and make it through my day because she was my life. "Please just promise me you will never try to kill yourself again…you are my everything, baby girl, and you know you can always come to me no matter the problem." Amelia looked me directly in the eyes. "Mum, I promise I was just so scared I didn't know what to do." "Good, or else I will kill you myself" I smiled; it was a joke, an attempt to lighten the situation that seemed so bleak. And then Amelia's smile lit up her face; I had not seen her smile like that in a long time, and here amongst all this pain and turmoil, getting a smile from my baby meant so much to me.

Perhaps now we had hit rock bottom; the only way might be up; we had to hope because, without hope, we had nothing. CAMHS had sat with Amelia and gave her a safety and Coping plan, strategies for when she has an urge to self-harm and pointers to things she could do to stop her acting on the impulses. There were telephone numbers and websites all people there ready to help her, like a cotton wool bandage prepared to soak up the emotional pain.I was impressed that she seemed to think the techniques she discussed with her new CAMHS worker would help. I always thought that kind of stuff was bullshit, but we had nothing to lose. Breathe in, breathe out, but she seemed open to it all, as long as she didn't cut any more of her beautiful arms. I mean, those scars would be there for a long time.

The reason that Amelia got a placement so quickly was down to the fact that she was a quiet girl, a victim, and I was so glad she wouldn't be carrying the label of gang member. You see that's the thing with professionals they have the power to label you either good or bad and then it sticks. Nina reiterated, "We've been lucky to find somewhere so fast teenage placements are always a bit tricky to find, but Amelia is a good kid; she's not as complex as some others. I mean, she doesn't have behavioral issues or violent tendencies" I swallowed my hospital coffee, ready to walk home; praise the lord, I don't have a child with behavioral issues or a tendency to want to harm others; thankfully, she only wants to hurt herself, well thank goodness for that. For once we look good on paper. I left the hospital and walked the 2.8 miles' home in the rain so nobody could see my tears falling, and nobody would have cared if they had. This was London; you were invisible until you had something worth taking, and I had nothing left to give.

18

Amelia- Hertfordshire The County Of Opportunity

Can you ever really begin again? can you ever really get out of the lifestyle you have been so indoctrinated into? Let me tell you, you need a fresh canvas because otherwise, you are painting on a spoiled canvas, and the darkness is just going to seep through.

My original canvas was black and bleak, and trying to paint it pink or white would not work. The darker color was bleeding through to leave it a tepid Grey. I needed a new pure white canvas. I felt so damaged I could never see a way out; this must be some trap. Good things never happened to Girls like me.

When I first knew I was going to Hertfordshire, I was scared, and I had only known that place from my county line shit. I remembered girls like Katy with their semi-detached houses and stuck-up attitude. Imagine going to live with a cunt like that.

The social worker sat me down with her smiling face to impart the good news, a foster placement with a lovely couple, and it would be just me in the placement. A home in a rural location, four bedrooms and a lot of land, and they had decided I was worth taking on? What's the catch? I kept thinking, is the husband a paedo? Is the wife after cheap labour and will have me clean the place up? Why would people whose lives were so perfect open their world to others whose lives were damaged or flawed? Surely we could infect them with our bad luck and chaotic lifestyles.

The other surprise was that this was the Social worker's last day at Newham, so my case would be transferred to another Social Worker. Another face, another person for me to re-tell my story. I shut down after hearing that. What was the point in even beginning to attempt to trust them anymore? To them, it was a job, but they didn't realise this was my life, another stranger making decisions about what happened to me, and judging me by what I was on paper, never knowing the real me. Especially not this cold-hearted Bitch. I could tell she was glad to get her ass out of there; yeah, enjoy your leaving meal tonight and sip that red wine in the expensive Italian restaurant telling everyone what a Saviour you were for working in the East End.

Mum trusted Nina, but I didn't. I thought she was a little too happy for my liking. I just hoped she hadn't fucked Mum over signing the section 20 documents putting me into care because I'd soon escape if it were a trick. I wasn't a prisoner; if I didn't like where I was going, I would run away, but to where I don't know because, at this point, there would be no way I could go back to the flat. Mum said some shit about getting a hotel room temporarily, and I knew that was bullshit, but she would try. I knew that much. When a safe place is identified, the hospital wants you gone; no more, Mr Nice Guy, pack your bags and get out! They need the beds. I was no longer sick, was I?.

I was occupying a paediatric hospital bed because my life had gotten out of control, and I didn't have the proper family support to see me straight. Not what the NHS is for really is it? to occupy a bed for a social crisis. The doctors always announced loudly on their ward rounds, "She is medically cleared" like I had no right to even waste their time by existing.

The social worker informed me we were leaving that same day. She helped me pack the few things I had, we had to wait around another hour for all the paperwork and discharge letters to be printed, and then I was on my way, sitting in the front seat of a nice car again, heading out of the city. Onto the congested roads of the A13 with the smell of hospital still clinging to my hair and body. All my clothes were in these big bags with Hospital property written all over them. I felt like a prisoner being released from jail. During the drive there, I clutched my bags and hardly listened as the social worker made polite talk. I wished she would have just shut up and let us be silent. I needed the peace to compute it all.

The closer we got to Hertfordshire, the greener the surround-ings became. I opened the windows to smell freshly cut grass, golden fields, and so many trees it smelt earthy. It was a sunny day, the type of day where you feel upbeat just because the sun is in the sky. It heralds a bright day, and everyone is in a good mood when the sun is out. Not too hot yet for tempers to rise. It was just perfect. If the tower blocks were all you knew all your life, and you grew up surrounded by sirens and cheap chicken shops, then such smells and sights were blissful. I inhaled the scent of fields and cleaner air, and I could imagine running wild through them, alive and not just penned in by concrete jungles.

If she had opened that car door, I would have run and run, not to escape but to feel the grass on my bare feet. How would a horse galloping free with no constraints feel? This was what a prisoner must feel like when they are finally released from jail, able to see the world again for the first time, but this was freedom from a life of blocks and grime. I had still been trapped and imprisoned but just in a different way.

We drove down a bumpy, potholed path called (Church Field Path- Unadopted) I wondered what that meant. Perhaps the kids taken here couldn't be adopted fuck knows. We pulled up on a gravel drive to a massive house with a beautiful racing green-coloured door with a brass knocker. Beautiful wisteria plants bowed to us, all immaculately trimmed, and an enormous garage to the left of the house and so many windows it looked like a gorgeous boutique hotel. I had only seen homes like this on the TV, it was impressive, and I suddenly felt a bit out of my depth.

My foster Carers opened the door so quickly you could tell they had been waiting for us, ready to pounce, when they heard the car pull in. They greeted us with warm smiles as if we were family members returning from a trip away, that welcoming embrace. You know, when you have that instinct whether someone was good or bad, well, these guys were good, you could tell. Even though I knew to proceed cautiously, Rose and Fred West looked kind at some point.

Rosa was a lady in her 60s with short dark hair; she radiated motherliness from her plump bosom and a beaming smile, and her husband Mario, a kindly man with curly grey hair, stood next to his wife, welcoming us into their home. My social worker led the way inside, leaving me with my NHS property bag still standing on the doorstep and a little afraid. If I'm honest, this house was beautiful. I had never seen anything like this in my life.

The social worker's voice went up an octave; she felt she had to impress them too. "How lovely to meet you again, Mr. and Mrs.

255

Siracusa, and this Is Amelia, who you have heard all about" I smiled as I was thrust forward on display; here she was, the little freak from the East End. I suddenly felt scared as if by looking at me and seeing me, they would realise I had no place here with them in their home. They would be better off fostering a pretty baby that would be easy and less risky than me, the mixed-race girl from East London who had self-harm marks up her arms and a fucked up background.

This beautiful home was alien to me. It smelled of home cooking. When I entered, red plush carpets led upstairs, a dining room to one side and a living space to the other. Rosa showed us into the large open-plan kitchen, with a rustic wooden table in the centre and family photos on the wall. I looked around, not quite believing how big and wonderful the house was. It was huge. I glimpsed outside from the Kitchen Window and saw a vast garden with many things growing, a large greenhouse, a lovely rattan garden set, and so much space.

Home-cooked cakes, biscuits and juice were all laid out on the table in front of us as if we were here for a pre-booked lunch. I felt scared; Surely it was me that was supposed to be trying to impress them and not the other way around. We all made small talk, and then it was time for the social worker to leave, and I wondered if this was when the curtain would fall, and the bad things would start. Would they start shouting at me or making me do things I didn't want to do? There is no way I would live in luxury for nothing, right? Everything had a price.

Rosa and Mario showed me to my room, carrying my small hospital bag of clothes containing my essentials. The bedroom overlooked the beautiful garden. From up here, I could see how well cared for it was with Green lawns and the sound of birdsong; it was like I was looking out onto a TV screen. My room had an en-suite with a small shower, toilet and wash basin. The bedroom was old-fashioned but beautiful.

Rosa took my clothes, telling me she would run them through the wash to get them fresh for me. She told me to make myself at home and then pop down when I was ready. I lay back on that bed, feeling like a queen. The bed sheets smelled of washing detergent; this was luxurious to how I had been living, and as I closed my eyes, I thought of my Mum, and guilt washed over me. She was still on the block; I had left her to it, deserted her; I had run away, to play happy families with people that were not my actual blood. But I couldn't go back. I just prayed that deep down she understood, but if I went back, things would be so much worse for me, and I'd never get out of there alive.

Peace can be hard when you are so used to living your life to a backdrop of noise in the city or the noise of the people in the block; there was never any silence in Newham.

I knew the sounds of my neighbour's door being kicked open because the police had broken it down months ago, and now it needed a good push to open. I lived to the soundtrack of bass music pulsating through the ceiling from the guy that lived above, next door to Peter that played his reggae music full blast all day. There were always voices coming from somewhere, and now I was in a room surrounded by silence, with no one living above or below me and just the sounds of nature coming in through the windows. It was unsettling at first.

That first night Rosa fussed around me, making me hot chocolate, asking if I wanted more to eat, helping me fold my clothes into the wardrobes, and washing the damp ones. Since I was Rosa and Mario's first foster placement, they seemed on edge quickly to jump to my every whim; this was a learning curve for us all. One thing that radiated from them was compassion;

in some ways, Rosa reminded me of Glenda, those strong salt-of-the-earth women who always knew what to do and say. They know how to cook and make everything alright; they would fix your crown without telling you it was crooked.

My Mum never really had that aura; she always seemed to prefer other adults to tell us what to do. I know she loved me fiercely, but she wasn't the Mothering type who would own a sewing box or bake cakes. But Women who are not good parents are sometimes the ones that were never shown how, and that was certainly true of my own Mum. She never had a lovely house and warm upbringing, so how would she know how to do all the nice things ordinary Mums would do? I couldn't blame her. She did the best with what we had.

Silence and green spaces meant time to contemplate everything that had happened. It's hard, especially when you can't bear to think about the painful things you've done. I had a warm home with lovely people, but I felt strange. I felt like an impostor. I ate three meals daily breakfast, lunch and dinner my whole life. It was always one or the other either a big lunch or dinner but never three home cooked meals daily. I had never had soft towels or properly branded toiletries, and for the heating to be left on if I needed it? Maybe this was just the first week, and then it would go to one meal a day and shit. If it did, I still wouldn't mind because this house was still paradise.

I loved looking out the window and not seeing the city, but a garden which was so green and beautiful. I never knew such places existed outside our world. I knew they had to be real, but I never thought I would have the opportunity to inhabit them. I never thought I would end up in care either, but that's the way life goes sometimes. After spending my whole life with my Mum with everything on the cheap, the branded toilet tissue and foods all felt luxurious.

Foster care was like being taken from an Ibis hotel to the Ritz I'd upgraded everything, food and life. I accompanied Rosa to the Supermarket, where she loaded the food into the trolley without having to tally up as we went along. We never had to choose what items to return; everything I chose, she happily put in the basket. At first, my body still craved the sugar and the beige fried food I had been raised on, and I wondered how I had sustained all that shit for so long.

Rosa and I sat together a lot in that open-plan kitchen; she didn't pry; she just cooked at her massive cooker, ironed my clothes and did everything a Mum should have done. I was happy to sit there, mesmerised at how she chopped vegetables and made pasta sauce, the most delicious meals ever, Rosa and Mario were Italian, and most of the food they made was from scratch. They had so many vegetables growing in their garden; it was a different way of life. Sitting at the table and soaking it all up for a while was nice. Rosa and Mario never made me feel less of a human being for not knowing how to make my bed correctly or fold my clothes away; Rosa just showed me and smiled; she was lovely, and I couldn't help but wish I had been born into a family like this.

Then guilt would hit me, poor Mum still in that awful block. Even though I'm not religious, I prayed so hard that we would be back together soon. I wished Mum could have moved in here with us, but that's not how it works; it was just a shame, and that's all because I wanted Mum to experience this way of living. Mum could have used some of this nurturing in her life. It made me think it's a shame that this respite care couldn't be extended to my Mum because we could have had a different way of life together here. Rosa could have taught my Mum how to do so much.

I would spend time with Mario in his lovely garden. He was growing courgettes, cucumbers, sweet peas and all types of tomatoes. I was in awe of this and would often wander with him, losing myself in the land, pinching out shoots of the tomatoes and picking the ripe ones to take inside to have with salad or make into sauce. Being outside with Marco made me feel good. It was a time to concentrate on the magic of how things grew, and I hoped that, like the plants, now I was in a suitable environment, I could also grow.

The fresh air and clean living soon reduced the nightmares and flashbacks. They occasionally returned if I smelt a specific smell. Rosa cooked steak one night, which triggered me as that was my meal with Malachi before I was raped; just watching the meat cook made me want to puke. Rosa and Mario never cooked steak for me after that, and they also went without it. Lasagna was another meal that triggered me as that was the meal we had been eating just before my dad committed Suicide. It was the meal I threw at the wall to distract him from the phone and the video of me. So whenever I Replayed that night in my head, I thought of the lasagna dripping down our wall and then Dad falling to his death. I appreciated their sensitivity and did not pry why I couldn't be around Lasagna or Steak, which was a big ask for Italians.

I had a new phone given to me by Mum, so I had no access to my previous social media and my contacts, which was a relief. I didn't feel tempted to see what was going on or face any of the threats that were undoubtedly put out against me. My dad's death had, with all intents, given me a slight reprieve from all that, but I had still been raped. I still left Peters flat to the youngers who probably fucked him up and took advantage of him more now I wasn't around.

I still had scars on my arms that reminded me every day what had happened. I hated to look at anything to do with babies. If they came on the TV, I would turn it over, the guilt I felt for taking that abortion pill was killing me inside, but I knew deep down I didn't have a choice; I couldn't have been a good mother. But it would take a while for me to feel ok about being around tiny babies.

When Mum visited, she always seemed on edge; she would sit on the sofa with her hands clamped together. She never accepted more than coffee, milk, and no sugar, as if taking more would be greedy. She was still thinking people were out to get her, and trap her. I could now see clearly how her upbringing impacted how she raised me. Everyone in my Mum's life had hurt her, abandoned her or made her feel that she wasn't worthy; everyone had let her down in one way or another. It was no wonder she didn't trust very freely. If something was given, then we were led to believe it could be taken away again quickly. But Rosa and Mario would always give us space and make Mum feel welcome.

They even had the kindness to parcel food up for her, which I knew she would eat when she got home because my mother's whole stance was I don't need help; I can do this, but it's become pretty obvious now that, no you can't, and sometimes you do need help. "Are you happy here?" She asked me as we walked outside; I had been there a few weeks by now. I had settled in quicker than I ever would have realised. "Yes, Mum, I'm just sorry, I still can't go back there." She nodded and exhaled through her nose, a noise that meant she was holding back the tears. She blew out from her mouth as if she was exasperated. "Don't worry, I get it, it's pretty lovely here, and they seem nice.

You're not missing a lot back on the block. They have moved a few families out and are considering demolishing the block again. Even though we have heard it all before." I smiled and cuddled my Mum; she felt skinnier. "I hope so, I would love for nothing more than to see that place turned to rubble, but Mum, let me show you something; come with me."I led her over towards my little section in the garden where Mario had let me start growing tomatoes and sweet peas, I had put the sweet peas in a wigwam trellis, and I had a crop that I knew I had to pick soon as they were becoming ripe with the glorious sunshine. I wanted to show them to Mum before I picked them, I had achieved this small crop from a few tiny plants, and I loved watching them grow. They flourished with my love and also the excellent warm environment. Like my life, I was a tiny seedling but had no chance to grow in such a dark environment forever in the shade. I could see how things would have been different if, as a child, I'd been raised here. Not Saying my Mum didn't love me, but sometimes love is not enough.

I felt bad for thinking that way. "Did you grow this?" she looked so happy for me that she laughed, and at that moment, I wished I could have taken a picture and captured it because, for the first time in years, at that moment, she looked carefree. Her face was starting to tan from the recent sun, and her hair was longer and thicker somehow, as if not having me around didn't drain her so much, but she was not eating right; that's why she looked so thin. I smiled; I was so proud of my crop; look at me, an inner city hood rat growing her own Veg. "Yeah, I did; pick some you can cook with them" Mum smiled at me. "I wouldn't know where to start, Amelia; I can't say anyone has ever shown me how to cook with fresh tomatoes before".

And then it hit me. My Mum was as much a victim as I was. She hadn't been raised; she had been dragged up by a human being that had deserted her and let her down. How the fuck could we expect a life that was full of promise and roses when we were growing in the dark.

19

Louisa- Lost But Now I Am Found

On the train back home from Cheshunt to Stratford, I sat alone in that carriage and felt my world falling apart. I felt lost like I was leaving part of myself behind. My baby, whom I had tried hard to do everything for, looked happy and healthy for the first time in forever.

Amelia had been given a taste of normality, a fridge full of food, an adult at the cooker each night cooking real food, not just shoving frozen food into the oven for 30mins. And most importantly, she had an adult that had given her time and space to be herself. I had somehow lost her in the struggle to make ends meet and work.

Amelia had become a stranger to me; my baby could no longer confide in me. I wasn't present enough; I was happy to leave that to the school and the streets, and looked what the fuck had happened.

Her clothes now smelt freshly laundered; we would wash our clothes in the bath then hang them over our balcony or, in winter, hung up on a clothes rail in the living room, so we always smelt a bit damp, a bit poor. Cheap washing powder and cheap everything. Freshly laundered clothes that were tumble-dried were plush. They smelt and hung on you differently.

Rosa and Mario's house was warm, the environment friendly, and it highlighted the coldness and depravity we had been living in for so long. It wasn't until we were out of the cycle that I could see how my childhood had impacted my ability to parent Amelia. I wasn't shown stability; all our foundations were built on quicksand, and the more we built, the quicker we sank.

I had never been part of anything stable; I had spent so much of my life always hoping for something better, just a secure clean stable home and not housing unfit for purpose. I had always had Glenda and Fatima; even though they were not family, they were the closest thing to family I had, but again their lives echoed mine, always struggling and hoping for something more, journeys full of abusive men, low incomes and surviving in a hostile world. This was not the right way to raise a child and live a life. Now I wonder what would have happened if my Mum had got help and more support. Would she have loved me more? Would she have tried to be a better mother rather than constantly running away from her responsibilities, blotting out the mundane life with drink or drugs?.

My Mother had never spoken much of her family or her upbringing, only that her Dad was an abusive bully and her Mother was cold and distant and never really liked her. So I guess it was no surprise when she found out she was pregnant with me; she didn't know how to be a mum. It's hard now, though, to think that she just cut me out of her life for getting pregnant, making the same mistake she did. I could never shut the door on Amelia ever! My love for her was just too strong. I wished I could call my Mum and ask her why? But I guess that will be for another day.

For now, I had to do what my instincts told me I had to do for my baby, and that was no matter what, I had to get her back with me somewhere safe with me and better than we were before.

Those first nights alone back at the flat were awful; the flat was so empty and quiet. I slept in Amelia's bed and found her room's smell comforting. I was told not to call her for the first few days and give her space, but she had a new number, and I messaged her to say I love you, and I'm thinking of you. Imagine how that felt, my baby I raised living in a stranger's home as that's the only place she could be kept safe. It couldn't get any worse than that for a mother, trust me.

I looked around her bedroom, still painted in the bubble gum pink we had chosen years ago. It still had the marks left from the blutack where her posters used to be. The room still smelt faintly of vomit, and the perfume sprays she loved from Victoria's Secret. I lay there in that tiny single bed night after night imaging everything she had gone through and me not knowing. It cut me like a paper cut; no matter how many times I tried to forget, I was continuously reminded of the pain. How could I have never known my little girl had been subjected to such evilness or depravity? I had not even talked with her about sex because she would bash me away when I mentioned it, saying she knew about it all. The school had given her lessons, and to discuss anything like that with me was just wrong, pure wrong and embarrassing.

She forgot, of course, I had been young once. I was just like her, thinking I was tougher than I was and looking for a way out. There was so much time that we could never get back, so many years of surviving and not living, but you didn't realise it then. You are trying to put food on the table, struggling to manage your bills, and in survival mode. When you get time to sit back and think about everything, that's when it floors you. It's like PTSD; it will hit you when you're out of the battle and sitting on the bus on your way to work. It will grip you when you're trying to sleep in the middle of the night.

As a parent, you want to do your best that's all you ever wish to do, but sometimes you have to equally wake up to the fact that sometimes the best you are doing can be the worst thing and do more damage.

I have never had this motherhood shit down to fine art at all. I wish life would come with an instruction manual at times. I have never been the type of Mum to have Wet Wipes and organic rice cakes in her bag.

I feel like I have been a Child trying to parent another Child.It was an evening in July when I was sitting on a plastic garden chair on my balcony looking out into the light night sky, pondering life and how some people manage to sail through this world without trouble in the world, while others got all the shit luck. When I heard my mobile ringing on my coffee table, I ran inside to answer it just in case it was Amelia or Glenda making contact.

The Social Worker who was allocated to us a new one called Michelle, her name flashed up on my screen. They always chop and change, but this one seemed ok, just like Nina before her. Michelle was a tall black lady with dreadlocks down to her backside and a kind demeanour; she never looked like she judged me. She had visited me here at home and brought her own Peppermint tea, and she seemed ok, but I was still wary.

I was slightly worried about why she called me after work because it was about 9.15 pm. Panic went through me. Was it Amelia? Had something happened to her? What was wrong? "I've been trying to reach you all day, Louisa." I was momen-

267

tarily afraid. "I've been at work. I've told you there is never any mobile reception in that place. What's wrong? Is it Amelia?" She laughed, and I felt relief Amelia must be ok. "No, No, my lovely, I have good news, and I am calling now because I wanted to let you know; we have found a place for you both out of the borough in Hertford, and I know how well Amelias foster placement has been going and how much she enjoys that area; she has embraced it." I went back outside and stood overlooking the city that once held so much promise for me.

When I was younger, I had looked across at the city development and had hoped, one day, that I'd be free of tower block constraints. I never realised we would achieve it through my Child's pain. "You still there, Louisa?" "Yeah, sure, sorry, I was just lost in my thoughts for the moment...so a new flat, you say?" "It's nice; that's why I'm excited for you. I know Amelia has a college placement near this location and the chance of a new job with Mario, so this is great news." I exhaled with relief; this wasn't a call to give bad news. I could be with Amelia again in a new place. I didn't need to be scared of a fresh start. It was the only option we had we had to take it. "It's a two-bedroom, ground floor flat in a quiet residential close. It has a little garden and its Housing Association, so a secure tenancy and reasonably priced; we can always claim Universal Credit until you get a job. Honestly, as soon I saw it, I knew it was for you. I fought hard to get you to the top of the list. I know it has not been easy, Lou, for you to live there without Amelia and all that has gone on for you both. I think it's going to be perfect for you...a fresh start back with your Daughter." I could feel tears welling in my eyes, and I didn't know what to say. "I'd like it very much". Was this real? Would I wake up back on the sofa and realise this was just some crazy fucked up dream. I pinched myself to ensure I was awake.

"Can you come with me tomorrow? I'll drive you Louisa, and we can have a look, as the Housing officer is keen to get someone in there asap. It will only need a little doing to it as the tenant there before is moving abroad and leaving most of the stuff behind. It's all nice and in good condition." I was trying to get my head straight; tomorrow was Saturday, and I knew Michelle worked Monday- Friday. "But tomorrow is Saturday. I'm not working, but it's your day off too." She laughed. "It's ok. We can say this is an emergency but a good one, meet me at the bottom of your block at 11 am, and we will go there first thing tomorrow; we don't want to lose this one, ok. We won't tell Amelia until we have visited and you like it, ok." I was stunned. "Sure...yeah, of course. Thank you so much".

I hung up the phone and double-checked to ensure she had called me and that I was not dreaming. Was this a social worker doing something good? What was the catch here? Where was the trap? Then I realised what was I running away from?. What could be worse than the situation we were already in? My Child was in Foster care; she had tried to kill herself, and her Dad had jumped from this very same block we inhabited. We had to get away from here. This was not home; this was just bricks and mortar that contained so many tears and nights of pain.

But Change was scary. A new area was a big step. I wouldn't know anybody, but maybe this was perfect; this was our time. This was for us. I looked around at the home I had tried to make clean, tidy, lovely, and homely. We could paper over the cracks, but we could never really hide the damp smell of rotten wooden windows with bases so worn they never shut correctly. No, we couldn't end up any worse off than we were. I had to trust the people that it had been ingrained into me not to trust. Because if I had been removed from my Mother, my life could have been normal; I may have just stood a chance. I had to do this for my Daughter, not me, but for her.

The drive to the new place was full of the usual small talk between two women who didn't know each other that well; we talked about the weather, cooking, motherhood, and safe subjects to fill the silence.

The moment we drove into the small close, it was like a dream: a circular close with flats that went up only one story. The ground-floor flats had patio doors that opened out onto well-kept gardens. You could tell this was a place with residents who cared about how it looked and maintained it, from the pretty flowers and shrubs to the garden bird feeders and colourful wind-chimes hanging outside the doors. This was a nice place; no rubbish was strewn anywhere, and it breathed respectability. This was a space you could envisage calling home, a place to look forward to returning to. Not just a shell to house them, an area where nobody gave a fuck about their surroundings because we never thought it was worth it.

Could this be a home for me and Amelia? Would they not look at me and believe that the likes of me did not belong here in this space? .We were met at the door by a friendly-looking woman in her early 50's she had bleached blond hair piled on top of her head, a leopard skin headband, and bright red lipstick. She smiled and introduced herself as Laura, the warden for the block. The first thing I noticed was that inside the entrance had carpet; now, I've never had carpet inside; maybe when I was young, some dirty leftover scrappy thread bear shit, but this was plush. She chatted as she walked us past doors that looked clean; there were no strong smells of weed or music with the heaviest bass line blasting through the walls. "Here we go" She opened the door to a well-lit hallway, and we went inside.

To the left was a small kitchen with a small pine table- perfect for two. The two bedrooms were great sizes, and the living room was spacious and overlooked the garden area. "It's a quiet block, the neighbours are all lovely, and I'm on-site Monday -Friday as the warden here as we have an over 55s block just across there" She pointed towards another block opposite which was just as abundant with flowers, Gardens looking like they belonged to a Garden centre. "So this block is for the under 55s?" my heart was racing, hoping there would not be a fuck up, and it wasn't the right age category for us. "Yes, that's right, lovely, for wonderful women just like you who need a new start" I looked from her to the social worker. "Like a refuge?" Laura shook her head. "No, not a refuge exactly. We don't offer round-the-clock protection and security but let's just say a lot of the women here have not had the easiest starts, but now they are all on the right tracks".

Many of these women had left abusive men and relationships; my direct neighbour next door was a lady called Lisa, who had escaped an abusive man; the other lady to the left of me also had the same story. I did not doubt in my mind that I would accept this chance. I could imagine sitting with the open patio doors, reading a book, chatting with Amelia, and being Normal! Having a life that wasn't full of constant living on the edge. I had to make this work. I don't care what job I had to do to pay for it, this was our chance at a new life, and I was going to grab it with both hands.

After I viewed the flat, we sat in Laura s little office to discuss the details. I would sign the contract, and they would help me fill out the benefit claim forms and Universal credit online to help me with the rent. But I knew there was a prominent general hospital a small bus ride from this place because I googled it last night.

Now the joy of working for a large outsourced company that cleans for the NHS means there are jobs all over the country, and transferring from one to another is easy when you're in. And besides, my supervisor felt deeply sorry for me and the shit I had faced in my life; it was time to make some calls and see if I could get a transfer.

When I had signed the contracts for the tenancy, which would begin in three weeks, I sat in the Social Workers' car, laid my head against the back of the car seat and cried. Knowingly Michelle placed a hand on mine. "It's your time now, Lou. You can do this" Her grip was firm, and I wanted to hug her, but I didn't. "I just keep thinking something will go wrong, they will see they have made a mistake, and it all be taken away from me" Michelle squeezed my hand tight. "You know there is a saying it can't always rain. I know you've had some pretty rainy days and troubles lately, but now Lou, there is a brighter sky, so go with it. It is yours and Amelia's time now."

We were now driving to tell Amelia, who was at Mario's restaurant doing her little Saturday job getting experience in the restaurant trade. She had dropped entirely out of doing her GCSEs but had enrolled at College for a catering course, and I was so proud of her. Because, for once, she had faith in herself. Kendra from St Giles had a massive part to play in this. She visited Amelia regularly and helped her look at options she could take. Vocational routes where she could work and study. Amelia needed another young person to show her she could make something of her life and support her when she felt she couldn't. The charity St Giles's motto was about turning a past into a future, and they certainly did that for Amelia.

Mario didn't work at his restaurant anymore but still popped in and sat at the bar drinking espresso coffees and keeping an eye on his business. This family had a soft spot for Amelia; perhaps they could see in her what they had when they came to this country, with nothing but determination and grit. Mario had allowed Amelia to learn the restaurant trade. He was happy to have Amelia as a project; they had an incredible bond.

I asked Michelle to stop as we reached the little restaurant with its small wicker tables outside. I just wanted to stand still and watch my baby without her knowing I was there. The high street was full of boutique clothing shops, butchers and Grocers, not a £1 a bowl fruit and veg on a dirty table in sight. These were proper shops, and they had lovely windows. This was like an old-fashioned town with clean streets; again, you could tell people had pride in their high street.

I looked towards the restaurant and could quickly identify Amelia; she was the only mixed-race person there, gliding between the tables, smiling and laughing easily. She moved like a ballerina, elegant and wistful.

Michelle allowed me the time to take it all in, and when I was ready, she linked her arm to mine, and we walked towards my baby. Amelia's face when she saw me broke into such a joyous smile she ran straight towards me, enveloping me in a hug that was so tight she could have broken my bones. She had grown taller and looked plumper with all the food they had given her. Mario, who was always there on Saturdays while Amelia worked, immediately got us a table and was fussing around ordering coffees and asking if we would be staying for lunch, always the most welcoming host.

Amelia sat with us, a worry creasing over her face as I told her I had news. I could see in those moments the fear as I so often lived with those thoughts, too; whenever anything was going well, you would wait for the wrong things to hit. You didn't ever really allow yourself to be happy because you were always waiting for something to go wrong.

I smiled as I waited for the coffee to be placed before me. "I've just been to view a two-bedroom flat about a ten-minute walk from here." Amelia looked between me and the social worker, and I could see the confusion in her little face. "What do you mean? A place for you and Me?" As I smiled, the tears I was trying to hold back released like a dam. I couldn't hold them in. "Yes, me and you, a place to be a family again. You will be living back with me." "Your joking? Are you being serious?" She looked back and forth between me and Michelle. "You Serious?" "Yes!" Michelle laughed. "Yes, Amelia, a home back with Mum, not in Stratford or London, but a new start for you both, here in Hertfordshire.".

Amelia jumped up and threw her arms around me, hugging me tight. Mario made his way over, his instinct to protect Amelia already kicking in to ensure that everything was alright, and at that moment, I loved how he had looked after her and still felt such a sense of loyalty and protectiveness for her. Ok, they were paid to care for her, but I could see from his eyes that he genuinely cared for her wellbeing. "Oh my goodness, Mario! Mum has got us a place ten minutes from here, can you believe this? We will be together again!" he watched us hug, and I could see tears in his eyes.

He was one of the kindest men that I had ever met. "This is the best news. I am so happy for you both" Mario had tears in his eyes, and I suddenly realised at that moment there were good people in the world; you just had to find them. Amelia was like a whippet running back towards her new colleagues to impart her news, rushing back out again. I had not seen her as excited as this in years; the last time was when someone brought a large paddling pool for the estate kids. "I can't believe this; tell me I'm dreaming, Mum... I'm just in shock." I smiled. "You're coming home; this is the beginning for us, Amelia. This is what I wished for you all those years ago when I brought you home from Hospital when one side of the skyline was Grey, and the other was blue. It's time for the blue skies now, not the Grey." I held her in my arms, and for the first time in my life, I felt it might just be alright

20

Louisa-Austerity Cuts, Cost Of Living Crisis

I decided that the only things I would bring with me from the flat would be my battered suitcase of memories, all the School photos and painted pictures from Nursery that Amelia had done. All our clothes smelt of the life we were leaving, and I believed we had to start afresh. Nothing in that flat could be used again, and to take anything with us was almost like a bad omen; it could stay where it belonged, second-hand and not worthy of coming to a new beginning.

I didn't want the past to taint the future. Amelia's bed covers were still blood-stained from her abortion, as I had to wash them in our Bathtub, and the stain wouldn't budge. I didn't want her to see the covers and have to re-live that traumatic time.

So many items from that flat would be a massive trigger of some traumatic times, her Dad's suicide and god knows what else that I didn't know about.

Maybe one day Amelia might feel able to tell me, but for the moment, it had to be shut away and packed away for another time. I wasn't stupid I knew that you carried your scars and memories of the past always with you, it was like a heavy bag and after a while your arms grew tired. I knew that in time Amelia would be able to maybe sit and tell me but for now we just had to look forward.

I can remember closing the flat door for the last time and feeling bereft; so many memories were inside this flat. Even the marks on the door told stories, boot prints that had been Jerome's when he had tried to kick his way inside. Scratch marks, again from his attempts to break in, a small blood stain from Amelia's abortion where she had bled as she was taken to hospital. Memories of walking in here for the first time, heavily pregnant, trying to make a home from other people's leftovers. Sofas that were not mine, curtains mended to make do, a table that we found, it was all makeshift and only ever meant to be temporary, but that temporary had lasted us for 16 years.

There were so many memories in that flat, and they went through my mind, Amelia's first Christmas, the tiny little tree we had, and a Turkey from Iceland that Glenda cooked and sliced up into portions, sharing with others in the block. We ran up and down the stairs with plates of food, doors open where people would walk in shouting out "Hi only me!" Everyone was in it together, we had such a sense of community, and now it felt like I was locking it out. I was going again into the unknown.

But I knew that with every step I took, it was for the sake of my child. We couldn't reside here. We needed to be strong and move on. It's natural to fear the unknown; Uncertainty has never been a friend of mine, yet for so much of my life, I've lived this way on edge. It gets tiring after a while. When I shut that door for the last time, I almost felt that I would return back one day; it was crazy, but it was like this new life was being dangled in front of me, but I had a feeling in my belly it might all come crashing down, and we would be back, I was bred to expect disappointment.

Some people call this impostor syndrome, where you can't believe something good is happening to you. That's what I feel now. We were like butterflies trapped in a net; this time, that net needed cutting, and we needed to be free.

I'm not sure how I had envisaged my moving on to be, perhaps with a lovely man and a lovely new house, a new relationship, and the safety of a man to help me. Not with a daughter in foster care who had been involved in gangs, a back street abortion pill and an overdose.

I still questioned if I was doing the right thing. I'm not being funny, but East London was my safe haven. It may have destroyed me at times, but this was my home. No, I told myself stop being so fucking stupid pull up your big girl knickers and get on with it. East London will always be my home, but in reality, by being here, we could never move forward and go on to anything better.

I moved into the flat the day the tenancy started. I was lucky my supervisor had easily transferred me to the local hospital in Hertfordshire, same uniform, the same rules, just different colleagues, and that hurt.

My colleagues had become like family; we all knew each other and worked together for many years. We had trauma bonds from so much. Our kids all went to the same school, and our lives revolved around our block and our community.

I felt like a new kid starting at a new school, the odd one out, the newbie, but I knew I had to get on with it for Amelia's sake. This was not about me anymore.

I spent that first night in the new flat awake because there was no noise. The silence was eerie. The silence made me feel alone; it scared me. I decided that I would drink chamomile tea rather than lying in bed and sit outside on my step because I had a small garden for the first time. I can hang the washing out; hooray, and my feet can touch grass! The fact I had chamomile tea made me feel immensely grown up.

The foster carers gave us essentials like chamomile tea, which Amelia liked at their home. They had visited in the day with a hamper full of everything we would need washing up liquid, bleach, and sponges. Rosa had all bases covered as if she knew I wouldn't be capable of remembering such things and she was right.

I signed the paperwork to return Amelia to my care, and that was so amazing it was like I was being given my life back, my life was beginning. I opened the door that led out into the shared garden, the night sky was so dark, and I could see all the stars above me. I had never seen the sky so clear and bright before because there was no light pollution, so the sky was properly there for the first time. I breathed in the scent of trees and grass and countryside. It was like a new perfume; I inhaled it as if it could somehow cleanse me, I couldn't get enough. I had never had a garden, so this was big. This grass that I could feel tickling my toes was mine; this was my space; it felt fucking good.

I sat on the step outside the patio door for 15 mins contemplating everything that had happened. It was like I was out of the war zone, so I could finally look back at my life. You must get away before you can sit and process everything because your brain switches to survival mode when you're so intent on surviving. It does not allow you to overthink, or you would crack up and go insane. Now having the time to sit and contemplate was overwhelming. I was grateful, away from the madness and chaos that had become my life.

The tranquillity made me feel scared to be at peace. But I was here, and we deserved this. I still had my anti-depressants Fluoxetine, and I didn't think I would give them up anytime soon as they were still taking the edge off some of my anxiety and making my mind feel a bit clearer. I had just changed GPs and had my first consultation with the new one. I could tell by the look she gave me she couldn't believe the trauma we had been through. She signed the prescription and agreed I should continue on the medication until I felt ready to start weaning down.

I looked around the clean kitchen with the nicely painted walls, jars of spices, and all the nice kitchen things Rosa and Mario, the foster carers, had kindly donated to Amelia to help her with her new cooking course, and I felt like I was living somebody else's life. I felt a little fraudulent, I was still waiting for the phone call to say it was a mistake, and soon we would be told we would have to return to Stratford.

The change in Amelia was unbelievable. Foster Care had turned her into such a well-adjusted lovely girl in such a short space of time, and it saddened me to think it had been years since she was carefree and genuinely happy. I can't tell you when it all went so incredibly wrong. I wish I knew because then I could have tried to stop it. I had tried but ultimately failed; the thought of all those years of struggling left me empty, for so much of Amelia's short life had been ruined, and it was all my fault.

How many times had I not been there? How often had I missed her school plays and assemblies because my stupid zero-hour contract job would not allow me? I had missed out on so much by trying to provide, and I wasn't giving anything but an unstable, hostile environment.

Amelia looked clean and healthy, and she looked like a proper teenager. She was radiant. Kendra from St Giles visited us in our new home, and she also couldn't quite believe the difference in Amelia; they had kept in touch by phone, and I was so glad that she was visiting us so she could see how much of an impact she had had on our lives. If she hadn't broken down the barriers enabling Amelia to trust in an outsider, I hate to think of where we would have been. Kendra helped us so much by showing us that we could overcome these challenges and had a right to a life free of violence and disruption from all we had been through. She was such a fantastic inspiration to Amelia. I could never say how much she helped us in those early days. She made us see that our abuse was not our fault; we were vulnerable. We were Children that had been taken advantage of when we were at our weakest point. We now had the right to reclaim our lives and live! For the first time in forever, we were free, and there were no men to keep us in fear, no fear of reprisals. We had lives where we could try to be whatever we believed we could be.

Our new start didn't just end there; I was applying for a course with the Open University. Yes, me, who left school with nothing, was returning to studying. Kendra had inspired me because she told me she was doing a degree this way and had left school like me with only a lousy report next to her name. She made me think that I could do it because she was; she inspired me. Amelia was more excited for me than I was. "Mum, seriously, you have to do it. I never thought I would go to college, but I am." I looked into my daughter's eyes and knew she was right. I had to try, at least. I only had one life. I had actually to live the rest of it and not just survive.

If I failed, I failed, but I had to try at least. So I applied to study K100 Introduction to Health and social care. I could use the hospital computers and the old laptop Amelia's Foster Carers gave her. After my cleaning shifts, I would go to the hospital library, log on, and do my Uni work in the evenings. Sundays me and Amelia loved to go to the local library, where we both became obsessed with reading. Amelia on any cooking books she could get her hands on and me on health-care and nursing textbooks. We laughed at how our lives had changed the boffins!

I applied for every health care assistant job that would ensure a step in the door and even more of a move in the right direction. Don't get me wrong; I still had impostor syndrome moments where I couldn't believe this was my life. I had a few nicer clothes as the charity shops in this area had some branded things cheap as anything. I was joining the Marks and Spencer crew, albeit it all second-hand jeans and shirts, but I looked the part -grown up, in control, and finally an adult. I was working and studying and had a nice kitchen to cook in. I was living for the first time in years.

And you know my front door well; I could close it shut. I never had to put a chair under the door handle; we could breathe.

21

Louisa-End Note

They say time flies when you're having fun, and there is some truth. My life had changed so much. I now had a clear path with no shit or rubbish. There is not a day that doesn't go by where I don't think how lucky I am, I have a clean, safe space, and I'm in a job I enjoy.

I'm in my final year of Nursing; I qualify next September and will have a graduation. Yes, little old me from the council estate with a Mum who hated me and left school with nothing will wear a mortar board on my head; pinch me, I'm dreaming.

For the first time, I feel like a proper Mum; I never rush to work or run to make fast food. I'm not rich, not by a long shot my salary is basic, and we still go without. But Amelia and I are content, and that's worth more than anything money could ever buy. Amelia is passionate about frugal cooking and has set up cookery sessions in the restaurant she now runs, where she teaches younger people how to cook on a budget and eat healthily. Yes, my baby left college with her Chef and Hospitality management qualifications. She was now managing one of Marcos's restaurants in Hertford, a vibrant bar/restaurant with a flourishing young clientele. Amelia was like a new person.I hate to think what would have become of Amelia if we had stayed in Stratford. Her scars ran deeper than the marks on her arm, and I knew that one day we might have to embrace them, but for now, we were distracted; we were moving on.

Amelia still had regular counselling sessions, and I didn't ask her about them; it was enough that she could tell me she was feeling fine. Every anniversary of Jerome's death, we raise a glass to him, and Amelia has a Rose Plant in the garden and a little stone that she painted with his name on it. She will never forget Jerome, nor should she; I pray that the pain of blaming herself for his death has eased.

Meeting up with Glenda and Fatima three years later was quite strange- I managed to track them both down by making a few calls through Lana, one of the cleaners I kept in contact with at Newham Hospital.

These two women had been like Mothers to me, and I wanted them at my graduation because I knew that this would mean as much to them as it did to me. And I was desperate to hear from them and see how their families were doing. These were not just friends; they had become my family. So Glenda in her Nigerian dress, Fatima in her headscarf, and me with my tight jeans and jumper from M&S look quite the odd mix as we sit together in Amelia's restaurant in Hertford.

This is predominately a white middle-class area full of Italians, and low and behold. I was surprised to know Fatima could speak Italian! She had lived there years ago. There was so much crying and hugging when we met up; as soon as these women held me, I was back on the block again when they held me it was just like the past few years had not happened they still had the same smell and perfumes from years ago. Amelia had provided

284

a spread of foods for them to try. "It's all Halal", She proudly declared. Gosh, I loved my daughter so much at that moment. With her hair twisted up in a bun and her bow headband, I could see how Glenda and Fatima now see her as a grown woman, a powerful one.

No more Amelia from the block, who was young and restless with no options in front of her other than drugs, gangs and teenage pregnancy. Fatima and Glenda looked around the restaurant in wonder; the last time Fatima had seen Amelia was huddled under the covers in the children's ward with a blanket over her head, not speaking. And the last time Glenda had seen Amelia was the night she packed her bags and fled the tower block with Leon in tow.

Our shared time in that block had taken us in many different directions all our lives sharing different trajectories, but one thing remained, our love for our children; no matter what they did or how much pain they caused us, they came first. The crazy thing is we looked the other way so much. I don't quite know if it was to protect them or us. How many of us took the envelope of money from our kids to make ends meet? In that way, we were complicit in Gang life.

Fatima and Glenda may not have known as much as me, but I chose to look the other way, which Is something I have to live with every day. I blamed myself for Amelia falling prey to these Gangs. I was the lucky one; I had got out and managed to get on, but as I was to learn, they were not so fortunate. Glenda returned to the UK alone seven months after leaving Leon in Nigeria; she had been moved three times since we left the block. Glenda's temporary accommodation took her to Rainham, where white racists drove her out of the one-bedroom flat they occupied; sticking an African family next to white Skinheads was never a good plan. The flat they occupied had dog mess pushed through the letterbox and racist graffiti plastered all over the walls outside, and a firework through the letterbox.

Luckily, nobody was seriously hurt, Glenda had to fight to move and was now back in Newham, in a one-bedroom flat in Forest Gate, Upton Lane, which was small and cramped, but again she had her front door and was back with the community she knew. Glenda Was now living in one of the houses that overlooked West Ham Park, she lived in the basement flat, and the landlord and his family lived upstairs. She laughed as she said she had gone from tower blocks to almost residing now underground.

Her eyes spoke of untold sadness as she told me Leon had stayed in Nigeria, she didn't have to voice the unspeakable, but I could tell from Fatima's face she knew what had gone on. Leon was a killer and could never sit foot back in this country. Leon was engaged to be married to a girl from the village who was called Simone, and Leon would never step foot back into the UK. He had never really gotten over killing Adimchi; it had stayed with him; the boy still had night terrors and panic attacks. He was never a cold-blooded killer. He was a young boy caught up in crazy shit that got out of hand.

Glenda's Baby boy the apple of her eye, the one she had sacrificed so much for, and he had lost his way. There was no way back for him. Julius, the level-headed one was now an accountant and married to an English girl called Emma, his wife worked as a teacher, and they had a beautiful little boy who Glenda doted on; her grandchild became her reason for carrying on. A woman who attends church every Sunday with such strong Christian Values, how does she look in the mirror every day or go to church knowing a child she had given birth to had taken a life?

Fatima had lost two of her boys, Mohammad was serving life in prison for Kidnap and murder. Her youngest boy Farid had just been convicted of murder, rape and burglary, and his trial was coming up. Fatima had her daughter and grandchildren to carry on for, but her pain and loss were palpable—a mother still without her sons. How can you be such a good woman and raise such a bastard of a man? Fatima was a devout Muslim; she prayed daily and gave so much of herself to whoever needed it. I couldn't comprehend how any child of hers could have done such evil things. Fatima cried as she told us, "I prayed for all my life for better things; we travelled so many miles, most of my children were born in exile, we had years of living in refugee camps full of hunger, pain and all that time I struggled to get out for my children" tears began to fall down her face and Glenda and I both reached out so we all held hands.

Broken women with broken dreams, but we never gave up. "My babies that were born in the UK were the ones who had the golden ticket, the British passport, they were born in a UK hospital, they had access to schools, opportunities, everything… and look what happened, they both became involved in things way above their heads, and here I am now with the two British born babies spending the rest of their lives in jail."

Fatima's pain and sorrow were etched onto her face; her children's pain was her pain. It wasn't just them paying the price for taking a life; it was the mothers too. Most weekends, she would travel to the prison, a tiny Somali lady in her headscarf still carrying her prayer beads and cleaning NHS floors; because she was a good woman, there was no bad bone in that woman's body, and she would never give up on her Children.

We had all been to hell and back one way or the other there

was not a day that went by without us questioning if we had done things differently, would our children's lives have followed a different path? Fatima and Glenda would often ask whether or not their children's lives would have been different if they had stayed in their homelands, which is something we would never know.

The British-born children were the ones that fared worse. They had their tiny little feet planted onto the ground of opportunities, free education, and accessible health care, and even if money held you back, there were still chances if you worked hard enough and wanted to achieve. We would never truly know nature or nurture or a product of our environment. We may have come from different cultures and backgrounds, but one thing we had in common was Motherhood. I am still determining what the future will hold for us. I pray it's a happy one. I have shed enough tears over the years to last me a lifetime.

Does poverty make your child a killer? Are you a bad parent if your child picks up a knife or a gun? Are you the lowest of low if that wad of Money your Child brings home feeds you that week? We can't blame the Mothers because we are all trying our best. Some of us fight against the tide, pushing us back down the stream, while others get to sail on calm waters with a safety raft around them.

My love is for the Mothers struggling against that tide, but always know those tides can indeed turn and change. Motherhood, the biggest blessing and the biggest curse all rolled into one. It can make you, or it can break you. I'm just glad it made me.

AMELIA END NOTE

It's unbelievable I do not recognise the person I used to be, I catch myself sometimes remembering those days, and it makes me feel like I can't breathe. I had extensive counselling from CAMHS, which helped me. I developed strategies to help when the feelings got too much.

I'm lucky that the scars on my arms faded, except for one that was quite deep, but I don't look at that as a failure. It's a sign of survival.

Going into foster care was the best thing for me. I could take a break and contemplate life and what I wanted to do. I'm not saying that option would be suitable for everyone because I know that some placements are not good fits and they can cause more heartache and breakdown. I just won the lottery with my Foster Carers.

Studying and getting my Catering qualification was my proudest moment; I was blessed that I was able to find a career that I genuinely loved. I was again fortunate that my Foster Carers owned restaurants as they took a chance on me to bring all I learned to prove to them I was worth something.

My passion is teaching younger people how to cook; I run three sessions a week and host many charity bake-offs and charity nights to raise money to give back to St Giles, the charity that helped me.

I want to say that no matter how bad your life is, there is a way out. It may seem that, at times, there isn't, but rainy days can't last forever, the sunshine will come

The grief I carry about losing my Dad still weighs heavy on my heart. And the video of my rape is still on the web.

As for my abortion, that's something that I will live with until the day I die. I know I chose to take those pills and end that life, but it was not an easy decision. I had been raped and scared, I didn't know where to turn, but I prayed every night for that life I took. I will never be able to accept what I have done. I may live with it forever until my dying day, which probably hurts me more than anything I've ever done.

I hope Leon is living the life he deserves now in Nigeria, and I'm pleased he has plans to marry. I hope she looks after him and treats him well. I long to try to contact him, but I know that would not be fair to him or me. Nothing good could come from it, we both had to move on, but I would never forget him.

Whatever happened to Malachi and Deano, I don't know. I can't believe that I thought these men were powerful once because they are not, they are bullies that rely on Younger Children to take advantage of, and that's not right.

In sharing my story, I hope you know that no matter who you are and your background, you can rewrite your story and make some good chapters. Your book is your life. You have the power within you to change the story. Nobody has the right to make you upset or afraid, as that says so much more about them than you. Keep strong. Your time will come.

Printed in Great Britain
by Amazon